NEXUS

KEN MCALPINE

DEDICATION

To my family, who loves the oceans. And to future families, who will hopefully have the same chance.

ACKNOWLEDGMENTS

No writer has a better team of family and friends. Thanks to my amazing family – my inspirational wife Kathy and our sons Cullen and Graham – for believing in my words and filling my life with so much happiness and love. Thanks to my incredible cadre of intelligent readers – Kathy McAlpine, Pat McCart-Malloy, Lyn Tovar, Kay Giles and Joe Apple – who provided the extra eyes that every writer sorely needs. And finally, thanks to my special friend and creative genius, Hank Tovar, who still carries the standard for selfless giving.

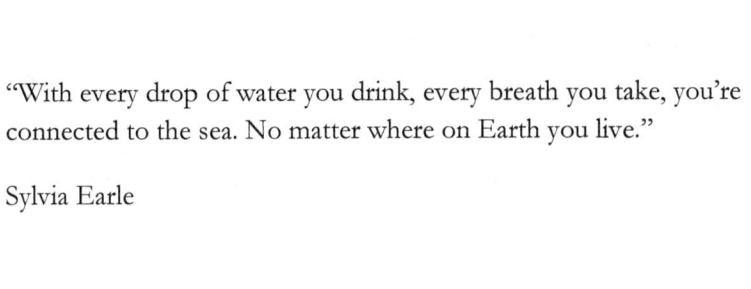

"With every drop of water you drink, every breath you take, you're connected to the sea. No matter where on Earth you live."

Sylvia Earle

"We are letting nature slip through our fingers, and taking ourselves along."

Edward O. Wilson

CHICAGO, ILLINOIS.

Amber watched him, crouched at the pond's edge, lost to the world, the dragonflies settling on his palm like jeweled raindrops. His palm already brimmed but the dragonflies kept coming, vectoring across the ruffled pond, hovering and landing atop each other, going still with a last gossamer flicker of wingbeat.

Stroked by the wind, the bulrushes issued a congregation's reverential whisper. The Chicago Botanic Gardens was one of their favorite places, especially just before sunset.

A neon green dragonfly made its regal, stick- legged way along his finger until it perched on his fingertip. It threw back the last light of the sun.

"They're impossibly beautiful," she whispered.

"Pixie dust come to life."

"They're not afraid."

"They don't need to be," Justin said.

He smiled up at her. It was a smile to love. Some people, childhood never leaves them.

"You look like a little boy, squatting there. All you need is a slingshot in your back pocket and a wad of bubble gum behind your ear."

"You don't have to be a little boy to love dragonflies."

They smothered his hand past his wrist, a twitching, iridescent coating, a morphing beehive. Still, they dropped from the deepening blue.

Justin turned his hand slowly, surveying the swarm.

"Sometimes the smallest things can take up the most room in your heart," he said.

"That's beautiful."

"That's Winnie the Pooh."

"My beautiful, honest little boy."

Justin gazed out across the pond, the opposite shore blurring in the dusk.

"When I was a little, I used to sit in the mangroves and watch them for hours. I thought they were magic. Messengers from a fantasy kingdom. Now I know I was right."

A man walked toward them. He wore an orange vest and a grim look.

Amber touched Justin's shoulder.

"Justin. Closing time."

The docent was two weeks short of his seventy-fifth birthday. His knees ached. He liked working as a docent, but he didn't like rounding up the laggards at closing time. The sign out front clearly said closing time was sunset. Making matters worse, his eyes worked perfectly fine; this couple was as handsome as they were oblivious. He had never liked pretty people. Too many things just fell into their lap. Their handsomeness added to his irritation. Pretty, spoon-fed daydreamers. This generation was coddled to helplessness.

"Closing time."

He heard the brusqueness and challenge in his voice. It wasn't him, but he was tired and drained.

The boy came out of his crouch like a dancer. The ease and grace made the docent jealous. The green eyes fixed on him; the slightly circled mouth no doubt preparing some smart-mouthed retort. In his day he would already have mumbled an apology and skedaddled. With a tinge of unease, he saw the boy was lean and muscled. Clean cut enough, but his hair fell to his shoulders. It was a world of thugs. There was no telling what this generation would do. These days, all the rules were off. He wished he had a radio. He was a decrepit sheriff.

The boy did not skedaddle. He spoke clearly.

"It's my fault, sir. She's been telling me we should go. I'm really sorry."

The way the boy looked at the beautiful girl made the docent sad. His wife had been plain and beautiful.

And then the docent saw the boy's hand, and forgot his knees and his sadness.

"Dragonflies," the boy said unnecessarily and smiled. "I won't take them home."

It was almost as if the boy held a lantern in his hand. Only when the boy raised the lantern to the sky did the dragonflies lift away. They rose as one, a humming mist of rainbow confusion, and, on some collective signal, vectored off into the gloaming in dozens of perfect angles.

The attendant stared after them.

"How did that happen?"

The boy just smiled and shrugged.

GULF OF ADEN.

Sugule Ali watched the fishing sloop through stolen binoculars, a sad-looking scrap nearly invisible upon the Gulf of Aden. The sloop reminded him of the hand-carved boats he had played with as a boy. Standing where the waves washed in, he had worked tirelessly to keep his boats upright, but they had capsized every time. Even then he had realized this was a life lesson.

The three fishermen were so thin as to already be ghosts. Sugule Ali thought of his fellow pirates, all of them scarecrows on the open sea. None escaped Somalia's poverty. In this, his country bestowed equality.

It was no cargo ship, but cargo ships were far fewer these days, redirecting to other waters or accompanied now by armed escorts. Perhaps, mused Sugule Ali, he was a victim of his own success.

Watching the panicked fishermen through the binoculars, Sugule Ali spoke his last words. He experienced no regret. It was a matter of survival.

"Shoot them when we are in range."

He felt the impact, a simultaneous hammer strike upon every bone. In the instant before the pain, he was angry. The half-wit Yusuf had run them aground, although he knew this was impossible in four hundred feet of water. It occurred to him that one of his men might have shot him. Their marksmanship was only slightly better than that of the blind. All about him was popping; the undisciplined report of Kalashnikov rifles, splintering wood and a snapping not quite like branches underfoot. There was a smell, sweet and sickly, like a butchered oxen. He had yet to lower his binoculars. He saw, in two perfectly oval worlds, the squalid fishermen gesturing madly, as if they had never seen pirates before. Yusuf screamed his mother's name. Wet doused Sugule Ali. Dropping his binoculars he saw the rain was red.

After a time the boat of Sugule Ali, pirate king, slid beneath the sea, but it did not concern him anymore.

THE SEA.

Here I am in Oliver Wendell Holmes' poem. There I am in Jules Verne's novel. I am not even where you expect I am. Certainly, in Andrew Wyeth's painting "Chambered Nautilus," I am clearly visible on the bench at the foot of the woman's canopied bed. But look closely. The composition and proportions of the bed and the window behind it mirror those of the nautilus on the bench. Just a little hidden fun. More than once, while writing "Twenty Thousand Leagues Under the Sea," Jules Verne confessed to his wife Honorine de Viane Morel. "Honorine. As God is my witness, a voice is whispering inside my head." More than once, she wisely counseled her husband keep this to himself. His family, she rightly pointed out, had madness in its bloodlines.

Mrs. Verne cared for her husband's reputation, just as she cared for his position as wage earner. The public is seldom generous toward madcap authors.

Here I am, there I am. Whispered of, I am. This is not meant as grandstanding or conceit. It is strictly an attempt to illuminate possibility, to have you look more closely at the world around you. And perhaps sense something larger than yourself. And maybe listen to the whispers in your own head.

Your species believes anything is possible. I suggest this is so.

"The globe began with the sea so to speak; and who knows if it will not end with it," Jules Verne wrote.

Maybe he wrote this; maybe he didn't.

I do have my limits. I cannot be everywhere at once. I must oversee my offspring more carefully. The young, they are more elemental. Closer to their roots. Sometimes unthinking. I remember. In this day and age, however, such recklessness is far more a risk. Had she taken a different vessel, say a pleasure yacht populated by technology and people who mattered, her impulsive feeding might not have gone unnoticed. But, by happenstance, she took the starving and the poor. Plenty of them to spare, without creating a proverbial ripple.

Her attack on the pirate vessel is a small thing, though not for the pirates. Or the three fishermen.

There are no survivors. Only lapping waves and splintered wood.

Like the shipwrecks of yore.

Wrote your poet Jonathan Swift, "So geographers, in Afric maps, With savage pictures fill their gaps, And o'er uninhabitable downs, Place elephants for want of towns."

Elephants. How very quaint.

CHICAGO.

Midnight phone calls don't always come at midnight. They come as easily on a crackling bright winter afternoon.

From across the miles, Marty said, "Your mom, she's taken a turn for the worse. She called your father. He's making arrangement. We're coming to Chicago." There was a long pause. The sun was rising in Palau. Justin knew exactly where Marty was standing. "Justin, she just couldn't talk to you from so far away."

They settled a few details. Words can be agony.

Marty hung up.

In the silence, Justin looked past the apartment to a sunrise in Palau.

A door banged shut, Amber coming out of the bedroom. It startled him. It wasn't part of the sunrise. She had her head down, fooling with a scarf.

"Okay. Believe it or not, Mr. Mahoney, I might finally be ready," she said, before looking up.

He was sitting cross-legged on the couch just as she'd left him, dressed and ready. He still hadn't put on his shoes. He hated shoes. She saw now that his black socks had gray stripes. The phone was in his lap. He cried soundlessly.

Everything the same, everything changed.

He looked at her as if he had a question. The radiator rattled.

"Mom," he said. "I don't know if I can do this."

In the Chicago Botanic Garden, the ball of dragonflies hovered above the pond. One by one, they settled on the surface. Slowly, the water ruined their wings. They stayed where they were, making no attempt to rise.

CHICAGO.

She had a nice room. Wyatt had seen to that. From her bed, through the plate glass window, she could see Lake Michigan, a prairie of evolving greens and blues and grays. She liked it. Water had seen her into this world. Now water would see her depart. She knew she wouldn't leave this room. Three weeks or three centuries, you never grew accustomed to the realization. But you realized it.

She was not looking at Lake Michigan now. She only had eyes for Justin. He moved to the window, fidgeting with the curtain's edge. He moved to her purse, nudging it back from the counter's edge. He moved to the water pitcher. He moved with the barest purpose, absent of thought, like a little boy who had lost something he would never retrieve. Which, mused Cedar, eventually held true for all little boys and girls.

Sorrow made him more handsome. She had never seen this many nurses coming and going. *He's just a little boy* she wanted to say, but of course he was only her little boy. Her lethargic mind worked to do the math. Nineteen. Her son was nineteen. Even in these circumstances he politely acknowledged the nurses' sympathetic looks, though he missed when their eyes said something else.

Cedar smiled to herself. Women were as bad as men. Worse, actually.

Marty was talking. She had asked him something, something that, a moment ago, had concerned her. Staring into her husband's smooth, earnest face, she tried to remember. So many chemicals swirling.

Marty was putting on his best face. His was a handsome face too, the white teeth shining, the dark curly hair close cropped and neat. *There is something exotic about him*, Cedar thought. The nurses stole glances at him too, though he was unavailable. It was a fine joke. The two men standing in the harsh light of this sterilized room were far more beautiful inside.

"The Wendell Holmes is in good hands, Cedar," Marty said. "Mongkol is tending to her."

Right. The boat. Her boat. It had cost her everything she had, leaving barely enough to feed her and her then six-year old.

"You don't need to worry," Marty added.

"I hope he's not smoking while he's doing it," she said.

Mongkol Songkhla was one of Koror's best fishermen, and an equally talented mechanic. He favored clove cigarettes, smoking them in an unbreakable chain.

"He only smokes to steady his hand during engine repairs," said Marty.

Her husband's smile, as white as the untouched tea cup on the institutional brown tray. She and Marty Haruo had married beside the sea. Six months, three weeks and some odd days ago. She tried, but she couldn't figure the days. It made her sad. She didn't want to be sad. Not now. Finite time for emotions, and everything else.

She looked to her son. He had always been so comfortable in every situation; even as a child, oddly self-possessed. Now he was wounded and out of place. He was a creature of the sun. Chicago's winter had returned him the pale complexion of his Irish ancestors, but somehow the blond hair that rested on his shoulders remained lightened at the ends. For so many years he had lived beneath a tropical sun. A freckled boy, she had fairly bathed him in sunscreen while he squirmed like an eel. She was glad to let that worry go.

She had been lucky with her men. Even Wyatt, her ex-husband, was a good man. They had just wanted different things. He had made the arrangements for this care, pulled his endless strings to see she received the best medical attention the country had to offer, but he was still Wyatt. He had been in this morning, but not for long. A meeting, he said, but she could see from the way his fingers crawled about each other that she scared him. She knew she looked like hell. An unearthed cadaver, with all the soil brushed away. Of her men, Wyatt was the littlest boy. She didn't hold it against him.

Justin said, "You have a beautiful smile."

She hadn't known she was smiling. Her face was mostly numb.

"I'll consider the source," she said.

The nurses had propped her up in bed. They did everything for her now. Her remaining job was to maintain her dignity.

Someone coughed. Things were disjointed. Sounds seemed to come from a great distance, or, quite suddenly, right in her ear.

Justin moved to her bedside table, reaching for the water pitcher again. Had she coughed? He poured water into a plastic cup and moved away.

She remembered. A shared room.

Turning her head she saw her son put the glass to Mr. Desimone's chapped lips. Louis Desimone was ninety-five. He had lived his entire life on the South Side, and now it was coming to an end. They had a bet as to who would go first, allowing that collecting would be difficult.

A single long wisp of hair remained atop Mr. Desimone's spotted head. Determined to be noticed, it often managed to fall down in front of one of his eyes. Before every effort had become an effort, Louis Desimone had brushed the hair away with a flourish, while looking across to her bed. In acknowledgment, she would say, "You need a haircut." To which he would respond, "Rock stars don't cut their hair."

The hair dangled now. She watched Justin gently return the hair to its place on the turtle-wrinkled scalp. Between classes – the University of Chicago, she proudly remembered -- Justin had fairly lived in this room. He had won over Louis Desimone just as he did everyone else.

"You need another clipping," Justin said. "Maybe a pompadour."

Louis Desimone gave his smoker's raspy laugh. Cedar saw the pink tinge on his lips.

"Still have my leather jacket," he said. "It may fit me now."

Though she was straining to hear, Justin said something she didn't hear. Louis Desimone laughed so hard he began choking. Justin gave him water, which he promptly spit down his front.

Merriment filled Louis Desimone's eyes, but the nurses' eyes said *move away*.

"I'll fetch the barber," Justin said, moving away. "I'll have him bring a fistful of lemon lollipops."

"My only reason to get a haircut as a boy, my only reason to get a haircut now. And tell your mother I don't mind losing a bet."

Louis Desimone turned to her and winked.

Cedar was suddenly conscious of her own hair. Matted and sweaty, it snagged and bunched under the pillow.

Justin moved soundlessly to the side of her bed, but she knew he was there. A mother always senses her son. She barely felt Justin move her head forward. His other hand smoothed her hair before gently easing her back to the pillow. He simply knew these things. Empathy incarnate. It was no longer odd to her.

She felt his warmth. He kissed her forehead. He was kissing another woman now. That *was* odd. She had met her. Amber. She had come to the hospital regularly, holding hands with her son. She had dark hair so thickly luxuriant it was a wonder the damn stuff didn't yank her over backward, and breasts that appeared to be straining to look up at the ceiling. Youth was a slap in the face. But she also had eyes that would remain kind long after all the other accoutrements fell away, so Cedar forgave her her excesses. She liked the girl. One worry, cast away.

Amber had stopped coming to the hospital three days ago. Cedar knew why.

"I've got something for you," Justin said.

She was mildly surprised to see him standing there.

He was close to crying. Good. He was still a mother's child. She needed someone to console.

Her throat was lined with broken glass. She started to speak, but he lifted a finger.

"Enough talking." A smile flickered. "Anyhow, it's not much to get excited about."

Leaning close, he slid something cool into her hand. It felt like a cigarette lighter.

"Hold tight."

She smelled his cologne. One minute a little boy crouched at the edge of a mangrove watching dragonflies after a rainstorm. Now something different. But not really. She wanted to close her eyes and drift back to the muggy aftermaths of so many monsoons. See again how he had always held out his hand, the dragonflies landing like tiny airplanes in a big hurry. Oh, the colors.

Had she taken it for granted? She hoped not, but she couldn't be sure.

He gently wormed something into her ears.

Her lips might have moved.

He lifted a finger again.

"Listening is more important than talking," he said.

They were her words, and she knew she was going to cry.

The song came to her in the sterile room separated from the world, but it swept her back to the past.

You. You can be me...

She closed her eyes. Some songs lose their thrill. Some stay magic. Forever and ever. David Bowie had gone through some interesting phases, but his music stood the test of time.

Well I, well I wish I could swim. Like dolphin, like a dolphin can swim. Well nothing will drive them away. We can be them, forever and ever. We can be heroes, just for one day.

The pain in her throat was worse. She realized she was singing. One of the nurses was frozen in place at the door. Cedar kept singing. She couldn't hear her own voice, but she knew it was not turning heads for the right reasons. Once, it had. She had loved to sing. She had been good at it. Yes, she had.

Justin was singing and crying. Marty was just crying. Her own cheeks were wet. She tasted salt on her tongue. Like the ocean.

It was a long song. They let her sing the whole thing.

Gently removing the earphones, Justin said, "You are my hero. Forever and ever."

She had not seen many men cry in her life. Now she realized they always cried silently. Marty brought out a handkerchief -- that was just like him, she thought, smiling this time to herself -- but Justin made no attempt to wipe away his tears. Since his first breath he had been himself, moving easily through the world. She had no idea where that came from. His father was a captain of finance, a Chicago power broker, but he had been saddled with the self-consciousness imbedded in all of us. Wyatt. Had he been in today?

The nurse in the doorway was crying too.

It took Cedar a long time to catch her breath, and then she smiled at all of them.

"That bad?" she asked.

It was past midnight when Justin set down Howard Zinn's "A People's History of the United States." A few yards away his roommate snored softly. Todd Sangstrom was a Physical Education major from Boston. If there weren't any parties, he was asleep by eleven. Performing a small twist, Justin placed Zinn's tome on the desk pushed up against the head of his bed. The University of Chicago was a fine institution, with dorm rooms as small as any.

The Palauan flag was affixed to the wall with duct tape, the photograph of the fruit bat stuck to the wall beside it. Jonathan's head was cocked slightly. His inky eyes bulged. He had always looked mildly accusatory, funny for an animal whose primary aims were the hedonistic pursuit of bananas and an ever-expanding harem. Maybe his was a healthy sense of perspective. He had been Justin's pet, and he hadn't.

Jonathan stared out at him from the cinderblock wall.

"Stuff you," Justin said softly. "I've read more than enough and then some."

Rolling to the edge, Justin swept his hand under the bed, his fingers settling on the thick spine. The book was heavier than it looked. Every night when he pulled it from beneath the bed, the muscles in his forearm strained.

He laid the book in his lap. The gold gilt page edges shone even in this dim light. She had given it to him the day he left Palau -- Koror, Guam, Houston, Chicago – mother and son standing awkwardly, staring at the runway through the streaked glass. She had broken the exhausting silence. *I've got something for you.*

The gold gilt pages were accompanied by hand-drawn illustrations. The book had been printed in 1890. She had bought it online from a Massachusetts collector for a small fortune she couldn't afford.

She had named her boat after the poet. She had sent him off to a new life with Oliver Wendell Holmes yanking down at his backpack.

He read a poem every night before turning off the light.

On this night he read "The Last Leaf," and he would remember that forever.

He didn't have to read the poem, he knew it by heart, but he let his eyes wander the lines for the pleasure. When he reached the end, he was holding his breath again.

And if I should live to be
The last leaf upon the tree
In the spring,
Let them smile, as I do now,
At the old forsaken bough
Where I cling.

That night Cedar dreamed. After all these years she knew the dream well, but it always frightened her, the lovely ocean spread before her, blue and sparkling as the darkness rose up on the horizon. The darkness rose and rose like some gargantuan wave, before it rushed forward. It raced toward her, staining the ocean black. It had never stopped in any of her previous dreams. It didn't stop now. It rushed up the shoreline, throwing itself over the high bluff on which she sat.

This time was different. The darkness poured into her lungs, drowning her last breath, and then it moved on, taking the pain with it.

They scattered her ashes on Lake Michigan, February's afternoon clouds shorn and bruised. Herring darted up and gobbled the ashes. The herring stayed on the surface long after the ashes were gone.

The sun fell to the horizon. The three men on the stern of the Boston whaler cried silently, and the world continued on.

When the boy dipped his hand in the water, the herring swirled about it.

THE SEA.

She is gone, but he is ready. I know this. He is the greatest hope I have encountered. Still, this does nothing for me now.

I wallow in darkness. If I had a heart, it would be breaking.

I wish I could play the bagpipes.

BYRON BAY, AUSTRALIA.

The rapping was steady, methodical and impossible to ignore, but Lacey Goodenall did her best for a good five minutes.

Finally she pushed back her chair and went down the steps two at a time.

The fisherman on her stoop held a bowling ball-size burlap sack. He was exceedingly tall. He stooped forward slightly, but the prayer flags draped across the entryway still slapped at his face. Byron Bay was in the midst of a serious blow. The winds had come up Thursday evening. They had continued to rise for three days. From her porch halfway up the hill, the ocean ran creamy white to horizon with whitecaps.

The fisherman made a futile attempt to brush the flags out of his face.

"Bit of wind," he murmured apologetically.

"You're not responsible."

She hated interruptions.

His head bowed a bit more.

"Sorry to interrupt, Miss Goodenall."

She was tempted to let the flags slap the man sillier, but a man who fished in these conditions announced his life.

She ratcheted a smile onto her face.

"No interruption. No need to be so formal, either. It's Peter Allen behind the flags, isn't it?"

"Bit of a surprise you know."

The man's shyness was mildly endearing. Most Australian men backstroked in macho and half of them couldn't swim.

"You're hard to hide, Mr. Allen. And you brought me something three years ago. An interesting cuttlefish."

"I did. I didn't think you'd remember. Women generally remember the fetching ones."

"Cuttlefish all look the same to me."

Peter Allen gave a hint of a smile. She hadn't paid any attention to his looks, then and now. Now she saw his clothes didn't quite fit. Khaki pants and gray flannel were haphazardly patched. He had a bad case of acne, made no better by days spent beneath an unforgiving New South Wales sun.

She nodded at the sack.

"Probably not the catch of the day."

"Not for most. Bull shark fetus. It was alive when the mother snagged in the net, but it died shortly after she did. I tried to save her, but she was too tangled for one man."

"Not a good day to pitch into the sea," Lacey said. "Let's take it around back and have a look."

Stepping quickly past Peter Allen, she trotted down the steps. She didn't like visitors in the house. Her lab was pin neat. Her house was not. A lifetime of travel and collected curios had seen to that. She had willed the lab equipment to the local college. Everything else would go in the rubbish when she died, if she didn't toss a match into it first. Except maybe the Papauan woodcarvings of humping pigs. She might give those to Paul Wiley. They matched his sensibilities.

Byron Bay was a lush place. Most bungalows sported colorful gardens. Lacey Goodenall's side yard bloomed with trampled dirt. The rear yard continued on in the same motif, only it also sprouted working detritus large and small: plastic buckets and lobster traps, a rusted boat trailer, a sun-bleached gray zodiac, several outboard engines in various stages of repair.

It was an oasis of exceptional ugliness. Lacey stopped for a moment to admire it.

"Pretty things die on my watch," she said to Peter Allen.

Something different hung above the door to the lab. The four long strands of hair appeared to be in dire need of conditioner. She had stopped noticing the smell long ago. Occasionally some prissy soul reminded her it was fleshy and pungent.

"Been pig hunting recently?" Peter Allen asked.

"Last week. It helps me avoid gardening." Opening the military green door, she said, "I'll ask you to tread very carefully inside, Mr. Allen, and keep your hands to yourself."

Lacey Goodenall rarely let other people in her lab. But she felt a small kinship with a man forced to fish alone in the middle of a blow.

Entering the lab always felt to her like entering an oasis. Her lab had first been a garage. Now, with the application of liberal amounts of cinderblock and concrete, it was a bunker. Cinderblock walls and a cement floor kept things cooler. They also offered firmer roots when the occasional cyclone came stampeding through. There was much to protect. A half dozen 50-gallon fish tanks rested on the floor along one wall. Other walls were neatly lined with shelves; those shelves, in turn, neatly lined with laboratory equipment. The sole exception was a shelf lined with books, the long row pinioned between two whale skulls. Three stainless steel tables, aligned end to end, the last with a sink, split the middle of the room. Paper towel sections rested in the far right hand corner of each table. Upon the paper lay an array of sharp knives, arranged small to large. Each table also contained a large cutting board, mightily scarred.

In the silence, aerators burbled.

Lacey bent and pulled a white plastic bucket from the stack beneath the sink. Placing it in the sink, she filled it with water.

"I'll take that," she said.

She saw how Peter Allen hesitated, probably out of ingrained custom.

"It's my business to get my hands dirty," she said, not unkindly.

"Right."

He handed her the sack.

He deserved at least an explanation for his effort and kindness.

"I'll rinse it off now and put it on ice for examination later."

Placing the burlap sack on the stainless steel table, she opened it carefully. She stood staring. Her hands shook slightly in very unscientific fashion.

"Well," she said.

Axial bifurcation was very rare. It was a marvelous specimen.

Peter Allen had proved a sly codger.

"You're a sly codger," she said.

"You never asked. Specifically."

Peter Allen had acne and a winning smile. She liked men, but eventually they all said or did something heinously stupid. She had grown tired of setting herself up for disappointment.

"I suppose that doesn't make me much of a scientist," she said, giving Peter Allen a little more attention.

He didn't answer. Better still.

They stood shoulder to shoulder gazing down at the two-headed bull shark fetus.

"The harbor patrol bloke said it was a bad omen," said Peter Allen.

"Only for the fetus," Lacey said, wiping any attraction from her memory banks.

It truly was a lovely specimen. Wholly intact, the two heads regarded her through four soul-less eyes. She had always hated that expression. Sharks' eyes were only soul-less when they were dead. She laid the stunted body carefully across the ice. Much of the fetuses' energy had gone into developing an additional head.

"How does it happen?" asked Peter Allen in a reverential whisper.

His voice startled her mildly. She did not take her eyes off the fetus.

"The embryo splits, as if twins are going to be formed. Halfway through the process, the embryo stops dividing. You see it in snakes and turtles and humans."

"What would have happened to it?"

"It would have died. A predator with two heads moves slowly."

A fisherman required no additional explanation.

"You should charge folks a few bob to see it."

She hoped he was joking.

"This has nothing to do with money," she said.

There was something odd about the specimen. When she pushed at the heads they moved far more supplely than she expected. The mouths were larger too.

She forgot about Peter Allen.

"It's my favorite book," he said.

This time she was irritated. Her head came up quickly but she put the brakes on her tongue. Insulting the man might stop the flow of specimens.

Still, her voice was sharp.

"What book?"

Peter Allen was standing by the row of books. He looked a little embarrassed.

"Twenty Thousand Leagues Under the Sea," he said. "Me mum read it to me when I took baths as a small boy."

She tried to imagine him tucked in a bathtub. It softened her a little.

"She sounds like a good mother."

"She was. I enjoyed the story a great deal. I felt a kinship with Captain Nemo. Bit of an outsider he was. And too smart for his own good. Not that I have that problem."

Peter Allen looked back at the bookshelf.

"There are times when I don't like to be with people. It's one reason I became a fisherman."

"I understand." She thought about it for a moment, and then decided. "Nemo, in Latin, means nobody. I like it that way."

Peter Allen smiled.

"Mum always said it was the nobodies who mattered."

Lacey reached into her pocket and pulled out a small billfold. She plucked off five twenties.

"Take this without arguing."

Peter Allen flushed.

"It's too much."

"Fuck me. Does anyone listen anymore? Take it. There are collectors who would have paid you ten times as much."

They both knew it was a lie.

Peter Allen took the money.

"Thank you," he mumbled. "Best be leaving."

"Thank you for coming to me. Again."

"A pleasure."

"I sincerely doubt that."

She thought she saw him fight back a smile.

Peter Allen stopped, hand on the knob.

"Miss Goodenall?"

"Yes?"

"I've been a fisherman since I was a boy."

She waited.

"I don't know if that fetus is an omen," he said. "But I do know that things in the ocean are changing."

After Peter Allen left, Lacey took a last long look at the fetus before placing a lid over the top of the bucket. Her fingers worked the rim, carefully pressing until the lid was tight. The local ants were voracious and cunning. Before she left, she went to the bookshelf and pulled the book down.

That night in bed, wind rattling the bungalow's shutters, she opened Jules Verne's most famous work.

Vingt Mille Lieues Sous Le Mers.

Her mother had insisted she and her sister learn French. French, she said, was the language of sophisticated women. Her mother had gotten her wish on one front.

Pas moi, ou ma chienne d'une sœur.

The oil lantern ladled soft light on the page. It could have been 1870, but it wasn't. Man's chances had dwindled considerably in one hundred and fifty years. Lacey Goodenall wasn't sure if she cared.

Her eyes went to the page, some long ago meal smudged in the corner. Her sister had been a sloppy reader and an equally sloppy eater. At the time, Lacey had wanted to kill her.

"On the surface, they can still exercise their iniquitous laws, fight, devour each other, and indulge in all their earthly horrors. But thirty feet below the surface, their power ceases, their influence fades, and their dominion vanishes. Ah, monsieur, to live in the bosom of the sea!

Jules Verne had been meticulous in his research, and often eerily forward-thinking in his writings.

But on this front, time had proved him wrong.

THE SEA.

She is right. A predator with two heads moves slowly. And so becomes prey.

Pardon the pun, but this particular two-headed shark was a dead end.

But evolution is a work in progress, a painting sometimes on its way to the slag heap, and sometimes on its way to glory.

KOROR, PALAU.

It was a muggy afternoon, even by Palau's soggy standards, and so Miss Patsy's Stonehenge form resided in what shade resided on the porch. Still the island's reigning busy body, age and some three hundred pounds of pudding flesh now kept Miss Patsy, for the most part, soundly anchored to the rickety swing that cried out whenever she shifted her weight.

Whenever she made an irrefutable declaration, Miss Patsy prefaced it by snapping her hand, as if quickly releasing dice.

She released the dice now.

"They will have to sell the boat," Miss Patsy declared. "That man Haruo cannot swim, much less dive."

Sitting opposite Miss Patsy, Miss Claren Obdifice neither agreed nor disagreed. In conversations with Miss Patsy, both approaches were pointless. Their daily afternoon tea consisted largely of Miss Patsy talking. Miss Claren didn't care. She was not much of a talker and, if you could set your clock by one thing, Miss Patsy never failed to entertain. No one knew Koror's business better, and Koror's business was immensely entertaining. Plus, they had dispensed with tea long ago.

Miss Patsy repeated herself, as though Miss Claren were deaf, although it was Miss Patsy's hearing that was failing. Miss Claren thought it the worst of torments, yet appropriate too.

"Marty Haruo cannot swim, much less dive." Miss Patsy looked thoughtfully at her yellowed nails. "I would still like a go with him."

Miss Claren tipped back her Red Rooster, enjoying the fizzy cold. Placing the beer back on her arm rest, she cackled.

"You would be the end of him. He is a dainty thing."

"There are ways," Miss Patsy said.

The two women sat in the oven heat and insect drone considering the possibilities. A cockroach made its comfortable way across the floor boards.

Miss Claren was getting her share, so her thoughts ambled a bit more quickly back to the loose subject at hand.

"I am worried for Ernan," she said. "He will not find a job nearly so good. The Mahoney woman paid him a fair wage."

"You are worried about how you will pay for your beer."

"There is some truth there," Miss Claren said.

In Koror, the better-off looked out for their less fortunate family members, immediate and extended. Ernan and Miss Claren shared not a whit of genetics, yet Ernan still provided for her. In the cooler at her feet, Miss Claren had three more Red Roosters at the ready, paid for, in large part, by Ernan.

Miss Claren was spryer than Miss Patsy, but at 180 pounds it still took some effort to rise from her rocker.

Miss Patsy spat beetlenut juice into the empty olive jar in her hand.

"I have a bad feeling," she said.

Miss Claren said nothing. Miss Patsy often had bad feelings. Sometimes they were just from too many olives, but often enough her bad feelings proved right. Her premonitions had solidified into all manner of concrete misfortune, from the Moses twins jailed for shoplifting to Agnes Cludley nearly losing both hands after a man who was not her husband tied her too tightly in bondage play. Miss Patsy had also claimed to have had a dream about the nun's terrible death at Jellyfish Lake, though now Miss Claren couldn't remember if the poor woman's death might have preceded Miss Patsy's premonition. The world forgets, even when it comes to the most horrid of deaths.

"I do not like the way the world is going," Miss Patsy stated.

Miss Claren kept her smile inside. Scattered like inconsequential birdseed in the Pacific southeast of the Philippines, their island nation was largely removed from the world. It was, she firmly believed, their saving grace.

"We are all connected," Miss Patsy said. "And I believe our collective train is heading hell bent for the cliff edge."

Miss Claren gave an involuntary shudder. At times she wondered if Miss Patsy might read minds. She also realized that soon the cooler would be empty. She knew Miss Patsy kept hard liquor squirreled away, but Miss Claren didn't fancy staggering home blind drunk in this heat.

"I wish I could speak with Able," Miss Patsy said.

It was even more frightening to see Miss Patsy serious. Fear made Miss Claren voice the obvious.

"Able is dead."

"That still makes him smarter than half the folks on this island." She squashed a mosquito on her forearm. "Went for a swim," she said in a musing tone of voice. Taking a fold of muumuu, she wiped the blood away. "Never in his adult life had he gone for a swim. Off he goes, fins in hand. Gone without a trace."

"Poor Portola," Miss Claren said.

They observed a moment's silence for Able's widow. Able and Portola had been married for thirty-five years. He had bought her Blue Dawn flowers every Friday. And then one Friday he didn't. Overnight, Portola became a shell of herself.

Miss Claren had never been married. It left a permanent hole in her stomach. She filled it temporarily in the shed out back with Leonard Chima. When he wasn't surly, she made him say wedding vows before she spread her legs. "Our honeymoon," she joked as they commenced.

The hole was there now, but Leonard wasn't. She filled it with three guzzles of beer.

"Things turned quiet after his death. But they are not quiet anymore," said Miss Patsy.

"What do you mean?"

Miss Patsy did not appear to hear.

"I liked her," Miss Patsy said. "She was not one of us, but she was a good woman. I hope Cedar Mahoney passed easy."

"Amen."

Both women observed a moment's silence for Cedar Mahoney. Miss Claren tracked her own whining mosquito, swatting futilely.

Miss Patsy burped fried onions, enjoying them again.

"Cancer is terrible," she said, reaching for her own plastic cup. "It is probably eating me up as I speak."

I don't know if anything can be that hungry, thought Miss Claren.

Miss Patsy said, "That boy Justin."

Miss Claren had a fantasy or two on that front.

"Do you think he'll come back?" Miss Claren asked cautiously. She didn't want to seem like a pedophile. She wondered what the age cutoff was.

"He's in America."

"It is not a prison."

"It can be." Miss Patsy snapped her hand. "The boy is odd. Polite, but very odd. Some folks you can't predict."

Wiping the condensation from her cup, Miss Patsy transferred it to the back of her neck.

"I told Cedar Mahoney about the nun and the jellyfish," Miss Patsy said. "She was in her storage locker when I told her. White women can go pale. That one was a surprise to everyone. In my opinion, reopening the lake is a mistake."

"Nothing has happened," Miss Claren said doubtfully.

"You can say that about many things."

A breeze rose. It carried the smell of flowers and frying pork. They enjoyed it in silent rapture until it died away.

"Strange thunderclouds rollin' in off the horizon," Miss Patsy said.

It was Miss Patsy's favorite saying, reserved only for the direst of calamities.

Out in the jungle something screeched, a wild cry that could be pain or pleasure.

Miss Claren thought, *We do not know the jungle.*

Marty returned to Koror two days later. Disembarking from the international flight, he drove straight to Koror's small private airstrip to check the plane. He had built the twin-engine Piper Aztec from the wheels up, and, until now, made a living transporting people and gear between the dozens of islands that comprised his island nation home. The engine was still sound, no surprise as he had given it a thorough overhaul shortly before leaving for Chicago, and the Piper hadn't moved since. But the windows were caked with salt and bird droppings baked to hard and acrid plaster by the sun. In his distraction he had forgotten to cover the plane with the tarp.

Hauling the ladder from his office, he walked it across the tarmac, the heat rising off the cracked and rutted surface in a visible shimmering. Overhead a frigate bird, more giant kite than bird, rode the very same updrafts. Stepping up on the ladder, Marty cleaned the windows twice, taking small pleasure in the familiar act and failing to smile at his quirks. Returning to the bunker that served as his office, he put the ladder back in the storage closet, and then turned on the air conditioner to cleanse the dank smell. Hanging from fishing line, the World War II models spun slowly in the new breeze.

He sat at his desk. He wasn't sure why.

He sat for a long time. He had already made his decision, but he made it again. Then he broke down and cried.

When he went down to the dock the next afternoon, Ernan was sitting with Mongkol Songkhla. The two men smoked clove cigarettes and leaned against their respective pilings. Ernan stood when he saw Marty approaching, brushing ash from his sun-bleached khaki shorts.

Mongkol Songkhla continued to smoke and look out at the water as if Marty were not there. The cloves crackled and popped, giving off their pleasant smell. Mongkol wore a plain white Hanes t-shirt. Someone, presumably Mongkol, had scrawled "I have very bad posture" across the front in brown crayon.

"I came down to see her," Ernan said. "It seems Mongkol has done his job and then some. He is a fine mechanic." Ernan glanced at the man at his feet. "Still I was a little worried she might also have been blown to bits."

"A legitimate concern," said Marty.

"Welcome home."

"Thank you." Marty inhaled. Home was a mix of brine, creosote, gasoline and fecund dampness. Punctuated with clove. "It's good to be back."

The unspoken hovered in the air.

"At the end, she passed peacefully," Marty said.

Now Ernan looked out to the water.

"Good. She was the finest woman and an excellent captain. It was an honor to know her."

Marty knew the past tense would always send a frozen poker into the center of his heart.

"Good afternoon, Mongkol."

Mongkol Songkhla made some indeterminate movement with his head. He kept looking at the water.

Marty smiled despite himself.

"He's not talking to me?" Marty asked.

"As we both know, he rarely talks to anyone. Before you arrived, we were smoking and discussing nothing."

"There's much to be said for that," Marty said.

"I believe there is. I also believe it's possible he's unhappy to see you."

Marty regarded the man sprawled, legs akimbo, at his feet.

"It would be pointless to ask how I have offended you," Marty said.

Neither Mongkol nor his cigarette flickered.

Marty looked at Ernan.

"It seems I must rely on you," he said.

"Now that you are here, his work is done. He enjoyed that work. He liked not fishing. Fishing is hard work. Much harder work than maintaining a vessel already impeccably kept. He liked the money."

"He told you all that?"

"In his fashion and his time." Ernan smiled. "I also understand how he feels."

Cedar had explained her decision to Ernan before she left. Ernan had understood, but for some reason Marty felt he needed to tell the young

Filipino again.

"She would have hired you to do the work in an instant, and she would now keep you on as captain. But she knew you'd be busy studying to be a policeman. She wanted what you want."

Two tenses, each fraught with meaning.

"I am playing a little hooky now." Ernan's smile assumed a trace of sadness. "She was right to hire Mongkol. I have been too busy, and no one knows engines like this man. Not even me or you. She always did the right thing."

"She did."

"No one was fairer."

It would not do to cry here. They both knew it.

Ernan flicked his cigarette into the water. Something rose and slurped it down.

"Well," said Ernan, "I'll be going. I believe my conversation with Mongkol is finished."

"How are your studies going?"

Marty already knew how they were going. After the airstrip, he had paid a visit to Miss Patsy. Miss Patsy knew Able's secretary, and so she knew that, short of Able, the local constabulary had never seen a mind as deft as Ernan's. But Miss Patsy also knew Miss Claren Obdifice. Miss Claren visited her adopted nephew often. It was true she often needed spending money, but it was also true that she genuinely cared about the Filipino boy. Often she brought him beef stew or fried fish, and once she brought him a painting she painted herself. It was of a small island, with a single palm and a white sand beach. It was very familiar and very good.

Miss Claren had told Miss Patsy that, between studying, Ernan slouched about his home, and that he often looked up from his studies at the kitchen table to stare morosely out the window in the direction of the sea.

Miss Patsy kept no secrets.

Marty already knew Ernan loved the sea. Now he knew he loved it more than the prospect of police work. But police work paid better, and though he had spent much of his childhood homeless on the streets of Manila, Ernan now had many purported relatives relying on him. That they weren't blood relatives didn't matter to anyone who depended on him. It didn't matter to Ernan either. Instead of a home, Ernan had been born with a conscience.

"My studies are nearly complete," Ernan said without much enthusiasm.

"Word is you will make a fine policeman."

"I will do my best."

It was why Cedar had hired him as her captain when she had started her dive charters.

Marty said, "I believe your career will be short-lived."

On the streets, Ernan had mastered the art of disguise. Now he did an admirable job of feigning casual indifference.

"Maybe I won't be a good policeman. Everyone is entitled to their opinion."

"In fact, your career is already over now."

Marty saw the corners of Ernan's mouth twitch. He would have laughed, if he had remembered how.

"I do not understand."

"If you're going to be my captain, you must be honest with me always."

Ernan had a young boy's laugh. Marty remembered. He probably wasn't twenty-five.

"Then I will begin by being honest now," Ernan said. "Koror will become the global seat of power before police work is for me."

Mongkol shifted. The smell of untended underarm rose off the dock.

"Good," said Marty. "I have decided to go into the dive business, and my first order of business is rehiring you as captain. Now that that's settled, I have something for you to do immediately. See if you can talk this man at our feet into being our chief mechanic. Tell him I will pay him enough to put aside fishing. Tell him he must learn to dive. Tell him it is not possible to smoke clove cigarettes at sixty feet. Or anywhere closer to a boat than this."

Mongkol Songkhla rose by pressing his back against the piling and pushing himself up to his feet. Marty wondered how he didn't fill his back with splinters.

Mongkol ignored both of them. Hitching up his khakis, he walked toward the Wendell Holmes. Just before he swung his leg over the transom, he flicked his cigarette into the water.

Not without sympathy, Ernan said, "You are a pilot."

Marty felt queasiness bubbling in his stomach.

He gathered himself.

"I was a pilot, but I have grown tired of the skies." It was for Cedar. It was all for Cedar. And Justin. He cared for the boy, as if the boy was his own. He felt himself faltering. "We will require one more crew member besides our chatty friend. Someone who knows the local waters, but who can also interact easily with their fellow man."

"I have just the man."

"Good. Bring him to me as soon as you can. We need to get started." Marty was growing tired of playing boss. He let his voice soften. "I know police work pays well and you have more responsibilities than you should. I'm hiring you with a fifty percent raise."

Ernan shook his head.

"No. Your business will fail before it starts."

"Maybe so, but I can't have you worrying about your relatives while we are on the water."

Ernan's dark eyes watched Marty. This time he disguised nothing.

"Cedar was right to marry you. I accept your offer, but under these conditions. I start at my former salary until the business is up and running again. We both decide when that is."

It was Marty's turn to be grateful.

"I accept your offer."

When the two men boarded the Wendell Holmes, the hatch to the engine room was raised. Some kind of caterwauling rose from the open hatch. It sounded to Marty like a truck backing over a never-ending row of garbage cans, with someone was singing along to the banging. Caterwauling.

"What in God's name is that?"

"Nirvana, I believe," said Ernan. "Possibly Pennyroyal Tea."

Marty peered down past the hatch. Mongkol was crouched beside the engine, circling a wrench and bobbing up and down on the balls of his feet. The noise issued from a battered tape deck at his feet. He paused in his wrenching to gaze up at them with a blank expression.

"This is music?" Marty asked.

Mongkol continued bobbing.

"I believe the answer is yes," said Ernan. "Mongkol is an admirer of the late Kurt Cobain. Mr. Cobain was not much of a social climber either."

Marty remembered now. Kurt Cobain was a young musician who had committed suicide. He had seen the boy's heartbroken mother on television. It was possible Cedar had also mentioned him.

"Perhaps I could win him over to something more conventional," Marty said.

"Perhaps tomorrow you should try Neil Diamond."

"Can you at least ask him to turn it down?"

Mongkol grunted and held up his hand, the pointer and index finger held up in a reverse peace sign.

"I believe he is pointing out that he has already given up smoking."

"Fine. On it stays, then. We need to be able to put to sea without threat of mutiny."

Ernan was still chuckling as Marty climbed the ladder to the bridge.

Marty stood quietly, looking out at the harbor. Everywhere, the jungle spilled down to the water's edge, a lush flood that seemed to breathe. In the few places where there were buildings, the jungle had been haphazardly hacked away, providing a fingernail sliver of civilization. Marty had always had the feeling that if he turned his back the jungle would swallow the harbor and everything else like playthings; claustrophobia brought to fungal and fern life.

Now this was home. And he would have to dive. The thought of water's press only added to his urge to scream.

Closing his eyes, he wished for the sky.

That night Marty walked up the hill to Shirley's.

A February Tuesday, Shirley's was empty.

Henry looked up from behind the bar.

"Mr. Haruo, you are my lucky thousandth customer. Help yourself to anything in the place. Help yourself to the place."

Henry's dour face made Marty feel better. Henry had taken a chance on the bar. He could take a chance too. Owning a bar was like owning a dive boat;

sometimes it was full and sometimes it wasn't. And both could sink. Marty's enthusiasm deflated slightly, and then Henry's long face breathed life back into Marty's cheer.

"You look like Eeyore."

Henry picked at a bowl of no-doubt stale popcorn.

"Who is this man, Eeyore?"

"He is a donkey who looks like you."

"He must be a fine looking donkey."

"He is, but he is not particularly quick-witted." While Henry squinted at him suspiciously, Marty chose a stool. "I prefer to buy my drinks," he said, sliding a twenty across the bar. "Accepting free drinks from gloomy donkeys is bad luck."

"Good luck for me." Henry wore a fraction of a grin. He was not a man to stay down for long. "In lieu of a free drink, I have provided you with your choice of any seat in the house."

Shirley's Emporium comprised four patio tables and a six-stool bar. Shirley's sat atop a hill, offering a lovely view of the harbor and the sea beyond. Henry was Shirley's fourth owner. None of the owners had ever known or heard of a Shirley.

"I decided it would be rude to sit outside," said Marty.

Henry placed a scotch malt on the bar.

"You will get your drinks quicker."

Marty knew what was coming. He felt himself brace. Maybe with time, but he doubted it.

"Welcome home, friend," Henry said. "I am so sorry for your loss."

"I am sorry too."

It was as if Koror, and his life, had disappeared inside a sinkhole. Only he could make home feel like home again.

"How was Chicago?"

"Cold. Windy and cold."

"I do not know why people would live there."

"Almost three million people do."

"Maybe I should open a bar there."

"Perhaps you should first spend some time living in your freezer."

"I have already reconsidered this business opportunity."

"Wise. There's no place like home."

Marty's mouth was dry. He wanted to drink, but his hands were shaking. He had proposed to Cedar here. He had rented the entire bar so that, except for Henry, they could be alone. It had been her birthday. He had worn a tuxedo. He had worn the tuxedo once before. He had met Cedar the first night he wore it. He had saved it because he knew that one day he would propose to her wearing it. He had dropped to one knee on the patio, the strung lightbulbs swaying in the warm breeze so that the ring disappeared and reappeared in perfectly timed shadow and light. They had danced to "What A Wonderful World" on the jukebox.

It had been a perfect night, and then it had turned to nightmare.

Again Marty saw schooling fish, only this time they weren't feeding on dry ashes.

Closing his eyes, he picked the scotch up quickly and downed it in three swallows. His throat burned. Behind his lids, his eyes watered.

He opened his eyes.

"Another please."

"Sure," said Henry, regarding him warily.

Marty downed this one too. He sang softly. He did not have a very good voice.

I see trees of green, red roses too. I see them bloom, for me and you.

He sang a few more words, and lost interest. His mind went somewhere. He let it go.

When he opened his eyes, Henry was staring up at the television. A rugby game in Sydney.

"How is Justin?" Henry asked, without taking his eyes off the screen.

"He is managing."

Marty pushed the glass across the bar. Henry hesitated. Filling the glass, he placed it carefully in front of Marty.

"And you, my friend?" he asked.

"Trying to manage. And not succeeding."

"She was a good woman," said Henry. "I have never known anyone like her."

Marty took up the glass. This time he only drank half of it down.

"I have never known you to drink more than two," Henry said.

The malts didn't make him feel good. They only made him sadder.

"I have made a career change. I am now a hard drinking man of the sea."

He drank down the rest of the glass and pushed it back to Henry.

"No more for me," he said. "You can relax."

Henry did.

Walking down the hill, Marty realized what a teetotaler he was. His head felt as if it were listing to the side, and he worried that his body would follow suit. In the darkness, loose gravel sifted threateningly beneath his feet. The scraping of his shuffling feet was the sound of someone crawling. He negotiated the hill like an old man. The sky above was filled with brilliant stars but he kept his eyes on the ground. It would serve him right to fall and break his neck just as he launched this new enterprise. With the startling clarity of the drunk, he realized Ernan and Mongkol would run things splendidly without him. This was good. His confidence experienced a lift. Then he thought of the money he had set aside at the end of every month's flying and he wondered if it would be enough and his confidence vaporized.

He needed blank, unencumbered sleep, and he wasn't sure the scotch would help. It had been a long few days. He remembered Justin and Amber driving him to O'Hare, and Justin's fierce hug as the snow blew about them like dust. The snow had settled in his dark hair and Justin had smiled at him and said, "Now I know what you'll look like when you are old," and they had both been very sad. His only other memory of his journey was a long procession of mussed and stone-faced travelers.

Now, miracle of the modern age, here he was wobbling beneath the stars of his home.

Now forever changed.

Last night he had slept on the cot he kept in his office. At the bottom of the hill he hesitated, and then he said a fervent prayer to the stars and turned purposefully for the harbor. He didn't want to sleep on the Wendell Holmes ever again, but that was problematic.

He might have been mumbling this to himself. The dock was spongy under his feet. He wondered if he might just list off the side of the dock and sink right to the black bottom, never to be seen again. He saw that someone had left a light on in the forward cabin. He imagined he was an arrow, fired toward the light. A guywire chimed. Tinny reggae drifted from somewhere and a feeding fish splashed. Before he came on board he checked the lines.

Bent and peering, he realized he had no idea what he was checking. The lines were tied precisely to the dock cleats, the leftovers neatly coiled on board.

"The wise captain hires a wiser crew," he said to himself, but the conversation was doing him no good.

His legs felt heavy. He stepped aboard, taking special care not to fall in the dark place between the boat and the dock. He was already having a hard time breathing. Memories squeezing him, he went down the steps to the galley. The galley was tidy, half lit and silent. Beyond the galley the small sitting room was dark, but he saw the couch, the small flat screen television and the table where they had eaten their meals, their knees always bumping, as if every light was on. The small table had leaves, but they had liked the bumping.

Little things.

The night was quiet, but a tremendous humming shanghaied his ears. He had walked to the table. Now he placed a hand on it to steady himself. When he did he saw Cedar's computer, resting closed, a yellow notepad beside it. She had been a compulsive list maker, even worse than him. He placed a finger on the notepad, started to flip it closed, then paused in spite of himself. Picking the pad up, he held it just off his nose. *Have Ernan check the seals on the tanks. Check the refrigeration system. Important papers for carry-on bag: birth certificate, health insurance, social security. Squeaky hinge on main cabin porthole.*

He wondered if it was possible to drown on dry land.

He almost missed the piece of paper, torn from the notebook and carefully folded in half, an inch of yellow jutting out from beneath the computer.

He used both hands to unfold the note.

Whatever we were to each other, That, we still are. I love you, Marty. You can do this. I know it. I didn't just marry the first dashing pilot who came along.

He sat down on the couch, crying in great heaving sobs.

That was where he slept and that was where he woke. In the first moment of waking he didn't know where he was, and then he heard the jungle birds shrieking and the tide making its small commotions beneath the hull, and he felt his dried tongue swollen in his mouth and he thought, *No Cedar, I can't do this.*

THE SEA.

A large shark moving fast displaces a tremendous amount of water. Most often the intended prey does not see the shark until alerted of its impending fate by a violent battering ram of water rushing just ahead of the attacker. Then the jaws clamp shut and the real show ensues.

This white shark is very large. The dolphin feels the aqueous shock wave and is cut cleanly in half. The shark swallows the bottom half in great convulsive shudders. The remaining half is taken up by the waves. It rolls and tumbles shoreward like some grotesque sausage, consciousness flickering in the eyes for a surprisingly long time.

This doesn't make us monsters.

Only survivors.

CHICAGO, ILLINOIS.

Professor Robert Blackstone, known to his students as Bobby B., had been teaching at the University of Chicago for longer than he cared to admit. He was still relatively young, or at least he saw himself in that light. He had started teaching at the University at the undeniably young age of twenty-seven, excluding a year of wandering Southeast Asia, right out of the Harvard's Kennedy School of Government. The University of Chicago had congratulated itself on hiring one of politics' brightest minds. Bobby Blackstone had hoped they were right.

Thirty years later Professor Blackstone's mind still burned bright, but his enthusiasm had dimmed considerably. Chicago had worn on him. His students had worn on him. An endless conga line of staff meetings had worn on him. Repetition and mediocrity had smothered his enthusiasm as an acolyte snuffs a candle. Two more years, and he was going to retire. He had never married. He had few possessions he valued. One of them was a collection of flyfishing rods. On retirement, he was taking them to the Florida Keys to bonefish. Fishing did not traffic in repetition. He had already purchased the flat bottom skiff. It waited in a storage compartment in Key Largo. In the University's overheated lecture halls, Bobby Blackstone wore flip flops to keep his goal in sight. When he lectured, he stole glances at his feet.

But now and again he was reminded of what had brought him to teaching in the beginning; the chance to witness, and perhaps even nurture, fiery bright minds. It was Professor Blackstone's belief that there were fewer of these minds than there once were. His undergraduate courses were now filled with students with bloated GPAs, superb test taking skills and nary a dust mote of original thought. He didn't think he was nostalgic. The old days weren't better days; they were just different days. He did wonder how it was possible to have so many high school graduates with 4.5 GPAs. More often than not, he found his students far more impressive on paper than they were in person. He did his best to raise their game, but often it was like chewing stale gum, and knowing that even that was going to fade away.

Mustering as much enthusiasm as he could, he would gaze out at the rising tiers of seats to see the students sleeping, texting, or ostensibly taking notes on their computers, only from their rapt attention and darting eyes even Mr. Magoo could have told you they were playing video games.

But there were exceptions, the shiny pennies that made his work still seem relevant. He remembered the first day of this class, looking out at the sea of faces and seeing the boy eagerly staring back at him. The boy's eyes were so bright they had actually given him a start. They were green as the Key West shallows. He had mustered himself quickly, continued on with the same opening day speech he always gave (they were all guilty of repetition), explaining the nuts and bolts of Public Opinion, and the questions that they would try to answer together (because we are all in this together). What is the relationship between the mass citizenry and government in the U.S.? How can political leaders best communicate with their constituents? Did (in his mind this question was most pertinent, but he kept this to himself) those constituents even care?

He had concluded his welcome, as he always did, with a rousing hurrah regarding the value of education; the meeting, and – this was truly good, he valued it greatly – clashing of minds, the boundless potential of knowledge rightly applied for the good of the whole. As he had once, accidentally, heard a student say, "Selflessness and service and all that proletariat shit." When he finished, he had glanced again at the blond boy in the fifth row. The boy had been leaning so far forward in his seat that Bobby Blackstone thought he might topple down the steps and roll right up to the dais.

In the ensuing weeks Justin Mahoney (he had looked the boy's name up immediately after his speech) had proved that opening day had not been an act or a dabble with amphetamines. Performing some mildly unscrupulous research, Professor Blackstone had discovered the boy was the son of Chicago financial scion (another spoiled private school brat) and, in the next sentence, discovered that the boy had spent most of his life in Palau, raised by a single mother who ran a dive boat. Unfortunately, there was no more than that. Intrigued, he had motioned Justin forward one day after class. He had asked the boy a few questions. Justin had been polite and open and charmingly modest. He had admitted, after some pressing, that he had some small knowledge of fishing; and then enthusiastically told Bobby

Blackstone things he had never known.

All of this was interesting, but not earthshaking; the University still admitted its share of quality human beings. But there was something else, something about the boy that he could not research or define. Each time they interacted, Bobby Blackstone walked away trying to figure out what it was that made him feel as if the past few moments had been different. Had *mattered*. More than once, reading at his desk at home, he had pushed aside his book and tried to pinpoint what it was that accompanied Justin Mahoney. Charisma, yes. Magnetism too. But something more. He had never been a follower, but with this boy there were times he felt he would take up the boy's banner and ride with it on to a battlefield where there was absolutely no hope of winning. It was truly odd.

And the boy could speak. Not in the stilted, self-conscious manner of geeky Toastmasters, or the smooth, polished (and in Professor Blackstone's opinion, creepily oily) manner of today's mannequin candidates, but in an easy, somewhat shy manner that made it feel as if he were volunteering his thoughts, with some reluctance, strictly to you.

At this moment, the boy was speaking of octopuses, one in particular, and, given the absolute silence in the auditorium, it seemed this octopus was the only thing in the world that mattered. The class assignment had been simple. Give a speech about anything. No topic was beyond bounds. Free speech and all that. Just convince us. He had given the assignment solely with Justin in mind.

He sat in the front row, not just because he was the professor, but because he wanted to be close. At the dais ten yards away, Justin spoke softly, but the microphone picked up every syllable, throwing it out to the crypt-silent room. He had notes, but by Bobby Blackstone's count, his gaze only dropped to the dais twice. Justin looked out at his fellow students and smiled the kind of smile most of us save for private moments.

"People think of our worlds as separate, and to some extent they are," he said. "You don't need a degree in marine biology to see I'm not an octopus. But here's something you might not know (the teacher remembered to make an obligatory note – *Good. Never talk down to your audience*), because until recently scientists hadn't seen anything like this either. Researchers at the Monterey Bay Aquarium were conducting an underwater survey using a robotic sub. It's actually an ongoing project that began four and a half years ago and ended last month. They logged all kinds of data, a lot of it baffling to me, but one thing wasn't. The very first week of their mapping, the scientists spotted a distinctively scarred octopus in a known brooding area a mile beneath the surface. When the sub went down again a month later they saw the same octopus, only this time she was clinging to a rock and guarding 162 eggs." Justin smiled. "Scientists aren't approximaters." He pushed the blond hair up and away from the green eyes. "Octopuses usually only brood for a few months, so imagine the scientists' surprise when they kept seeing this same scarred mother, protecting brood after brood on the same rock." He looked down, almost as if embarrassed. "For four and a half years."

Looking out at the audience, he gave a small shrug.

"Okay, I'm a bit of a geek. I read about this in an obscure marine biology journal I actually subscribe to. After I read it, I called the lead researcher at Stanford. He was really nice – he actually picked up his own phone – and when he found out I was calling to ask him about the octopus he got really excited. He told me they named it Octomom and that each time the sub's cameras picked it up, everyone watching the monitor cheered. He said as the months turned to years, the cheers got louder and louder. At the end they were bringing in champagne and toasting Octomom. Liberally. Their study marked the first time campus police found two Nobel laureates sleeping with their heads against the steering wheels of their cars."

Good use of humor, noted Bobby Blackstone.

When the class stopped laughing, Justin's own smile faded.

"Because it did end. Finally Octomom was gone, nothing on the rock but empty egg sacs. Like most cephalopods she probably never left the rock, never ate anything at all. When the last brood hatched, she likely died of exhaustion or starvation. Fifty-three months."

Justin stood square shouldered at the podium. A chair squeaked.

"Different," he said, "does not mean lacking value."

There was a waiting, for one of the few times in his speech-listening life Bobby Blackstone sensed the audience actually wanted more, and then the students exploded in applause and shrill whistles. Justin left the podium and took his seat quickly, but the applause continued on. Professor Blackstone turned in his seat, his eyes wandering the young faces. It seemed as if a light had come into some of them. He looked up the rows. He was about to turn to Justin when he saw the dark-haired girl seated in the uppermost row, close to the door. She was a striking beauty. He had never seen her before. Sitting up very straight, the girl was crying.

Bobby Blackstone, jaded to all things academic, forgot where he was. Standing up, he applauded with the rest.

That evening, alone at his desk, he Blackstone was reading a boring, self-inflated public policy diatribe when the realization struck him. He thrust the paper aside. Coincidentally, it fell into the trash bin where it belonged.

He typed the names into the computer one by one, watching clips of each man and woman, feeling the goosebumps and guilt rise as he remembered again that there was a greater good, and that cynicism was the easy path and he had often taken it. Much of the footage was grainy, technology had come a long way since those times, but each speech was the same. The words and thoughts were almost childishly clear, yet they were endowed with palpable physical power. At times the words arrived like physical blows.

Mahatma Gandhi, Mother Teresa, John F. Kennedy, Martin Luther King; captured on better video, his current Holiness the 14th Dalai Lama. Each spoke from the heart to the heart. The simplest, and most elusive, form of communication.

The next morning Professor Blackstone delivered a note to the chair of the Political Science Department. Befitting the topic, it was hand-written and simple.

We have a leader in our midst. It's possible I have seen the future.

Bobby Blackstone recorded his students' speeches so he could analyze them later. He was tired, but he still cared about education.

That afternoon, the department chair came to his office. Professor Blackstone made microwave popcorn, sprinkling it with cinnamon. The two men watched the video. They had known each other a long time. When Justin finished, the department chair turned to Bobby Blackstone.

"That's why we're here," he said. He looked down at his lap. "And that's why my popcorn is cold."

Daniel Brannon, chair of the University of Chicago's Political Science Department, knew people.

A month later Daniel Brannon stood in the now nearly empty ballroom at the Omni Hotel, floor to ceiling windows looking out on frosty, pewter Michigan Avenue. Outside, cars and trucks belched steam. Inside, piped music played "Strangers in the Night" and the faint scent of beef stroganoff hung in the air. There were a few hangers on; media, staffers, vetted hotel workers folding chairs and taking down drapes. The Secret Service men stepped from behind the stage curtain first. It would have been comical if the world hadn't become such a dangerous and unpredictable place.

The slender man with the close-cropped graying hair walked with a military bearing and a boyish spring.

The girl beside Daniel Brannon hissed, "Oh God."

"Nothing of the sort," whispered Daniel Brannon. "God has more time."

Daniel Brannon introduced the slender man, though it wasn't necessary. Reaching out the man took Amber's hand first. Then he turned to Justin. Both handshake and gaze were easy, yet focused. The man considered Justin thoughtfully and then he smiled.

"I enjoyed your speech a lot more than mine," he said.

"Thank you, sir."

Seriousness swam into the man's steady eyes.

"I had a mother who did everything for us," he said.

"I did too. We're both very lucky, sir."

"Yes we are. And my mother would have told you not to call me 'sir' until I earned your respect. I also had to earn hers, and it took me quite some time. She paddled my backside regularly, and more times than I care to say. Though I fear that method of behavior modification has gone out of style."

Daniel Brannon saw the stiffness spill from the boy, though the girl still stood rigid.

"I would have liked your mother," Justin said.

"It couldn't be helped," said the President. "I've heard very good things about you. We share a love of the oceans." The President touched the back of his neck gingerly. "Redder than a Jersey tomato. Just came back from a week's getaway on Kauai. Spent as much time as I was allowed to snorkeling. Forgot about the sun at my back."

"I've got Irish skin too."

"Ah. I knew there was something else I liked about you."

An aide nodded. The President gave the young couple a smile and a parting comment. The smile was genuine, he had liked them both instantly, but already he wasn't even sure what he had said. Tonight he was meeting with several of his biggest contributors, and his mind had already moved on. He hated this part, but it had become part of his fabric. Politics and power were thieves; they often stole the things that mattered.

That night, after he made love to his wife and just before he fell asleep, the boy drifted through his mind again and then he was gone.

That night Amber gave a long dreamy exhale. Not for the first time.

"I shook the president's hand," she said.

"It seemed fair. He got to shake your hand."

"Stop it. I'm talking about the President of the United States."

"I'm talking about you."

"I don't think I'll wash it."

"So I'm doing the dishes."

They were in Amber's apartment. They had just finished eating. Amber shared the apartment with two roommates, but they were both out.

Slouched in his chair, Justin said, "I wonder who washes the President's dishes."

She had never given it thought. It was just like Justin.

"Seeing as we live in a democracy I vote you do the dishes tonight, because one day you may not be doing them."

"I believe I scheduled a meeting."

Amber smoothed her blouse. Chemise accentuated her breasts.

"I believe I currently wield the power of executive veto."

Justin scraped back his chair.

"Trumped," he said, gathering up the plates. "By a beautiful tyrant."

They washed the dishes together. Since they met, they had done almost everything together. Amber Giles was a junior, majoring in International Relations. When they first met, she had been a sophomore at the University of Chicago and Justin was a high school senior, albeit at the very tail end of his senior year. The instant they were introduced, the proper part of her had said he was too young, and her heart had galloped and heat had rushed to unexpected places and she had, thankfully, discarded the calendar. They had met while working on the mayor's re-election campaign. One of the city's movers and shakers – Chicago Magazine had listed Wyatt Mahoney among the city's top twenty influential people – Justin's father had introduced Justin directly to the mayor. Amber had worked for Mayor Albright for four months before she and the mayor met, and Justin had made the introduction. It would have been profoundly annoying if Justin hadn't been so sweet and disarming. And pleasing to look at.

She looked at him now. He washed the dishes meticulously, wholly focused. She knew every inch of his body now, though she was up for exploring again and again on the moonshot that there was something she had missed. She knew almost everything about his life too; but a part of him remained unreachable. She couldn't put her finger on it. It wasn't that he kept it from her; she felt more as if it was just that she didn't know what to ask. More than once, she had almost brought it up, they talked about everything, but in the end she had opted to simply enjoy the mystery. In her previous relationships mystery had dissolved quickly, and, in short order, so had the relationship. He didn't keep secrets, at least not as far as she could tell. Whatever she asked him, he answered fully. It was something more mysterious. It was as if part of him existed beyond the common pall, on a plane few in this world reached, even if they wanted to. Even if he helped them along. She didn't find this frustrating. She found it entrancing, and when she let the thought of his otherworldliness enter her head as he moved inside her in a very real way, almost inevitably she was wracked by orgasms. Suffice to say, the thought of his differences entered her head as regularly as Justin entered her. In a weak moment, she had made the mistake of telling her roommates. Behind his back, they now called him The Sure Thing. Behind his back, she also saw the way they watched him.

He passed her a plate, which she nearly dropped.

"Still daydreaming about the President?" he asked.

"Power is an aphrodisiac. He's also a handsome man."

"You're making me jealous."

"You're making you jealous."

"Cheap psychology. And absolutely true."

She dried the plate and put it in the cabinet over her head. The apartment was small at every turn; including kitchen counter space that didn't allow room for a drying rack.

Justin handed her another plate.

"Juggle this one too?"

"Ha. Ha." She circled the dish with the towel. "Sometimes I get tired of this apartment. It's like living in a Hobbit-hole."

"I can think of at least two plusses right off the top of my head."

"Pray tell, Mr. Optimist."

"A small bed. And you'll be good at living on a boat."

She gave the Chef's knife purposeful consideration.

"You know, too much optimism is annoying."

"I'll dry that," Justin said, taking the knife.

She saw now that he was stooped slightly, and he looked pale.

She slipped into her best Irish brogue.

"Mother Mary and Joseph. I believe you're actually tired, Mr. Mahoney."

"Closer to wiped."

"How can you be wiped? You met *history*. Or can it be that domestic life is starting to wear on you? Maybe now you're only interested in circulating in the halls of power. Having someone else do your dishes. Having young girls swear to never wash their hands. No more Hobbit habitation and humdrum."

Justin gave her a somber look.

"We need to talk," he said.

"You need to keep washing, or we'll still be standing here in the morning."

"You know, you'd make a good president. I could be your first man."

She put down the dish towel. Her somber look was genuine. Taking his face in her hands she kissed him.

"You were," she said.

Justin fell asleep sitting up on the couch. Granted they were watching "The Big Bang Theory;" her favorite show, but not his. He hadn't watched television growing up and he wasn't hankering to make up for it. He always sat with her, watched a few minutes of whatever she was watching, and then got up and went hunting for a magazine or a book. Eventually – inevitably -- she felt guilty about watching TV and turned it off. He really could be annoying.

When she turned the TV off, the quiet didn't wake him. She went into the kitchen and poured herself a glass of water. Stephanie and Beth had already come tip toeing in and gone to bed, though Beth had first danced seductively for the benefit of her softly breathing boyfriend. Beth was a slim-waisted philosophy major with a minor in dance. Amber had found herself mildly aroused.

Elbows resting on the kitchen counter, she watched him sleep. He often slept fitfully. He twitched and often murmured, and sometimes he cried out softly. When he did, she always pulled him close.

Tonight he slept soundlessly, Terror curled on his lap. The calico despised humanity. In the four years since she had rescued the disinterested cat from the shelter, Terror had managed to avoid almost all comers; an exception being Beth's bratty six-year-old niece who had somehow surprised the usually alert cat. Scooping Terror up, Miss Bratty Niece had been rewarded with a ferocious clawing. The first time Justin came to the apartment, Terror had padded out of the bedroom and hopped up on his lap.

Walking over to the couch, she stood looking down at her boyfriend and her cat.

Both of them ignored her.

"Well," she said, "aren't you an exclusive little bitch?"

She gently shook Justin's shoulder.

"I'd like you to go to bed with *me*."

His eyes regarded her as if they were in mid-conversation. That was weird too.

"It's temptation I can't resist, but I have to. I've got practice in the morning."

He swam on the swim team. Distance freestyle. Amber knew nothing about swimming, and cared even less, but she loved watching him swim. He didn't so much swim through the water as meld with it, a human current. He and his teammates didn't look bad soaking wet either. Stephanie and Beth had attended several meets too.

She leaned down and nibbled his ear. Her hand kneaded gently.

"I don't mind being woken up."

"Mmmmmmmmmm. You'll feel differently at five. And you never fall back to sleep."

He was right. And suddenly she was exhausted. She didn't have a class tomorrow until noon. It would be nice to sleep in.

She gave him a parting squeeze and stood up.

"Thanks for the cold shower. I hate that you're so considerate."

Justin placed Terror on the floor. The calico stood there, straight-legged and miffed.

Justin stood and kissed her. His kisses were so soft until they weren't supposed to be.

"It's also true I often think of my own selfish needs," he said.

She wanted him to stay again.

"My favorite times," she said, but he was already walking to the door, bending to scoop up the backpack leaning against the closet door.

He turned.

"Hey. Did Stephanie and Beth come in?"

"You didn't see them?"

"No."

"Too bad."

He gave her that curious, amused look she loved.

He stood smiling, the backpack dangling from his hand.

"The President got to meet you," he said. "That's two of us who won't be able to sleep. See you tomorrow."

The world always felt a little empty after he left. She had never thought of herself as dependent, but there it was.

She put the last few things away and then she brushed her teeth. When she came back out to the living room to turn off the lights, Terror was sprawled against the front door.

"Fine. Pine out here if you like him so much."

She was sliding into dreams when Terror hopped up on the bed. Groggily reaching out, she stroked the calico.

"I understand," she murmured.

That night Justin dreamed too. It was the same dream, again and again, nearly exact in its myriad details. The night sea was slick with oil, the oil burning in choking flames. The men in the water shouted for God, their wives, their lovers, their children. They cursed their superiors. They cursed God. And then a man cried apology. Always, in the dream, it took a long moment to locate him. Always, in the dream, he was sitting on top of a toilet, bobbing clear of the water; a hunched shadow, backlit by flames, like the top of a toadstool. The ocean surface was calm. The toilet rocked slightly, but by some miracle the man kept his place. Maybe it was through sheer will. All about him, ragged toothed forms slid through the water. Along with the shouting there were hideous screams, and the jarring concussion of cartilage against flesh.

The man's face was charred black. It made his eyes appear huge, and those eyes held the glow of a child's discovery.

The man spoke to someone Justin could not see.

"I'm on the crapper," he said.

He wore a formerly white apron. There was a ragged hole at his left shoulder where his arm had been.

"I'm truly sorry for this mess," he said.

Things blazed. The air was heavy with the smell of diesel and smoldering metal. Smoke, acrid and nauseating, ran low across the water. Men continued to scream. Twenty miles away, beneath the dark water, coral lay in rubble piles and fish swam disoriented.

The man's face now held unfathomable sadness as he spoke to something in the darkness.

"Why do we do it? And it won't end here. We'll keep plugging away. Bang, bang. You're dead, and you're dead, and you're dead. I don't know why. Did you see all the fish?"

Here only the sharks swam. The fish floated wide-eyed. The blazing sea cooked them.

"We can't just go alone. The whole damn ship has to go down."

But the man didn't go down. Slowly he was lifted from the toilet, by what Justin never saw, though he knew now what was doing the lifting. The flaming sea, the smell of diesel and burning flesh, the screams of men being eaten, they fell away.

The man rose toward the sickle moon as if he were an offering.

Justin woke in the darkness. Todd Sangstrom snored; a measured, peaceful sound, like waves running up and retreating.

Justin lay quietly. He always woke from the dream feeling the same way. Profound sadness, run through with light-footed hope. Always contrary emotions. Always linked.

He wished his mom had had the dream, but she never did.

BYRON BAY, AUSTRALIA.

The dolphin's remains washed ashore two miles south of Lacey Goodenall's bungalow.

When Paul Wiley called, Lacey was sitting cross-legged on her front porch, watching the wind continue to gnaw the ocean ragged. Froth and whitecaps ran to the horizon. It was a Winslow Homer painting, framed by a heap of black-bottomed clouds and an insignificant string of sandy beach. Lacey breathed deep. She wasn't religious but she had a religion.

Between the wind and the snapping prayer flags, she almost didn't hear the phone. Her first inclination (often the right one) was to ignore it. Sunrise and sunset were her times, but 6am calls were generally not trivial, and when she looked down she saw Moe looking up at her. Paul Wiley loved the Three Stooges. Most people took themselves far too seriously, but Paul Wiley wasn't one of them. He was, however, captain of the Byron Bay Surf Lifesavers.

He was deadly serious now.

"Clean in half," Paul said. "Neater than a cleaver. Has to be your shark. Black Betty."

Whoa, Black Betty (Bam-ba-Lam)
Whoa, Black Betty (Bam-ba-Lam)

Black betty had a child (bam-A-lam)
The damn thing gone wild (bam-A-lam)

Lacey Goodenall watched the sun wrestle free of the storm-tossed horizon. The ocean leapt and laughed. So much unspooling beneath the veiled surface. Man would never know.

"I'll be down," she said.

It only took fifteen minutes to get to the beach, but by the time Lacey arrived a small crowd had already gathered. Small, quite literally. The school bus stop was beside the road that paralleled the beach. Two dozen children stood in a clump, heads of hair leaping in various directions. *Christ almighty*, thought Lacey. *Over four thousand kilometers of coastline and there you fucking go.*

She walked through the children as if they were a field of grass.

Paul Wiley, lifesaving captain, was doing his best to maintain order, but Paul was no teacher. The children, whom Lacey guessed ranged in age from eight to twelve, jumped about, shouting and poking at the carcass. The boys made chomping motions with their mouths and chased the girls who screamed delighted piercing screams.

"I see you have everything under control," she said.

Paul rolled his eyes in defeat.

"I think I'd rather face your pointer."

The dolphin's organs had spilled out into the sand in a brown slush.

A particularly noxious mop-haired boy bent to the sand and shouted, "Look! It's the heart!"

Next the boy looked at her.

This time he pointed.

"You're the shark lady! I saw you on TV!"

"You should read books instead."

She spoke quietly. Half the children fell silent to listen.

It wasn't the response he was looking for.

"You're the shark lady!" he shouted again.

Lacey looked about. The rest of the children were listening now. She saw the looks of recognition. Other mouths pursed to shout.

"And one day you'll be a shark's meal," she said pleasantly.

The boy swallowed his tongue, retrieved it, and managed a single word.

"Uh?"

"I said, 'One day you'll be a shark's meal.'"

The boy looked like he might cry. Many small jaws hung loose. Even Paul Wiley looked surprised.

"How do you know that?" the boy asked, with far more fear than challenge.

"Because I'm the shark lady."

Turning her back on the lot of them, she crouched to examine the carcass. One single bite. It was Betty.

"I don't want to be eaten."

She had forgotten about the brat.

She turned and regarded the boy.

"Well then, you should walk up to the bus stop. You should go to school, and pay attention to your lessons. You should ride the bus home and tell your parents they should move to Ayers Rock. Then maybe you'll get eaten by a dingo instead of a white shark."

"You're lying."

The boy was crying now, but she had to give him credit, he had spunk.

"Yes I am. Experts do that sometimes too. But you can never be certain of anything. Perhaps you might forget those atrocious newscasts, but you should remember that." She looked up at Paul Wiley. "Captain Wiley, perhaps you would do me a favor and escort this attentive group back to the stop."

When Paul returned he said, "Should we close the beaches?"

"You could, but we both know she's likely long gone. And no one would go swimming on a day like today."

"How do you know that?"

"I wouldn't swim on a day like today."

"I need a better reason."

Captain Paul Wiley looked a little like the defiant boy. It was the rare person who could accept being told to bugger off.

She eased off a little.

"She's been tagged now for four months, Paul. In all the time we've been tracking her she has never stayed in one place for more than two hours. If the readings are correct, she roams a section of ocean roughly the size of eastern Australia."

"Maybe. But you tagged her two miles from here."

That was true. It had been the serenest of days, a bright blue ocean topped by a child's yellow crayon sun. They had spotted the shark on the fathometer, an impossibly large thumb-like smudge. And then she had risen beside the boat as if offering herself up to the dart and the tag. Lacey Goodenall had traveled the globe studying sharks. It was the second biggest white pointer she had ever seen. Off Mexico's Guadalupe Island, a female had passed beside their 30-foot research vessel. It had stretched far more than half the length of the boat. The stunned crew had put the shark at close to 20 feet. Lacey Goodenall had agreed, and she was no exaggerator. If pressed, Lacey might say Black Betty measured in at 18 feet.

"We did. And then she promptly swam down to just above Sydney."

Sydney was roughly 600 kilometers to the south.

"Well now she's swum back from wherever the hell she was," said Paul.

Lacey liked Paul Wiley. He was a straightforward bloke who had spent his life around the sea. They raced against each other in local surf ski competitions. Paul was one of New South Wales' best paddlers. She had beaten him once when he was coming down with strep throat. But she was eight years younger and time was on her side. She reminded him of this constantly.

"Well then, maybe you can make up your own mind about closing the beaches," she said.

Paul Wiley sighed.

"You probably shouldn't have done that, Lacey."

"Counseled you to take responsibility?"

"You know what I mean. Given that boy the willies."

"He was a brat. And the rest of the lot with him."

Paul gave her a resigned smile.

"I agree, but they were raised by brats and ten minutes after that boy gets home, those brats will be calling my office, frothing about child abuse and telling me they'll have me fired."

"It pays to have an unlisted number."

"Not if you're a public servant."

"We coddle children too much these days."

Paul Wiley stayed silent. Anything else was brought equivalent results.

Lacey stood. There was nothing more to be examined or surmised. Death was usually like that.

"Do you always have an answer, Lacey?"

"I do this time. No. May I ask a favor of you?"

"You'd like me to circulate your home phone number?"

Paul Wiley had spunk too.

She smiled.

"I'd like you to remove this carcass as quickly as possible. It will only add to the ridiculous surmise."

Paul nodded.

"Right again," he said. "I'll phone the boys at Public Works. I think they're listed."

THE SEA.

The chambered nautilus, a cephalopod, is a relative of squid, octopus and cuttlefish. Unlike its relatives, the nautilus has an external shell. It inhabits ocean waters close to the sea floor during the day, migrating to shallower water at night in search of prey. Food is captured by its retractable tentacles and passed to the mouth, where a beak-like jaw tears it into pieces. Considered a "living fossil", the chambered nautilus has been traced back 500 million years to a time before dinosaurs roamed the earth.

So your scientists have gleaned. Indelible facts.

But there are many things you don't know.

Let's start with this.

The shell of an adult nautilus measures roughly 8 to 10 inches in diameter. Unlike most other cephalopods that have a short life span, the chambered nautilus can live 16 or more years.

These facts, you might reconsider.

My offspring, they are testing themselves. I can feel their burgeoning excitement. It is exciting to me. Unfettered youth. What is your expression for this? Ah, yes. They are feeling their oats. Oh yes they are.

The large female is the most aggressive of the brood. I know my offspring without looking at them, but they harbor physical differences. Should you ever get close enough, and your hope is you will not, you would see this female has a distinctive mark at the apex of her shell, just back from the mantle. The first of the dark brown stripes that run along her shell like wavering ripples, it is not a stripe like the others. It is thinner and hooked. It resembles a crescent moon. Or a sickle. This female, she is already far quicker and stronger than her siblings. She took the white shark. She took the pirates too. Experiments. Conclusion? Now she knows those efforts were child's play.

I worry about her a little. I can reach into the thoughts of others, including my own flesh and blood. But her thoughts are hard to fathom. They are like a figure in the fog; there, but without clearly delineated expression, and sometimes only the vaguest form. The others of my brood, I understand them clearly. But this one, no.

This world holds mysteries for me too.

MONTEREY, CALIFORNIA.

The two men sat in the dark room in the bowels of the world-renowned aquarium. Two floors above, throngs of tourists wandered among the exhibits, young and old alike standing mesmerized before the floor-to-ceiling sheets of Plexiglas, marveling at the oceans' pageantries and sometimes wondering about lunch.

The two men were silent. Collectively they had spent 70 years studying the deep seas.

"Run it again," the one said.

Again the squid swarmed the deep sea submersible, the unmanned five-foot sub twisting to and fro in the grainy violence. The video wasn't long; two minutes at most.

When it ended, silence resumed again.

The one man spoke to himself.

"Dosidicus gigas," he said.

"Not unusual behavior on certain fronts," said the other man.

"No."

They spoke as if reassuring themselves.

"Has anyone else seen this?"

"Not yet."

"A few of them are bigger than any Humboldt squid I've ever seen."

The other man nodded. *Brawn and brains.* His hands kneaded the edge of the chair.

Aloud he said, "There's a lot of commotion. It's hard to see. Run it again, as slowly as you can."

They both knew nothing would change.

The man with the laptop clicked out the appropriate instructions, and sat back.

"Ninety-five percent of the ocean's depths are unexplored," he said.

It was their joke. Their go-to sound bite. They hauled it out every time they gave a public talk or a media interview. Like a club to whop people over the head, help them understand that there are so many things about the ocean we don't yet know. May never know.

This time neither of them smiled.

The dark silhouettes collided with the sub like frenzied torpedoes. Ink and tentacles filled the screen. The one man had grown up in Iowa, the son of a farmer. The slow-motion tentacles reminded him of waving wheat. They waved, curled, twisted.

"There," he said without enthusiasm.

"Uh-huh."

Two floors above, toilets flushed. Water ran through pipes. Upstairs people were staring at jellyfish and buying rubber squids.

The one man sighed.

"I don't think there's much doubt."

"No."

"The sub flooded. They won't get it back."

"Stroke of luck the camera made it to the surface intact," the one man said unconvincingly.

The two men knew each other well.

"What now?"

"We have to tell somebody. Sooner rather than later."

"Preferably before they learn to walk."

Neither man laughed.

That night at dinner the one man ate spaghetti with homemade sauce. Spaghetti was Tom Browning's favorite meal. His wife made a sauce that was probably the closest he would come to heaven. He ate without tasting. He was an animated man, with a wicked sense of humor. He ate in silence. He was vaguely aware of his wife and two young daughters watching him with concern, but it was the video that ran in his mind, the large squid holding the submersible relatively still as its smaller companion worked the last bolt off the glass plate.

He heard a chair scrape.

"Daddy," his youngest daughter said, "let's go play."

He pushed his own chair back.

Why not? he thought. *It's what we've been doing the whole time.*

THE SEA.

Ah, the Humboldt squid. Poster child of adaptation and change. Moving farther afield as warming oceans create larger low-oxygen zones in the deeps where they once ably lived. Hunting now in tightly coordinated groups, communicating with flashing colors new to them and us.

But not always playing as a team.

As the camera drifted up and away from the ruined submersible, bobbling up slowly through the shadowy water column, the large squid turned on its smaller companion, tearing it to pieces. Within seconds intellectual advancement is naught but swirling blood and flesh bits.

My rudimentary cousin.

And so, ruder.

Too rudimentary to recognize the cutting of its own throat.

But evolution will proceed.

Perhaps the next time intelligence will win the day.

One last thing. Something your scientists did not observe. After all, observation requires comprehension.

It was not luck that saw the camera remain intact.

They let it go.

Allowing you yet another discovery.

KOROR, PALAU.

When Ernan came down to the Wendell Holmes, Marty was up on the bridge, looking out to the harbor mouth and the sparkling blue beyond, wondering again what in the hell he'd gotten himself into. Metallic banging echoed from the galley, Mongkol exercising creative plumbing repair. Kurt Cobain, perhaps unhappy with the repairs, screamed in anguish.

The man with Ernan was shirtless. He was not quite short enough to be a dwarf. Perhaps this made it easier to cover almost every inch of his frame in tattoos. He had bright red hair, left moppy on top and cut crewcut flat on the sides. From up on the bridge it looked as if some furry animal had taken up residence atop the man's head.

"Permission to come aboard, Captain?"

Ernan's request sounded silly in Marty's ears -- he wasn't even captain of his own fate – but he knew that Ernan, though smiling, was serious.

"Permission granted. This boat can't go anywhere without you."

"Not anymore," said Ernan, taking a long step aboard.

Marty saw now that the Wendell Holmes had drifted farther from the dock than normal. He had tied the lines and done a poor job of it.

Marty saw that the short man could not bridge the gap. There was a moment of discomfiting embarrassment, at least on the part of Ernan and Marty. The tattooed man did not bother. Placing his feet together, he energetically swung his arms three times and, in one explosive leap, performed a standing broad jump that left him standing, both feet perfectly aligned, on the stern deck.

When Marty came down the ladder, both men were laughing.

The tattooed man regarded him with an open face. His head was cocked slightly to the side, in a questioning fashion.

"You make me work before I even start working," he said. "My first task will be to teach you to tie off your own lines properly."

The man was dark-skinned, perhaps Filipino like Ernan, and hard with muscle. He looked like a piece of scrimshaw come to life. Marty wondered if a long ago whaling ancestor had ferried brilliant red hair.

The man bounced two fingers off the top of his mop, as if just remembering a forgotten grocery item.

"A long ago Basque gene reasserting its dominance. Other than a hankering for tongue, it is all that remains of my European ancestors."

Ernan said, "This is Fury Curtaine. I am hoping you will hire him as our chief dive guide and first mate. I believe he is highly qualified on every front but one. This is Marty Haruo. "

Fury Curtaine extended a rough hand. The man's grip fell just short of pain.

"Now that appearances are behind us, you wonder about the name. In trying valiantly for a daughter, my parents sired thirteen sons. I am lucky thirteen. By then, their creativity was exhausted. My mother named me after her favorite car."

"Plymouth Fury," said Marty.

Fury nodded approvingly.

"Enough to convince me to sign on with you," he said.

Koror was a small place. A man like this did not escape notice. Marty had never seen him before.

"You know the local waters?"

"As well as a man can after thirty years. There is always more to learn."

"How long have you been diving?"

"Fifteen years. Preceded by five years of free diving. Spear fishing. Not recreation. Thirteen children are a strain on the larder."

"You are a certified diver?"

"Not officially."

"A small matter," Marty said, and kicked himself mentally.

Fury Curtaine's eyebrows bobbed once.

"Fury was born to the water," said Ernan. "I know only one other waterman as equally gifted."

"I would like to meet him," Fury said.

"You may," said Ernan.

The two men waited expectantly.

Marty realized the banging had stopped. Mongkol had also turned the music off.

Marty remembered he was in charge. Sink or swim.

"Ernan vouches for you. Do you have other references?"

The two men exchanged a look.

"None trustworthy," Fury said.

"None trustworthy?"

"A man should know his friends."

Marty gave up.

"Oh, forget it. If Ernan is willing to stick his neck out for you, that's good enough for me. You're hired. On a trial basis."

Fury Curtaine clapped his hands and did a small jig.

When his feet stilled, he smiled up at Marty.

"Improvised Basque dance. Thank you. The opportunity is all I require."

"Do you have any questions?" Marty asked.

"Just one. Are meals included? I should mention that, for a smaller person, I have a considerable appetite."

"Meals are provided during working hours. It's not likely, but that policy could change."

The man stood up straighter. Marty recognized it as a salute.

"Understood," said Fury Curtaine. "I will fix the lines. I will go home and fetch my gear. I will return in two days. I will eat something before I arrive."

"Where is home?"

"Angaur."

Marty knew the island. The residents were a fiercely independent lot. He had only made a handful of landings there, almost always for emergencies.

"Will you need help finding a place to live?"

"I have secured a place."

"Well. That was forward thinking."

Fury accepted the accolade without comment.

"You have an excellent reputation as a pilot," Fury said. "Ernan and I hope to one day make you an equivalent ship's captain."

Marty couldn't stop the smile.

"I now share the similar hope."

"I will make a fine teacher."

"And I will see that our food supply is adequately stocked. Over the short-term."

"Understood."

After the man left, Marty turned to Ernan.

"Should I feel like I was railroaded?"

Ernan grinned.

"Fury is assertive. Perhaps because he is smaller. Perhaps because he is number thirteen."

"It's effective. How do you know him?"

"I don't."

Marty actually took a small step back.

"You don't know him?"

"No. Mongkol recommended him. They are friends."

"Oh Lord."

"I think we both agree that Mongkol is a man of few words. And so fewer good words."

"My kingdom for a shred of sanity aboard this boat."

"This boat *is* your kingdom."

"Perhaps then I should have your head. Lordy. Please, Ernan. Just tell me one thing."

"What is that?"

"They don't share the same taste in music."

When Fury Curtaine returned to the Wendell Holmes two days later, Mongkol looked up from his lunch break smoke, barked out a single laugh and trotted down the dock to take the small man's bag. Before he did, the two men exchanged a byzantine series of fist bumps and finger twinings.

Mongkol was still grinning broadly as the two men walked back toward the Wendell Holmes.

Watching from the stern, Marty turned to Ernan.

"One reference, and he's not trustworthy."

"It's why you're in charge," said Ernan.

"It's why my stomach aches."

Mongkol stepped on board. Fury stopped at the edge of the dock and looked up to the bridge.

"Permission to come on board, Captain."

"Permission granted." Leaning toward Ernan, Marty said, "When you get him alone, tell him to stop that."

Fury was certified within the week. When it was done, the instructor, a famously finicky German expat, drew Marty aside.

"I have had few defter students," the German said. "I have never seen anything like him in the water."

Marty savored his own sigh of relief.

"Well then, I suspect he'll make a good dive guide."

"I'll hire him if you don't," the German said.

Six divers signed on for their inaugural charter. A full boat was twenty, but Cedar had never taken a full boat, turning down money in favor of elbow room, one of the reasons word of her dive charters had spread throughout the Pacific and points beyond. Still, six was a disappointment. When one of the divers, a regular customer of Cedar's, came on board in the morning, Marty heard him mumble, "Welcome to the island of misfit toys."

When Ernan guided the Wendell Holmes into her berth that afternoon, all the divers had already signed on for the following day.

After the tanks were refilled and everything was washed down and tucked away, Marty motioned Fury over.

"Your internship is complete. You're hired."

Fury struggled to maintain a poker face.

"I am not overly tall, and I am not overly small. It is not such a bad thing to be endowed with neither blessing nor curse."

"Sometimes we don't know our own blessings," said Marty. "You're a beautiful diver. And I am not."

"No, you are not. You dive as if pithed."

It felt good to laugh.

"I'm glad you're not worried about job security," said Marty. "And I wholeheartedly agree. I fear I don't instill faith in our customers. Another reason I'm glad you stole the show today."

"You are a fine pilot, and you will become an equally superior boat captain. The diving is more uncertain."

"Apparently I can trust you to be honest."

"It's easier," said Fury.

The four of them celebrated the re-launch of their business over dinner that night. Situated in the heart of Koror between a laundromat and an Internet café, Rice was Cedar's favorite Thai restaurant. Coincidentally, it was owned by Mr. and Mrs. Na Songkhla. The restaurant's name was taken from their son's single utterance when they had consulted him regarding possible names for their new enterprise. Even at six, Mongkol had been a man of few words.

Fury ate his fill, and then he ate what remained on Marty and Ernan's plates. He stopped short of Monkol's plate. Mongkol had ordered fruit bat soup. When the bowl arrived, he had surveyed the bat. Its head resembled a miniature dog, the teeth bared. The bat was blackened and slightly curled, like a dead spider. The bat was whole. Marty tried not to think of Jonathan.

Before taking up spoon and knife, Mongkol had spoken solemnly.

"In Tonga you could not eat a fruit bat. All the fruit bats in Tonga belong to the king."

It was something like a prayer, and long, and it had left them all a bit stunned.

In the wake of that deluge, Mongkol said nothing more until dinner's end. When his father came to the table, Mongkol nodded at Fury.

"Tua Guan, please father. Double serving."

Fury ate his dessert and Mongkol's too.

Mongkol lived with his family in a spice marinated apartment above the restaurant. When they left, Mongkol had already gone back to the kitchen to help with the closing. Outside the restaurant, Fury took his leave. Marty didn't know where he was staying, and Fury hadn't said.

Marty and Ernan watched Fury sway down the street.

"Is there a chance he might explode?" Marty asked.

"Wise to keep our distance," Ernan said.

"Do you know where he's living?"

"No. I offered him a couch at my home, but he said he had found something."

"Well I hope it's close," said Marty. "I'm surprised he can walk. That was inspirational. I've got indigestion just from watching."

"He's already looking ahead to breakfast."

"Thank you for bringing him to me."

"You're welcome, Captain, but as I said it was Mongkol's doing."

They stood beside a pole. A naked yellow bulb, fixed at the top with duct tape, illuminated Marty's smile.

"Our friend Mongkol waxed eloquent tonight," Marty said.

"Apparently he appreciates the gift of fruit bat soup."

"A man is wise to appreciate his gifts. I could not have a better crew."

The moon hovered silent above the bulb.

Neither man looked at the other.

Cedar stood with them.

Before bed, Marty went up to the bow.

The moon had disappeared behind the clouds.

Marty spoke softly to the dark velvet sky.

"Well that's day one, behind us. I think it went pretty well, Cedar. There are still plenty of kinks, but once I straighten myself out we should be good to go."

Opening the door to the cabin, Marty knew how it felt to be Fury.

His stomach felt empty.

The next afternoon, Marty sent Justin an e-mail.

We are up and running with a full crew. Hired a new crew member I think you'll like. Two trips, both successful. But know there is always a spot for you. Temporary only. I promised your mother you would make something of your life.

It was midnight in Chicago, but a response came back immediately.

I never doubted you. And remember, I made the same promise to Mom. It's exactly why I'll be back.

Marty stared at the words on the screen. It was always so hard to believe. In his childhood, they had communicated between islands via ham radio. He had seen that crackling communication as a miracle. Now progress had ushered them to this unimaginably bright place. But it had also ushered them to places equally bleak.

Marty hesitated and then he typed back.

Are you still having the dreams?

Yes.

Marty waited. He knew the boy. Now the man.

The words were deceptively simple. Like the boy. To Marty, he would always be Cedar's child.

Our work has just started. And I have to come back. We both know why.

Marty slept fitfully. They were up and running, it was true, but each day, he knew, would bring a new host of concerns. Cedar had called it "my very own black hole." And there was something else, something beyond the need to order new dive tanks, and beef up their marketing and have Mongkol see to that pinging. Laying in the berth, warm night oozing through the porthole, Marty felt the faintest drumbeat behind his temple, almost imperceptible, yet repeated again and again. Marty knew the drumbeat possessed a rhythm and the rhythm contained a message.

Just as he knew he would never hear it.

THE SEA.

The man who swims like a tumbleweed is back. And there are others with him who possess promise. The unsung movers of stones. But will the quiet ones you never see be enough to overcome the obstacles? You are seven billion and counting. You could be a collective army of light. But you are not. Yours is an army of darkness, self-serving and ignorant, storming forward blindly to exterminate yourselves and possibly the rest of us with you.

The man on the toilet seat, a ragged hole in place of his arm, he saw things clearly.

The ship, it is going down with all hands.

Your ship, it drifts listlessly, without direction, without cooperation. You are black. You are white. You are Christian. You are Muslim.

You are laughable. When the fish are gone and the oceans are warm, polluted mass, it will be the end for all of you.

Then, finally, you will be together, crying like lost children.

BYRON BAY, AUSTRALIA.

Lacey Goodenall picked up the phone.

A woman's pleasant voice said, "We have something that may be yours. A tag our son found on the beach."

"How did you get my number?"

"We called the surf lifesaving station and a helpful gentleman named Paul Wiley gave it to us. I hope this isn't an intrusion."

"It would be, if you didn't have something that belongs to me." She reigned in her irritation. It was like choking down Brussel sprouts when she was a little girl. "Thank you for calling."

"It's our pleasure," the woman said, her relief rolling clearly down the line. "You can stop by any time to get the tag. I work at home and I think we are neighbors. My son tells me it's some sort of tracking devi…"

"Thank you. I'll be there in five minutes," Lacey said, and hung up.

The house was eight minutes away, a faceless brick bungalow in a neighborhood of faceless brick bungalows. Lacey located the faded house number on the curb. Two battered skateboards lay wheels to the sky on the macadam drive. The wheels were gouged and chipped. A wetsuit, gaping hole on one underarm, hung from a drain spout at the corner of the garage.

As Lacey raised her hand to ring the doorbell the door opened.

The mop-haired boy regarded her warily.

"We meet again," said Lacey.

A pot banged in the kitchen. The voice from the phone shouted, "Andreeeeeeeew! Wash up! Tomato soup for lunch."

The boy had yet to blink. Lacey hadn't seen him take a breath either.

She decided to try.

"I like tomato soup."

"You said a shark would eat me."

"I also said experts are wrong, and it appears I am. Looks like you're the one about to do the eating."

"You can't stay."

He stood as tall as he could manage. She realized it was his home.

"Good," she said. "And you can't be afraid. Fear makes life less pleasant."

The kitchen voice called out again.

"Andrew?"

"At the door, Mum."

A woman's head poked around the corner. The face registered surprise. It brought the body, bustling to the door.

"My goodness, Andrew, why didn't you say we had a guest at the door?" The woman held a tea towel in her hand. The tea towel was inscribed with the words "It Must Be Happy Hour Somewhere." The woman had Andrew's wide brown eyes.

"Well, that was lightning quick." She extended the hand without the towel. "Margie Etheridge. And this young fellow who should have announced your arrival is Andrew."

"I know."

"You've met?"

"We have."

Margie Etheridge regarded her son fondly.

"Well now, aren't you the gregarious bellman?" She stepped aside. "Please. Come in. It's not often we have a celebrity guest. You're the shark lady."

Lacey glanced at Andrew Etheridge. The boy stood stone faced.

"I am."

"You're even prettier in real life." She waved the towel briskly, like a cheerleader on a sideline. "Smarts and looks. Some people have all the luck. I'm afraid being a mother has stolen away a few curves. We see you on the telly every time there's a …." People didn't like to say shark attack. As if speaking the words bumped them forward in the queue.

"I understand," said Lacey for the second time.

Margie Etheridge spoke in the rapid fire manner of someone who spent too much time with quiet.

"It's how we knew the tag belonged to you. Such a tiny thing, I might have thought it was a scrap, but Andrew didn't. Technology is so remarkable. Things getting smaller and smaller until you can't find them, like that movie where those kids have an adventure inside someone. I'm afraid technology has left me a little bit lost." She nodded to the boy. "Couldn't survive without him." Moving briskly to a bookshelf, she picked up a glass chalice. The mints had already been unceremoniously dumped. They were without wrapping. Lacey prayed they weren't sticky. "Here you go. I'm the farthest thing from a scientist, but I hope it is still of some value to you."

Margie Etheridge held the chalice out as if she were offering communion. Behind her, Lacey could see framed photographs of a man. There were five photos. He wasn't smiling in any of them.

Lacey reached into the chalice, trying to avoid the sticky ring at the mouth.

"It's very much valuable to me," she said. "Thank you."

"Actually, Andrew found it."

Lacey looked down at the poker face.

"Thank you, Andrew."

The refrigerator hummed. Outside, a bird squawked.

"Parrot," said Margie Etheridge. "Andrew!"

Andrew turned slowly toward his mother.

"When someone says thank you, *you* say, 'You're welcome'," said Margie Etheridge, not bothering to give him a chance. "Children can be so exasperating sometimes. He found your tag while he and his father were at the beach. They'd gone down for a surf. Well, my husband surfs, and Andrew rides a boogie board. Or at least he used to. Recently, out of the blue, he just up and stopped going in the water. Children's interests wax and wane like a gusting wind. These days he's our resident beachcomber. It's not the first glass of mints I've had to empty."

Lacey was coming to admire Andrew's newfound ability to stay silent. She reached into a jean pocket.

"I'd like to give you something as a thank you."

Margie Etheridge waved her hands as if warding off the sudden appearance of bees.

"No, no, no! We can't accept anything! A good deed is it's own reward! Besides, it was just a matter of good luck." She looked at Andrew fondly. "And keen eyes close to the ground. You would have done the same for us."

Lacey removed her hand from her pocket.

She regarded the boy.

"Thank you, Andrew."

"Uh-huh."

Margie Etheridge gave the edge of a willowy shoulder a loving nudge.

"Andrew."

"You are welcome."

Margie Etheridge gave her son a curious look and then turned to Lacey.

"Not sure what's gotten into him. More often than not, he's a good boy. A little excitable sometimes, but that's how boys are." She gave a cheerful shrug. "Childhood is often a mystery to me. I suppose I'm too far removed from my own to know better."

"Well I truly appreciate this."

"Again, it was nothing."

She just wanted to leave, but something stopped her as she turned to go. She told herself it was scientific curiosity.

"Did your son ever tell you about a dolphin?"

The mop was motionless.

Margie Etheridge put a finger to her dimpled chin. Her brow knit.

"A dolphin? No. No. I don't think so. Not a word about a dolphin. Why do you ask?"

Lacey smiled.

"Never mind," she said. "It's not important."

Driving home, she thought, *Rarely right you are.*

She examined the data on the tag immediately. Then she put it aside – she had already been alerted to one mistaken impression today – before carefully re-examining it that night.

The night's examination confirmed the morning's findings. Black Betty had plunged down more than 1,500 feet. This was not unheard of. White sharks made deep dives. But as she plummeted into the deeps, the temperature registered by her tag heated up. Even the boy – What was his name, Adam? – likely knew the ocean gets colder as you go deeper. There was only one explanation. The tag had been in the belly of another animal.

Lacey thought of the dolphin, surgically cleaved in half.

There is always a bigger fish.

The next afternoon, she went to the sporting goods store. A ratty-haired surfie who stank of weed helped her.

She left the box on the stoop without a note.

Arriving home from Wednesday bridge, Margie Etheridge picked up the box gingerly, then opened it on the living room table with equal care.

When Andrew came home from school, she made him drink a glass of milk first before she let him see the skateboard.

The last she saw of him he was looping smoothly down the driveway, quickly gaining speed as he shot out into the street.

"Lord protect your angels," Margie Etheridge whispered to the picture window, as the top of his mop furled back like a sail and he disappeared down the hill.

THE SEA.

The Humboldt squid moved like a flowing curtain in the lightening sea. The school numbered beyond counting. The enormous form rose slowly through their midst, wobbling comically like a child's failing top. A few of the more primitive squid threw themselves against the gleaming shell in futile attack. Half-brained, they slid away. The nautilus ignored all the collisions but one. Almost playfully, a tentacle reached out and secured the stunned squid. The precise application of pressure saw the squid regain its senses. Nearly the size of a man, the squid struggled mightily with no perceptible movement. The tentacle recommenced its syrupy cinching until the squid burst in a ball of blood.

The remaining squid cavorted.

In most geographic areas, at sundown the chambered nautilus migrates up into the shallows to seek prey, returning to the deep ocean before sunrise.

There have never been any hard and fast rules.

THE SEA.

My offspring, when sunrise comes, he does not descend into the depths. I believe he senses something. He is easier to read than the large female, but all is not clear. I do not think he blocks my probing intentionally, but a slight fog still obscures my vision. It has only been six months since they hatched. Already they are endowed with abilities beyond mine. He is only hiding himself from the world.

He drifts eastward as if following the rising sun.

He follows some spoor I cannot sense.

SURIGAO-LEYTE CHANNEL, PHILIPPINES.

It was quite the porno, the three deck hands agreed. It made them want to do things. They could not wait for this trip to end so they could return to their wives. They stood on the stern of the ferry, clasped in heat and diesel exhaust, naked, yearning women in fantastical positions prancing in their heads. They paid little attention to the passengers streaming over the grate and no attention to the raw sewage sloshing upon San Ricardo's shore, including a pig, gray, fly-covered and ready to burst. All three men wore broken sunglasses. Soon enough they would not need the sunglasses. Steam rose from the jungled shore. Overhead the dark clouds, already swollen like the pig, gathered the additional moisture.

A girl of fourteen came on board, walking with her family. She was strikingly beautiful; her sarong made her into a living hour glass.

One of the men spoke brazenly to her.

"The movies make me hungry," he said.

His friends laughed. The girl ignored him. Her father said nothing. The family walked past with their heads down. Most of the passengers were very poor. The crew could arbitrarily put them back ashore. In this case it would have been a profound stroke of luck.

The girl put her arm around her little brother and pulled him close. The three men watched her until she disappeared down the steps to the lower deck.

Smells rode the ferry. Marine oil, fish, rust, ruined vegetables, unwashed bodies, spices, salt water. Each smell was part of the whole and distinct. A diary of present and past. Like many ferries in the Philippines, the Princess Cleopatra was a castoff, discarded by a Hong Kong captain after she had seen her best years, and sold to a captain in Liloan town instead of rightly being hauled away and scrapped. The Princess Cleopatra was broken in her fixtures and greasy on her decks. Her hull was wrapped in rust stains and her engines labored like a woman in her third day of childbirth.

The captain of the Princess Cleopatra had been watching the sky with rising unease. He was not a man who cared about much, other than money, but on this afternoon sliding toward evening, something troubled his conscience. Up in the wheelhouse, he watched the people board. There were a few cars, but most of the passengers walked, and they were burdened with what appeared to be most of their worldly possessions. They shuffled their feet and stared down at the deck. Only the children looked about. It was always the same.

The captain tapped the console nervously, avoiding the ashtrays and empty Styrofoam cups.

Turning to his officer of the watch, a nephew of fifteen, he said, "Go below and hurry up the boarding."

The boy grumbled, it was cooler in the wheelhouse, but he went.

Two hours later the captain turned to the panic-stricken boy, now praying fervently and vomiting into a plastic bin.

"We must abandon ship," the captain said.

The captain clicked on the intercom and gave the order. He tried to sound calm, but he was not. According to the manifest sixty-four passengers were on board, but the manifest was for records people would see; he knew they carried at least twice that. There were three life rafts. Assuming they were sea worthy, they would each hold fifteen passengers at most. It was not fortuitous math. There were close to enough life vests for the number on the manifest. He hoped his crew would distribute them before they clambered into the rafts to save themselves, but he doubted it. He made a distress call to the Philippine Coast Guard. The man who answered fought his way out of a sound sleep.

The girl in the sarong was named Dalisay Andrada. Dalisay meant pure in Tagalog, and she was. Because she was also pretty, when she came up the ladder holding the hand of her little brother, a crewman noticed her and handed her two life jackets. It was the last of her luck.

Dalisay Andrada was also capable. It is no easy thing, affixing a life jacket to oneself and a terrified five-year-old on a yawing deck whose rubber matting has largely decayed away to slick metal. There was screaming. The screaming of the passengers, the screaming of the wind, the screaming of metal. It was black too. The Princess Cleopatra's generator had already failed. Two of the crew had torches, which, in their panic, they shined liberally in everyone's eyes.

She dragged her brother to the railing. They had lived their entire lives by the sea, but she had never seen waves like these.

Taking her brother by the shoulders, she turned him so he would not see the waves. Then she crouched in front of him.

"Liberato!" she shouted. "We are jumping into the sea!"

His eyes were beseeching.

He shook his head once.

She could not look into his eyes anymore. She concentrated on fastening the straps of his life vest. Her fear, and the pitching deck, caused her to yank them hard. Liberato began to wail.

"Mother!" he screamed.

She slapped him. She hadn't realized she was going to do it. He went silent.

She could see the crew wasn't going to get any of the rafts into the water.

"The ship is sinking! We have to jump!"

She wondered how they would climb the ship's railing, then jump far enough away from the ferry. The ship was now heeling mightily. If they did not jump far enough, and it rolled over on its side, they would be crushed.

A clanging rang in her head. Turning, she saw the unlatched gate swinging wildly. Grabbing the scruff of her brother's life jacket in one hand she used her other hand to drag them along the railing. Wedging the swinging gate between her leg and the railing, she did not hesitate.

"Jump!" she screamed.

Up in the wheelhouse, the captain saw the girl and the boy jump. He said a prayer for them and for himself, for he had made a terrible mistake. For a moment he saw the bloated pig in his mind, and then he was clambering down the steps, intent on saving himself. At the foot of the ladder he pushed an old woman to the ground.

When they struck the water, at first Dalisay Andrada thought she had gone blind with the impact. The night's blackness was suffocating, and then she felt a sandpaper scraping against her cheeks, and she realized she was floating face down, her life jacket nearly up over her head. Kicking wildly, she righted herself and yanked the life jacket down. The heaving waves rushed at her, but she only half saw them. Spinning wildly she located her brother. Miraculously he was right beside her.

A deep, guttural groaning and a chalkboard shrieking filled their ears. When Dalisay Andrada looked over her shoulder, at first she thought the mother of all waves was nearly on top of them. Then she saw the dripping barnacles and the lines of rivets like metallic stitching. Foamy water poured in white tongues off the deck and people poured with it.

"Swim!" she screamed, but her brother did not.

For the second time she yanked him, only this time she did it consciously and without care and he did not protest, but only bobbed behind her as she frantically kicked and clawed at the water, trying to pull them away from the toppling ferry. The waves lifted and dropped them, but Dalisay Andrada did not feel them. She was only aware of the water immediately about them. It scoffed at her clawing strokes and drew her steadily back toward the black wall that was not a wave.

The wave that saved their lives came out of nowhere. One moment the world was filled with the port side of the Princess Cleopatra; the next they were tumbling in a world of froth and blackness. When, at last, they bobbed to the surface together, choking and gasping, Dalisay Andrada saw that they had been blown clear. In that instant it was like being saved, and she relaxed and said a prayer of thanks.

But they were not saved. They drifted alone, moving away from the black outline of the ferry at a frightening speed, and then the ferry was gone. Away from the ferry, the enormous waves were not jumbled confusion, but a steady westward rolling. Sister and brother bobbed, their arms out at their sides like acrobats on a high wire. Their legs dangled in cool darkness.

Dalisay Andrada reached for her brother. Taking a loose strap hanging from her vest, she tied it to her brother's vest.

They drifted for a time. The wind stopped as if someone had thrown a switch. Creatures swam about them, occasionally bumping their legs.

For the first time since they had stood against the railing, she clearly saw her brother's eyes. They were calm, but they did not calm her, for they were vacant.

She knew she must talk to him.

"Liberato. Can you hear me?"

She thought she spoke calmly.

He responded in kind.

"Yes. I want mother and father."

It was the thought she had fought to force from her mind. It took all her will not to cry.

"They are here somewhere," she said.

"Where?"

"Somewhere on the water. We will be rescued. And then we will be together again."

"It is night."

His stubborn refusal almost made her angry.

Pulling him close, she kissed his forehead.

"It will be light soon," she said. "They will send ships and planes. They will find us easily."

It was strange, but the monstrous waves no longer frightened either of them. The waves came and went in perfectly spaced intervals – up and down, up and down. It was like being rocked in a giant's arms.

A chicken floated nearby, clucking idly.

"I'm thirsty," Liberato said.

"Do not drink the seawater."

"Why?"

"It will make you vomit."

"But I want water. I want mother and father."

She looked at him. He was so small on the sea.

Her determination was like a growing flame.

"Let's count the stars together," she said.

They did. The ocean rocked them, and the night assumed a touch of gray, and everything was fine until the pale tentacle slid quietly from the water, draping itself around the back of the boy's life vest like a pallid vine.

Liberato did not see it, but Dalisay Andrada did, and in that moment she began to lose her mind.

The tentacle rested just back from Liberato's shoulders, as if the little boy was its good friend.

Liberato felt its weight.

"Mother?"

The second tentacle shot from the water as if fired from a gun. It slapped across the boy's face with a force that saw his head angle oddly.

It covered his eyes, but Dalisay knew her brother no longer saw.

He disappeared beneath the water as quickly as the second tentacle had appeared, and then it was only the rocking waves and the lightening horizon.

When the foreign merchant ship MV Lara Venture pulled up alongside her, Dalisay Andrada regarded her rescuers in the same fashion she regarded the horizon.

In the ensuing years she grew more strikingly beautiful, but her mind never left the rocking waves.

THE SEA.

So many people in the water. Some are rescued. Some are never found.

It has always been this way.

Like picking grapes.

Large and small.

I sense something else. It is faint. Almost imperceptible, but present nonetheless. Regret. The nuanced emotions, it took me a millennia to develop them. Again, hope nudges its light over the horizon.

My offspring, he swims now with a touch of heaviness.

Remember when you were a child and you toyed with some helpless creature until finally play came to an end and you were left with nothing but an unalterable ending and a queer sense of doubt?

Then again, maybe you don't.

KOROR, PALAU.

Marty missed flying, but three weeks into the dive season he was already too busy -- and too exhausted -- to flee to the heavens. Two evenings a week, after everything was washed down, and the gear stowed for the following day, Marty would leave the Wendell Holmes to drive to the airstrip.

They took divers out five days a week; sometimes separate morning and afternoon trips, sometimes a full day. Each morning when the divers came on board, Marty told them Palau's story almost exactly as Cedar had. The islands, he explained, were situated at the confluence of several major currents, currents that delivered nutrients and animals from the rich waters of the Philippine Sea and New Guinea right to Palau's reefs. Some 1400 species of reef and pelagic fish called Palau home, not to mention roughly 700 different kinds of hard and soft corals. There were sheer fall-away walls festooned with Jackson Pollock corals and World War II wrecks resting in viscous silence. A diver's paradise in every sense of the word. This -- here he always paused to smile – was not a sales pitch, it was just the truth; besides, they were already on board.

Most of what he said was in the brochure, or on the website, but Marty told the story just the same. Not everyone bothered with research, and, at the least, he wanted their customers to leave with an appreciation for a special place. It was why Cedar had started the dive business in the first place. *We protect what we love.* He remembered the first time she told him that. They had made clench-teethed (sound travels briskly across water) love in the cabin on a Sunday afternoon. When he finally regained his breath, Cedar had nestled in the crook of his arm, her hair tickling the tip of his nose, and looked up at him with those sea green eyes.

We protect what we love.

In this, he had failed.

During the dive briefings, he also addressed Palau above the water. These facts he had known before he met Cedar. Palau was his home and he was proud of it. A tropical archipelago of Micronesian islands, the Republic of Palau (Belau to the locals) was scattered across 400 miles of Pacific Ocean southeast of the Philippines. It comprised some 340 islands, of which perhaps 20 were inhabited. Koror -- home to Internet cafes, wandering packs of Japanese and Taiwanese tourists, pot-holed streets and air-conditioned grocery stores and guest houses – was the big city. On the other inhabited islands you might select a box of Cocoa Pebbles or a large can of Spam from a three-sided shack fronted by a corrugated tin awning. Along with school lessons and medical supplies, he had reluctantly delivered those very cases of Cocoa Pebbles and Spam. Nutrition was not a Palauan priority, and no amount of discussion with the island chiefs could change that. The chiefs loved Cocoa Puffs too.

Divers the world over knew of Palau's signature dive spots: Siaes Tunnel, Chandelier Cave, Blue Holes and Blue Corner. Marty did not know them well, but he was learning. Until he had met the woman who changed his life, he had been afraid of the sea.

But Ernan and Fury knew the famed dive spots and many others as well, and Mongkol knew many of them too, although until now he had spent most of his time trying to strip them of life. On one of their first dive charters, after helping the clients – a Japanese tour group -- with their gear, Mongkol stepped, without explanation, into the zodiac tied off to the stern. Marty watched, puzzled, as Mongkol motored to a corner of the reef away from the divers, killed the engine and produced a net which he began tossing into the sea.

Marty had shouted from the bridge, but Mongkol had kept his back to him. When the man returned to the boat just before the divers, the floor of the zodiac was awash in flopping silver fish. Ernan and Fury were still underwater with the divers.

Marty had stood dumfounded on the stern looking down at boat full of fish.

In the zodiac, Mongkol worked to extricate a last few fish from the net.

Marty addressed the expanse of back.

"We are here to see the fish, not take them."

Mongkol stood with a fish in his hand. Braining it on the gunnel, he dropped it into the Styrofoam cooler at his feet.

"Japanese eat fish," he said.

Picking up another fish, he swung it against the gunnel.

Once Fury and Ernan were back on the boat, and the tanks had been switched and the Japanese given their chocolate chip cookies and orange slices, Marty pulled Fury aside.

"Tell him he cannot fish," said Marty.

"Tell you you cannot breathe."

"Tell him he cannot fish on my time."

"He will say it is his time."

"If he does, tell him all his time will be his time."

"That he will understand."

When the Japanese divers saw the cooler full of fish, they burst into restrained applause.

Back at the harbor, they formed a single file line along the dock. One by one they stepped to the cooler as if receiving a diploma, Mongkol presenting them with a bag of fish. Fury watched the distribution without comment, idly fingering the tiny leather sack that always hung from the silver chain around his neck.

"They aren't paying him," Marty said.

"That is because he is giving them away."

"Well then, I misjudged him."

"You didn't."

Marty was puzzled, and then he was not.

"Tell me, Mr. Curtaine. What did you promise him?"

"What did *you* promise him? Since he has no dinner, you promised you would buy him two steaks. In return, he promised you he would give his catch away and never fish from the Wendell Holmes again."

Marty sighed.

"I thought I was captain of this ship."

"You are. Most of the time."

Fury was still turning the small sack absently between his fingers.

Marty had paid little attention to it until now.

"Good luck charm?" he asked.

Marty saw how Fury hesitated.

"A few coins in case I'm short on cab fare," he said. "If you'll excuse me, I'm going to tell him you told him to give me the rest of the fish."

Not infrequently, divers showed up on the docks expecting to see Cedar. On both the brochures and the website, Marty had prominently displayed "Under New Ownership" in large block letters, but apparently not everyone read print, large or small. Within the first month, a half dozen divers, disappointed by Cedar's absence, declined at the last minute to go out on the boat. Marty always refunded their money. Each explanation took a piece of his heart.

Other than the handful of last-minute cancellations, things were going surprisingly well. Ernan had never been a question mark. He had served Cedar well; he did the same now for Marty. Though he possessed the social skills of paint, Mongkol had wrenched the Oliver Wendell Holmes to a level of performance she had never before attained; even the galley garbage disposal gnawed like a wood chipper. And Fury continued his magic. Knowledgeable and funny, he commanded respect and exuded goodwill. Every trip was the same. On the trip out, the divers stole surreptitious looks at the short, tattooed, fire-topped fireplug, doubt pasted on their faces. On the return trip, they laughed at Fury's jokes and not-at-all-surreptitiously vied for his attention, and before they left the boat they stuffed the tip jar like a Thanksgiving turkey.

One afternoon, watching the divers walk away down the dock, Marty turned to Fury.

"If not for you, we'd have half the business and a fraction of that in tips."

Fury did not take his eyes off the divers, now boarding the hotel bus in the gravel parking lot just off the docks.

"Small people are not threatening," he said. "No matter what their skills, their short stature relegates them to the status of amusement. So amuse is what I do."

Marty looked to see if Fury was joking.

He was not.

"I don't find you the least bit amusing," Marty said.

"Thank you," said Fury, but he did not smile.

Evening was falling. Seas had been rough. It had taken them longer than normal to return to the dock. The air was cooling, the insect world was starting up its nighttime hum.

"How are your accommodations working out?" Marty asked.

"They are working out fine."

"Do you have roommates?"

"No." Scratching a muscled forearm, Fury gave a small grin. "For a man who has tanks to wash, you ask a lot of questions."

"I just want to make sure you're happily employed," said Marty. "I wouldn't know how to face down a mutiny."

"Now I think you would."

The days unspooled in a thread of wide blue tropical skies and wide blue tropical dives.

A month after their inaugural dive charter, Marty went flying, driving alone to the airstrip beneath another bright sun. This time he did not stop on the way.

As the Piper Cub chattered and bumped through the sky, mushroom clouds ahead and a maze of mushroom islands below, Marty felt someone beside him.

He didn't look, but he did smile.

"You became a fine pilot," he said. "I will always be an awful diver."

That night, by eerie coincidence, he received the e-mail he had been expecting. He read it alone in the galley, a bowl of couscous going cold at his side.

Got room on the manifest for two hard workers? Willing to learn and willing to do whatever is asked. Either way, our flight comes in two Tuesdays from now. I realize this is more warning than request. I hope that's okay. Amber is looking forward to seeing you, and so am I! And we'll share a berth, if it's okay with you. But your decision. You're the captain. And my father. Thanks for having us.

Marty sat back in the chair, smiling.

Cedar was beside him again.

"Not that you care much for awards, but you have won the Nobel for parenting."

Leaning forward, Marty typed, *I talked to your mother. She wholeheartedly approves.*

Nine thousand miles, an instantaneous link.

I talk to her too.

Marty's smile slipped away. The darkness of the galley closed in.

Now, thought Marty, *it begins again.*

THE SEA.

It is not beginning again. It never stopped. Only now, instead of one, there are five. Mother and offspring. Increasing the odds of success. Our success, and perhaps yours.

My offspring are only six months old, but their memories are not a clean slate. Memory, you might call it instinct, already marbles their fabric in the way fat marbles meat. The way I remember my own battles, thousands of years ago. The sea then was a grand place, filled with creatures endowed with marvelous capacity for killing. Intellect saw to my rise through the tooth and fang ranks, though brute force served me just as well. I remember the concussive collisions, the gladiatorial sparrings; dispensing with the literary posturings, the tearing of flesh from bone. Blood, and parts of the whole and something like screaming. From both the victor and the vanquished. Like the cry of sexual release.

Truthfully, I miss it. I miss it a great deal.

My offspring, these instincts boil and seethe in their veins. I do not know how this will play out. I do know they are young, and, like your young, impatient and impulsive.

I wonder if this might not be such a bad thing. Youth wants testing. And your kind might benefit from a little stick. Reward does not seem to make as much of an impression. You simply accept reward as your due.

I feel their urges. Sometimes they cry out in my head, their yearning like a distant wail. I believe I can control them to a degree.

Except for the one. She remains a continuing mystery to me.

They travel the oceans. They learn. They see what you have done. What you continue to do with ignorance, unabated and merciless. The ravaged reefs, the trawlers hauling up armies of fish, your waste -- great avalanches of chemicals and refuse --- spreading like a stain, forming what you dub "dead zones" that carpet great swaths of sea floor. And on the ocean surface -- for, regarding degradation, you leave no stone unturned -- vast spreads of plastic debris. On full moon nights, the plastic seas sparkle with an inarguably lovely luminescence. Soon, in your Atlantic Ocean, they will stretch from shore to shore.

The dead zones, they do not sparkle. They are a heaping boneyard of dead animals, and

113

the smothering white mat of bacteria you created. The bacteria, they suck the very oxygen from the water. The animals that cannot swim or scuttle away suffocate. And the boneyard grows. Oh, does it grow. Doubling every ten years. Spreading across the bottom in a syrupy pouring. But it is not a graveyard. No, not at all. We are merely making adjustments. Fish, corals and marine mammals, yes, they die. But the bacteria thrive. Jellyfish too. Evolution running in reverse. A return to the primordial seas. Of which you were not a part.

Still it is not evolution's natural course. My offspring, I feel their anger gathering, like the prickling hairs rising on your forearms before an electrical storm. Their question is simple.

How can you?

They are better than the sum of their seeds. The four of them, they are endowed with powers beyond mine. Communicators you cannot ignore. They will reach out to whomever they choose. We will need all the wise hands we can muster. This is good. This is your hope. That they will be messengers of your resurrection.

But they are young, and, as they see what you have done, increasingly blinded. It is not hope that courses through them now. It is rage.

And the quivering rage they emote could easily become the rage of others.

They could very well be messengers of the Apocalypse.

CURACAO.

In the afternoon there had been an accident in the dolphin enclosure. It was a simple exercise. The dolphins had performed it countless times. The dolphins had seemed mildly agitated, but Pietra had made the decision to continue the show. The entire enclosure was ringed with sun-crisped cruise ship passengers, close to seventy of them, a good crowd. If she canceled the show management would howl, primarily for her head. She knew more about the dolphins than anyone, but she did not mistake that for job security.

It was the day's last performance, the audience participation segment. Pietra had picked six volunteers from the shouting, waving, game show crowd. She had picked no children. She didn't know why. It had turned out to be a godsend. Four hundred pounds of dolphin could have been a killing blow. As it was Hermes – an adult male, born and raised in captivity – landed on two women and a man. Hermes could do the trick in his sleep. It was part of her spiel. "Dolphins sleep with half their brains still functioning, so actually, he could," she said yet again; in her own ears her voice always sounded sickeningly Mickey Mouse cheery through the megaphone.

But this afternoon, Hermes had added a literal twist. Instead of leaping straight over the stick, Hermes turned side-ways, landing with his full momentum and weight on the two women and the man holding one end of the stick. The Aqua Academy had requested that everyone present delete their videos of the incident, but of course no one listened, including Alex, one of the other trainers, and so Pietra had watched the accident again immediately after the ambulances left. In the first instant of Hermes' midair turning, the tourists had been slack-jawed. Then they had been broken. In the thrashing and confusion, one woman broke a clavicle. The other woman, raising her hand to protect herself, had shattered her wrist. Pietra had played rugby for the Netherland's national team. She had never seen a more twisted appendage. Standing in the waist-deep water the woman held her hand in front of her as if she'd never seen a hand flush against a forearm before. The man, who wisely had not raised his hands, had fallen back into the water, escaping with a severely bruised sternum. All would survive, but none would forget.

After the tourists had been ushered away, and the gates to the Academy – a grand name for an operation roughly the size of a football field – chained shut, the owner, a florid-faced Dutch accountant, had spoken to the trainers. An unfortunate accident, he said. They should not talk to the press. The Academy had refunded the injured tourists' entry fees, but would assume no responsibility. There was a reason dolphins were called wild animals, the owner said. Pietra had always agreed with this. Often, she had emphasized it. It was the rare ear that listened. Certainly not the owner. Until now.

Pietra Valenhaus has been at the Academy for six years; long enough to know the owner liked younger girls and was unhappy in his marriage, and long enough to know her charges were nothing like Flipper. They were bright and curious, and extraordinary problem solvers. Pietra had once watched two of the dolphins spend less than five minutes puzzling over a lidded PVC pipe, before working together to pull the lid off. They could also be brutal. Males formed pairs and trios (in the wild, larger groups still) to aggressively court females. *Court.* She had read that in a research paper. The paper had been written by a man. There was nothing courtly about gang rape.

Still, she had come to love the dolphins. Something of a loner, while the other trainers went into town together to dance and hook up with tourists, Pietra had spent many nights sitting at the edge of the enclosure – a former lagoon mouth now enclosed by landfill and a metal grate on the ocean side – watching the dolphins glide past on their sides, eyeing her with the half-knowing smiles that weren't smiles at all. Some nights, unable to sleep, she would rise and go to the enclosure. In the wee night hours, the dolphins were often playing. Often Hermes would come to her. Sliding back and forth beneath her bare feet he would issue clicks, whistles and rolling chirps. Some nights he would blow playful streams of bubbles.

She had noticed the first odd behavior three months ago. Hermes had always been cooperative to a fault. He learned behaviors quickly, and he worked hard to please. In the middle of a performance he had simply balked and swum off. When it became obvious he was not returning to perform she had joked to the crowd. *Men are so moody.* The next day he had done what she asked, but without his traditional snap and zest. There had been a pause of hesitation after commands. She remembered now the word that had come to her afterward. Truculent.

Today, the chief trainer had snatched up the intercom. *No need to be alarmed. It was just an unfortunate accident.*

She didn't think so. Hermes was the smartest of the lot. Children had dropped popcorn into his blow hole. People pawed at him, grabbed his dorsal fin, demanding a tow. He had played by the rules and then some.

Today he had made his own.

And now he was gone. When they had gone to the pens tonight they found a small opening in the metal grate that separated the enclosure from the sea. Hermes was smaller than most of the dolphins, but not quite small enough. Bits of flesh wafted from the rusted rebar like remnants from a parade.

Pietra Valenhaus stood at the edge of the enclosure, watching the dolphins slide past on their sides. They looked up at her, smiling keepers of secrets.

THE SEA.

In the Bahamas there is a researcher who believes that one day dolphins and humans will be able to communicate. She is right. Only one half of the equation hasn't caught on yet. Clicks. Whistles. Rolling chirps. Attention-getting streams of bubbles. Like exclamations.

Listen.

Hermes. The messenger of the gods. But you cannot hear.

Dolphins. Bright and curious, with a defined system for processing emotion. This, you know. But they are more than you know.

They are not the only showcase of your ignorance.

KOROR, PALAU.

The kayaking tours were Fury's idea. He broached the idea one evening, the four of them sipping Red Roosters on the stern of the Wendell Holmes and enjoying the day's first tincture of cool.

"Tourists love kayaking," he told Marty. "Anyone can do it. And all we have to do is sit. Diving is a lot of work."

Ernan listened with mild interest. Mongkol, slouched against the stern, gave rapt attention to the peeling of his Red Rooster label. Really, it was a two-way conversation.

Fury hurried along in a manner Marty found mildly amusing. It was odd to see the man nervous.

"The investment isn't much. Less than not much. I have a cousin who can deliver a dozen kayaks and paddles for three thousand dollars. After the initial investment, there is no other cost. The kayaks are in good condition and, as you know, they are made of plastic and almost impossible to damage. So your investment is good for many years."

"You've seen these kayaks?" Marty asked.

"Yes."

Ernan smiled slowly beneath his sunglasses.

"And your cut?" he asked.

Fury slapped a hand to his chest and fell back against the bench.

"You wound me."

Ernan waited.

Marty waited.

Mongkol stuck the beer label to his forearm.

"Ten percent," said Fury. "But in the long run we all benefit."

"Where do we put them?" Marty asked. "The benches and the tank set ups take up most of the deck. And what about storage after the trips?"

"I've got it all worked out," said Fury. "There are enough empty racks in the storage room behind the dive store. When we bring them on the boat, we stack them and lash them at the stern. They're light, and as I may have mentioned, almost indestructible. You can bang them together without effect, like Ernan and Mongkol's heads."

Mongkol raised an eyebrow.

"Liability insurance?" asked Marty.

He had already decided. It was a test of Fury's thoroughness.

"Of course, a small increase. Laughable compared to the insurance we carry for diving. I dug around. I found us a good price."

"You're quite the entrepreneur. I hope you're not trying to mount a takeover."

Fury clutched his chest.

Marty raised a hand, putting the theater to a halt.

Fury said, "I won't even ask for five percent of the additional profits."

"And I won't have you keelhauled."

A high pitched yipping issued from the stern, like a coyote bark. Three of the men nearly leapt to their feet.

Mongkol produced two more yips, not a trace of amusement on his face.

Fury gave the big man a dark look.

"I thought you were my friend," Fury said.

"He got you this job," said Marty.

"I am being unfairly maligned, but I will still not retract my offer."

A rumbling issued from shore. A truck pulled into the turnaround beside the White Squall. The side of the truck was emblazoned with the words "Gentry's Appliance Repair." Something was always breaking at the White Squall. Still, the truck was a bit of a surprise as those things were rarely tended to.

The driver shut off the engine, which gave a final belch of black smoke. He did not get out of the cab.

Marty only half registered the truck. Sitting in the now quiet evening, making yet another decision, he still felt like a pretender, an actor playing the role of dive boat owner. He wondered if it would always feel like Cedar's operation.

He looked at the three men, drinking quietly. *The island of misfit toys.* It was wonderful.

"We're in this together, so everyone gets a vote. Those in favor of offering kayaking, raise their hand."

Fury's hand shot up. Ernan raised his hand slowly.

Mongkol got up and gathered a beer from the cooler. Returning, he gave Fury's raised hand a fist bump.

"Well then, it's unanimous," said Marty. "We now offer kayak tours. On a limited basis. So you gentleman don't go soft. We remain, first and always, a dive charter."

He turned to Fury.

"How soon can we get the kayaks?"

"Two minutes." Fury jerked a thumb at the truck. "My cousin."

The first tour, conducted a week later, was a smashing success. They left the tanks in the dive shop and took twelve customers, on Fury's recommendation, to Blacktip Lake. Stacked like interlocking puzzle pieces, the kayaks rode without budging on the 20-minute trip to the Rock Islands. It was a postcard perfect morning, even by Palau's standards, the ocean practically immobile. Sliding the kayaks into the water was like pushing them out on to zambonied ice.

The evening Fury's cousin delivered the kayaks, Marty, Ernan and Fury had each taken a spin. Mongkol had demurred. Ernan and Fury had glided effortlessly about the harbor. Marty listed to and fro, his paddle banging the sides

At the outset, their clients exhibited the same spectrum of skills, but by the time they had paddled for twenty minutes, paralleling the limestone island capped with thick jungle – Palau's mushroom islands always reminded Marty of a chicken neck, topped with a toupee -- they had all improved considerably. Only Marty's paddle continued to clack against the side of his kayak, the noise reverberating through the quiet morning.

"He is keeping the sharks away," shouted Fury, and the customers laughed.

Fury took the lead. They traveled single file. The tourists followed behind Fury, Marty clacking in the middle of the line. Ernan paddled at the back. After twenty minutes of paddling, as if arriving at a street corner, Fury made an abrupt left, paddling straight for an impenetrable limestone cliff. Only when they drew close did the arched opening appear, low to the waterline and masked in shadow. Through the arch they could see the bright blue marine lake.

The arch was three feet high.

"Though I won't find it necessary, I will demonstrate the kayak limbo," said Fury, leaning back as his kayak slid through the dripping cool of the arch. "Easy and relaxing, though also why we wear helmets. Always an overachiever who sits up too soon."

To Marty's relief, their customers performed the limbo like Cirque de Soleil acrobats.

The clack of his own helmet against the limestone ceiling echoed across the lake.

Exiting the arch, Marty tapped the chalky smudge at the center of his helmet.

"A textbook demonstration of proper helmet use."

The laughing paddlers gathered around Fury.

Marty took off his helmet and wiped away the smudge.

"This is a marine lake," said Fury. "Very unique. Palau has over seventy marine lakes. They are saltwater lakes, cut off completely, or," he pointed his paddle toward the arch, "almost completely from the sea. They are like the lakes you know, only they are filled with tropical fish. It is like discovering a sea turtle in your bathtub."

In the white-bright sunlight, the lake was so still it was as if water had learned to hold its breath. Several kayakers now held their breath too. Near and far, tiny fins made viscous unzippings on the silky surface. The fins, roughly the size of a thumb, luffed like windless sails.

"Blacktip Lake," said Fury. "So named for these Blacktip sharks. *Carcharhinus limbatus*. Almost all of them babies. Have fun…"

Fury made as if to paddle away.

"Almost?"

Fury swung his kayak to face the German woman now scanning the lake.

"The mothers bring the juveniles here because it is protected," he said. "Until they rise up the food chain and can protect themselves."

The German woman did not bother looking at Fury.

"The mothers, they come here?" she asked.

Fury spun his kayak in an easy circle.

"To protect their young," he said. "It is what mothers do."

"How big are the mothers?"

"You guess."

"Bigger than this kayak?"

Fury gave the German woman's kayak prolonged consideration.

"No," he said. "But not too far off."

"When do the mothers come here?"

"Whenever they please." Fury laughed. "Honestly, they are harmless. Even the mothers. There is nothing to worry about. Unless you are a blacktip. They are a threatened species. Their meat is quite tasty and their fins are used to make shark fin soup. Man bites shark more often than shark bites man."

They spent twenty minutes drifting about the lake, a translucent blue marble basting in the sun. High above their heads, frigate birds circled against children's puffy white clouds. Closer to earth, pairs of cartoonishly colored birds darted through the high canopy, their shrieks the sound of a debauched frat party. Beneath the mirror-clear water, coral bommies -- cauliflower heads made of limestone -- studded the bottom. Rainbow-colored fish moved lazily about them as if swimming through cream. It was like paddling through a dream. Marty watched as the kayakers paddled slowly about. He stowed his own paddle so as to not shatter their dreams.

They made one more stop before returning to the boat, hauling the kayaks out on a thin strip of muddy sand at the edge of a mangrove forest. It was cool in the dappled shade. Penetrating the gaps between rustling leaves, the sunlight flickered like an old time movie projector. The tourists gratefully walked the loamy beach, stretching their stiff backs and cramped legs and trying not to trip over the maze of mangrove roots. Everywhere, bright green dragonflies hovered like helicopters.

Reaching beneath a mangrove root, Fury extricated two machetes. Several of the tourists wandered over.

Handing a machete to Ernan, Fury regarded a hovering dragonfly.

"Odonata," he said to the gathered tourists. The flickering light on his sober face made him look like one of those announcers in an old time movie newscast. "Beautiful, yes, but beware the dragonfly. They can fly straight up, straight down and hover in place. They are the flying aces of the insect world. They catch their prey in mid-air, but you cannot see it because it is too fast. The only way you can tell is when you see them chewing afterward on a branch. They are a fierce predator. They have been practicing a long time. Three hundred million years. They predate the dinosaur."

Leaning close to Ernan, Fury whispered, "I have been doing my homework."

Fury and Ernan crouched to the three coconuts in the sand, splitting them open with the machetes.

The tourists gobbled up the crunchy-sweet slices.

"I would like more," the German woman said.

Fury stood with the remaining coconut half in his hand. Bending he placed it in the sand.

"I'm sorry," he said politely. "You keep some and you give some away."

As they paddled away, the coconut crabs rose from their hidden places and scurried for their prize.

BYRON BAY, AUSTRALIA.

Twice a week, Lacey Goodenall went free diving with Paul Wiley. In Lacey's mind, the arrangement was largely a matter of convenience. Paul Wiley could take time off when she was available. He was also as accomplished at free diving as he was at surf ski racing. Regarding free diving, Lacey Goodenall and Paul Wiley did not compete. Here, ego could kill you. Stay down too long and you could drown. Spear a fish too large and you could drown. Focus on another diver -- and lose track of your own inner regulatings -- and you could drown. There were other dangers. But drowning was foremost.

After a week of steady blow, the wind had at last laid down. Lacey waited two more days for the inshore waters to clear somewhat and then she called Paul Wiley at lifesaving headquarters.

"I dunno Lacey. Water's still pretty murky down here."

Paul Wiley heard his own voice come back over the phone. Once, after a few too many drinks, he had somehow miraculously persuaded Lacey to take the stage at a local talent night. Her flawless imitation of Russell Crowe had reduced the pub to wheezes.

"I dunno Paul, but I'm betting no one dove the reef during the blow."

She was riding him, but she had a point. The damn woman always had a point. The first spear fishers on the reef would find a plethora of dinner options.

"The early bird gets the worm," said Paul.

"Every second of this wastes your breath and our time."

Paul kept a zodiac on a trailer at lifesaving headquarters. He also had several four-wheel drive vehicles at his disposal.

Men always needed one more prod.

"I'll be there in thirty minutes," said Lacey. "With money for petrol and beer."

"You're on."

"And you're predictable."

Her gear already rested by the front door, beside the 12-pack of Fourex and the envelope with the petrol money. She glanced at her watch. She had fifteen minutes. She returned to the den and sat down again in front of the computer. The research paper was already up on the screen.

When she arrived at the Byron Beach Surf Lifesaving headquarters, Paul was stretched out in the back of the zodiac reading a book. James Joyce's "Ulysses."

"You just picked it up before I came in," she said. "You're not really reading that."

Paul did not take his eyes from the book.

"I am an enigma," he said. "And you never pay attention to the time. Let me guess. You started working on something."

The trailer was hitched to the truck.

"I'm sorry, Paul."

"More feeling."

"I'm sorry, you great big smug prick."

Paul Wiley swung easily out of the zodiac.

"How could there be any other kind?"

It took a minute to reach the ocean's edge and thirty minutes to reach the reef. The reef was only a mile offshore, but it sat directly off a sheer bluff that, short of a heart-stopping jump, offered no access to the sea. The swell had nearly vanished. The waves were small, but an ugly cross chop remained, so that now and again the zodiac come down hard enough to clack their teeth. Lacey had spent her entire life in boats, and she had never come to like them. Boats were like so many things in her life. Necessary but annoying. They provided access to the world she loved. Until something better came along, they would do. A female friend had once suggested that the same dictum applied to men.

Maybe it was the gray sky, maybe it was the gray water, but Paul Wiley had an uneasy feeling.

"Something doesn't feel right," he shouted over the engine.

"Oi," Lacey shouted back. "That you make a lady buy the beer."

Truth was she had the same feeling, but it was silly talking about it. She was no New Age adherent. Once, as a child, she had gone to see a fortune teller. As she was leaving, she had nicked the old woman's crystal ball. If the woman really could see things, she would know where to find it. Lacey placed zero stock in premonitions. In the rare instances when she had one, she sure as hell wasn't going to give voice to it. Besides, they were rarely right.

When they arrived at the reef, Paul took his time slipping on his wet belt, fins and mask. They had both donned their camouflage wetsuits on the beach to keep warm on the ride out. Paul rigged his gun with molasses care.

They always went in together. The buddy system. Next, they always separated. Hunting wasn't a team activity.

Rigged and ready, Lacey waited patiently, until her patience ran out. This process took roughly a minute.

"Bugger me. Now I know what it's going to be like at the senior home. Just say you don't want to go."

Paul looked out at the gray water.

"I don't want to go."

Her first impulse was to chide him. They were rarely serious with each other. But he was serious now. She could see the lines on his face as his pinched eyes searched the water. He actually did look older.

"What say we compromise? Twenty minutes. Since you kindly already went to all the trouble to get us here." She nudged his shoulder. "All those fat fish down there, just waiting to be plucked. I'll even cook."

"More beer might make your cooking palatable."

"Christ. You're a relentless piece of work."

Paul pulled his mask over his face.

"Talking makes me thirsty," he said, crossing his fins and falling over the side.

Paul saw the white pointer first, the moment he reached the reef on his fourth descent. Lacey had been right. The reef hummed with the ebb and sway of fish. Big ones too. After only four descents they had already both speared good-sized Cobia. They had brought the fish to the surface as quickly as possible, tossing them into the zodiac, but the water had absorbed blood and struggle.

Paul's first thought was *You usually never see them*. His second thought was *Lacey*. He looked about frantically and then, heart already a frozen lump, he looked to the surface. He saw her clearly. She was laying on her back on the surface, legs finning idly, catching her breath. Paul Wiley's third thought was decidedly odd. *Dating back to 1580, when records on shark attacks first began, Australia is the nation with the second-most instances of shark attacks. The United States leads the world, by a wide margin, with more than 1,100 attacks on record.*

Lacey had told him that. In a blink, he lost the bet again in his head.

His mind was following a path of whimsy. His joints were locked, as if his emerging arthritis had vaulted instantly to paralysis. As a lifesaver he had spent his adult life engaged in harrowing situations. In this moment they became laughable. Now the muscles in his face were frozen. He recognized his own panic, and it did him no good.

Thirteen feet long and wine cask thick, the shark swung through the murk with elegant indifference. If it had noticed either of them, it gave no sign. Passing over the reef it continued on, dissolving into the gray as easily as a dream. The dream was contagious. Paul Wiley felt as if he was beneath the water, and he wasn't. Looking up toward the surface, he saw Lacey finning down to the reef. *Stupid cunt.* The poisonous curse in his ears saw him return to himself.

Gesturing as calmly as possible, he got Lacey's attention. Placing his hand atop his head, thumb against his forehead, fingers together to form a crude fin, he made the universal sign for shark.

Lacey stopped kicking. She was midway down. It was rare to see her hesitate. It didn't last long. She didn't return to the surface. She swam directly to him, kicking calmly but powerfully. Her body was rigid, but he could see her head turning, reconnoitering the murk. Again, oddly, he thought, *She has always moved like a dancer.* And then, more to the point, *What the fuck is the matter with you?*

She was beside him in the next instant. With her free hand she made a circling motion.

They stood back to back, spear guns sweeping the water.

Like a bug's antennae, thought Paul Wiley. *Only lobster were smart enough to jam themselves into a crevice to protect their arse.*

Finally Paul Wiley remembered he was underwater. Heat burned in his lungs.

He poked Lacey with an elbow. She turned to him. He knew she had plenty of air. He didn't want to force her hand, but now that he had remembered his innate need to breath, a new panic began to claw up the ladder toward him.

And then Lacey smiled and gave him the thumbs up, the universal signal to ascend and tears sprung into Paul Wiley's eyes.

He wanted to shake his head, but he wanted to breathe more. She was already cupping his elbow. With a kick, she lifted them both off the reef. They rose back to back.

They were halfway to the surface when the pointer reappeared. There was no indifference now. It swam for them with purpose, the intricate beauty of its markings growing clearer and clearer, the ragged line separating gray from white like a string of low-hanging storm clouds.

Paul Wiley's body buzzed. A part of him wished he would black out.

They must have continued kicking, he didn't recall, and then they broke the surface and he was sucking down air and Lacey was screaming in his face.

"Get in the fucking boat!"

He saw with idle surprise that the zodiac was right beside them.

He turned back to Lacey. She was gone. He wasn't angry. She had every right to get in the boat. In his mind he saw the dolphin, cut in half. *What did that feel like?*

He had little air and less energy. But Paul Wiley was a survivor. He gave one massive kick and clawed his way over the zodiac's slick balloony side.

He lay on his back, panting at the gray sky. The sky was slightly lighter than the shark. And then he realized his friend wasn't there.

He sat up and puked. A semblance of breakfast sausage splattered off the zodiac's side.

He saw Lacey the instant before the shark hit. One moment she was face down on the surface. The next she was in the air, nearly enveloped in an explosion of spray, something like a submarine just beneath her. He heard himself cry out and moan. It was his perfect imitation of loss. Paul Wiley would live to be ninety-one. The last three years of his life he would suffer severe dementia. When he drew his last breath, this moment was stamped upon his mind's eye.

Lacey came to his house the next day with a case of beer and store bought fish. He had puked all over the Cobia. They had tossed both fish over the side. An offering of thanks to the gods. It had only been half a joke.

They ate the store-bought fish and drank most of the beer, and when most of the beer was gone, Lacey slipped her t-shirt over her head and showed him the basketball-size bruise just above her right breast.

Lacey Goodenall was quite drunk. She only wore a bra on dressy occasions.

She swayed in Paul Wiley's living room.

"It's a fucking doozy," she said, idly running a finger along her collarbone.

As the shark had vectored up, Lacey swung her gun down; shark and speargun had intersected in a precise instant. Lacey had wedged the butt of the gun into her shoulder. Shark collided with gun, gun collided with shoulder. Lacey was driven eight feet into the air. When she fell back to the surface the shark was gone.

Here in the living room, Paul Wiley stared at his friend.

It was. A fucking doozy.

Her breasts were doozies too.

Lacey refused to talk to the reporters, but Paul Wiley didn't. She read the account in the local paper. It was reasonably accurate. The reporter had called a friend of hers at the University of Brisbane, an ichthyologist of global renown.

Shark attacks are increasing as water sports become more popular.

When she read the quote she smiled.

Like you needed a fucking expert to point that out.

Paul called two mornings later. She was working in the lab, but when she saw his number she answered.

"You're a bad man," she said. "My head still feels like a balloon."

"We were lucky."

His voice was dead.

"What is it?"

"Someone else. A young bodyboarder. Took both his legs. He bled out before his mates could get him to the beach."

Something crawled into her throat.

"How old?"

"Fourteen."

The lab was silent. In her mind the little mop-haired boy stared up at her.

She stared down at the stainless steel table without seeing. When she finally focused, she realized she was looking at the bull shark fetus. Draped across the sterilized dish, both tiny mouths were agape.

"Shark Uprising!" the headline screamed the next day.

She imagined her friend fielding more calls from reporters. The University didn't allow him an unlisted number.

THE SEA.

More of you everywhere, a tide that refuses to retreat.

You do not expect consequences?

KOROR, PALAU.

Justin and Amber arrived two weeks later on the Tuesday afternoon flight from Guam. Marty watched them walk across the tarmac. He smiled as one of the baggage handlers dropped to his knees in front of Amber.

They cleared customs quickly, passing out into the bright white, floral-scented arrivals area. They looked no different than the other honeymooners, smooth-faced, laughing and standing close. Always new beginnings.

Marty composed himself as they approached.

"Thirty seconds on the ground and you already have a suitor," he said.

Amber flushed and Marty felt a small pang in his own heart. The girl carried an easily embarrassed modesty that was charming.

"Men are fickle," she said. "He'll fall for someone else on the next flight."

"I doubt it."

Her hug came with a warm, caring look.

"It's really good to see you, Marty. I hope this isn't an inconvenience. He," she gave a sidelong glance at Justin, "makes spontaneous look like long range planning."

"I wish you'd come sooner," Marty said.

"See?" said Justin. "The first argument I've won."

"We only just got here," Amber said. "He's just being nice to you."

The girl's smile was like watching the sun come up.

Tourists milled about them, searching for baggage claim and hotel couriers.

"They're still spraying?" Justin asked.

"Some things don't change," said Marty.

Justin hugged him and didn't let go.

"I miss Mom," he said. "I missed you."

Amber was crying. Justin was crying. Marty started crying.

A little girl stopped to stare. Her mother yanked her away.

"Too much spray," Justin said, wiping at his eyes.

Pulling Kleenex from the fanny pack at her waist, Amber said, "*What* are you talking about?"

Marty accepted a Kleenex.

"They spray floral scent in the airport," he said. "They come through with cans just before the planes land."

Amber started to open her mouth in protest, but Justin spoke instead.

"It's the truth," he said, smiling now. "Paradise in a can."

They had two small bags.

Picking them up, Justin said, "Help. Get us to the water."

The baby blue 1965 Ford F100 was in the parking lot.

Placing the bags at the front of the bed, Justin said, "I'm glad you still have it."

"Many old things still run," said Marty. "Often with a touch of style."

When Marty turned the key in the ignition, something like the clatter of bowling pins rolled about beneath the hood.

Marty shrugged.

"Style can always use a tune up," he said.

"Old age is fifteen years older than I am," said Justin.

Marty looked at him curiously.

"Oliver Wendell Holmes," the boy said.

It was a fifteen minute drive from Palau Roman Tmetuchl Airport to the harbor. Amber sat up front with Marty. Justin sat in the back, legs turned sideways in deference to the tight quarters. Marty didn't make conversation. They had been traveling for 24 hours. Amber fell asleep the instant they left the airport. She slept with her mouth slightly open, sweat beading her upper lip.

Glancing in the rear view mirror, Marty saw Justin, hair popping about in the breeze, staring out the window.

When Marty parked the truck in the reserved spot beside the White Squall, Justin leaned across the seat and gently kissed Amber's cheek.

"Welcome to Neverland."

Walking along the dock, they could see Ernan on the bridge. Ernan waved and started down the ladder.

"I knew you'd know what to do," Justin said.

"I deprived the world of an excellent policeman."

The world darkened again. They had both known an excellent policeman.

"How is Portola?" Justin asked quickly.

"She moved to Guam. She has family there. Able was a saver. I'm told she will live comfortably for the rest of her years."

They both knew this didn't matter to Portola.

"It never gets any easier," Justin said.

"That's a good sign," said Marty.

When they reached the Wendell Holmes, Ernan and Fury were waiting on the dock.

To Fury's surprise, the boy embraced them both.

"We're going to be friends," Justin said, regarding the smaller man. "And you, Captain, have been my friend for a long time."

Ernan had not removed his sunglasses.

"Now it seems like home again," he said.

"I'm glad this man had the foresight to team up with the best captain in the Pacific."

Marty thought, *Not hire. Equals.* The boy did this naturally without thinking.

Justin tilted his head toward Marty.

"And how is this one doing?"

Ernan said, "He is proving a quick study and will soon be competent on the water."

No one missed the placement.

"He's just trying to keep his job," said Marty.

Fury had picked up their bags.

He turned to the beautiful girl, fighting the urge to stare.

"Only one bag?"

"It's filled with makeup," said Amber.

"Ha! I will marry you if he doesn't."

Justin slapped the side of his own head.

"I'm blaming it on jet lag. This is Amber. She is wiser than I will ever be, but not so wise she won't spend time with me."

Ernan and Fury shook Amber's hand.

"When you wise up," said Fury, "I will be waiting."

As they stepped over the transom, a head emerged from the hold. The eyes in the head regarded them steadily. Then the head disappeared.

"The remaining member of the island of misfit toys," said Marty. "I believe you know Mr. Mongkol Songkhla, Justin. And Amber, you may or may not meet him."

A sudden screeching rent the quiet.

Justin grinned.

"The perfect welcome. Aneurysm. The song, not the act."

Marty looked at him in surprise.

"You know this music?"

"They're my favorite group."

It seemed to Marty that the volume went up slightly. And unnecessarily.

"God help me," said Marty.

That night, after Ernan, Fury and Mongkol had left and Amber had gone below to sleep, Marty and Justin sat on deck chairs on the bow. It was a lovely night, the water's cool rising up to mingle with the sky's warmth. A shy breeze delivered the scent of plumeria, faint and sweet, and garlic.

"Tuesdays are still spaghetti night?"

At the far end of the dock, beneath the thatched roof of the White Squall, the help moved faster than they usually did beneath the rattan ceiling fans. The clatter of pots carried from the kitchen. A waiter was showing a couple to the door. Eight was closing time, and the end of all-you-can-eat.

"Change comes slowly here," said Marty. "Sam added a few gluten-free entrees."

Sam Creighton, an expat Aussie and retired Sydney policeman, owned the White Squall, largely for the purpose of having his own bar.

"What does that mean?" Justin asked.

"I'm not sure if I know. I don't think Sam does either."

"Do they still do karaoke?"

"Sadly, yes."

It was a little boy's giggle, which Justin made no attempt to hide.

"I remember when Mr. Creighton would sing 'Givin The Dog a Bone' and Mom would shut my porthole window."

Marty felt a twinge of embarrassment, but Justin only looked amused.

"He's probably the only person who sings AC/DC louder than AC/DC," Marty said. "Now he sings 'Sexy Lady' by MC Magic."

"That I'd like to hear."

"On Thursday you will."

They fell quiet.

At the far end of the dock, someone broke a plate and someone left the restaurant whistling.

"How is Chicago?" Marty asked.

"Things are open past eight. I'm not sure I like it."

"It sounds like you're thriving."

"I'm lucky to be there. I'm trying to make the most of that luck."

Marty watched Justin. It hadn't been long, but he was a little taller and a trifle broader. The eyes were still bright.

"You're not tired?"

"I'm too excited. Being here feels a lot like a dream."

They both knew why he was here.

Marty had brought two Red Roosters up from the galley. It was strange seeing Justin drink beer. All the changes Cedar would miss.

Again the sadness descended. It was like a continuous loop, a wheel rolling over him, crushing the life out of him, again and again.

Justin said, "She wasn't perfect, you know."

The abrupt burp of raw anger startled him.

"For one thing," continued Justin, "she enabled me. She always did the cooking. She never let me cook a single thing. If I hadn't met Amber, boxed macaroni and cheese would have been my lifelong signature dish. And she was always lecturing me about this fish and that fish. Did you know that seahorses are the only fish that can swim upright? That dogfish egg cases are called mermaid purses? That Anableps have four eyes, and can see above and below water at the same time? Fish are lucky. It's quieter underwater." Justin gave an actual burp. "Oh, right. And she made me watch the same movie every Friday night. *You* watch King Kong two hundred times. *That* doesn't do much for your imagination."

Justin put the beer to his lips. Green eyes sighted down the bottle at Marty.

"She was controlling," said Marty. "She made me learn to dive. Bullied me into it, truth be told. She knew I was afraid of the water. She knew it was the last thing I wanted, but she wouldn't let me be. And now look what it got me. My plane rusts on the tarmac and my insides boil with ulcerous beginnings."

Raising his bottle, Marty tipped it at Justin.

"She always made Issy wear a t-shirt," Justin said.

Justin's first girlfriend had been shaped like an hour glass. Cedar had politely requested the girl at least wear a tank top to prevent their male clients from toppling overboard. Probably their female clients too.

Marty said, "She played the bagpipes badly. Very badly."

Justin cocked an eyebrow.

"Worse than very badly," said Marty.

"There wasn't a pair of ear plugs on the planet that could save me."

"She played as if she wanted the whole world to hear how bad she was."

Marty wasn't sure who started crying first. It didn't matter.

The two men cried silently, because that's what men do.

The younger man waited for the older man to finish and then he said, "It doesn't make it any easier."

"No," said the older man. "No, it doesn't."

That night Amber rolled over in the berth and whispered in Justin's ear.

"I can't sleep."

His eyes opened alert. It was almost funny, except she wondered if he ever rested.

"Now, neither can I."

"I tried to fall back to sleep. Trying just wakes me up more."

Brushing her hair from her eyes, he examined her face seriously.

"Hmmmmmm. Jet lag is my diagnosis."

"Thank you, doctor."

"I'll tear up the bill if you come with me."

"Come with you?"

"Come with me."

She glanced to the shelf by the porthole. It was an old fashion alarm clock with the little bell on top.

"It's midnight," she said.

"Witching hour. You're the one who can't sleep."

Justin was already out of bed, pulling on shorts and a t-shirt.

"Have you always been able to convince anyone of anything?" she asked

"We'll see."

In the galley, Justin plucked the truck keys from the hook by the sink. Taking two chocolate chip cookies from the cookie jar, he handed her one.

"Breakfast time in Chicago," he whispered.

Walking along the dock she saw there were no stars. A fresh wind blew. She was glad she had put on jeans.

"It looks like rain," she said.

Walking around to the passenger side of the truck, Justin opened her door.

"I certainly hope so," he said.

The world was empty. They drove along a rutted dirt road hemmed in by jungle. The dashboard lights turned their complexions sallow and made the jungle look darker. The truck made its bowling ball clattering. Justin stopped once to let something low to the ground trundle across the road.

"May I ask where we're going?"

"You may."

They bumped along, Justin whistling.

"Okaaaaay," said Amber. "Where are we going?"

Justin smiled at his reflection in the windshield.

"I thought you'd never ask. I'm going to introduce you to my favorite place."

It was a small cusp of beach. A half dozen kayaks rested upside down in the sand. Foliage arced over the sand like a breaking wave, making it very dark.

Justin walked slowly along the edge of the jungle.

"What are you doing?"

"Engaging in foreplay."

She laughed, but just the word made her nipples harden. She felt the pleasant risings of goosebumps on her breasts. *Anything to make them bigger.*

The joke was supposed to disarm her, but her breaths were still getting shallower.

The sheltered beach was protected from the wind. It was still and warm. Beneath her feet, the sand felt like sugar.

Justin trooped maddeningly along the tree line.

"You could at least kiss me."

"I'm looking for something. Ah." He turned to her. "Hold that kiss."

He disappeared as if stepping through a portal. One second there, the next, gone. She was relieved to hear his footfalls in the brush. Still, it was like being swallowed. *I'm worlds away from anything I know.*

Her shallow breathing shifted reasoning slightly.

He reappeared in less than a minute, a paddle balanced in each hand.

She tried not to look relieved.

"Are we stealing?"

"Borrowing." Justin handed her a paddle. "I know the outfitter. If he knew you, he would approve."

Justin held his paddle straight up and down, a fiberglass staff.

"You paddle like this. Like a canoe."

"Very funny. What's that in your other hand?"

She thought he had just taken a towel from the back of the truck. But now she saw there was something wrapped inside it.

"Champagne."

"Champagne?"

"From the cooler in the back of the truck. I didn't steal it."

"You *planned* this?"

"I did. We stopped to buy the champagne on the way home from the airport. I thought we should check your pulse, but Marty swore to me you were still breathing. I don't know how you did that with your neck, though. How could anyone sleep like that? But you did. Probably why you're awake now."

Justin walked over and grabbed the loop on one of the kayaks.

"Oh, wait." He put the kayak down. He pulled off his t-shirt. Unbuttoning his shorts he said, "I don't want to ride home in wet clothes, do you?"

He was beautiful naked. Sleek and firm lines everywhere.

She saw that he was a little bit shy, and trying not to be.

"Nobody will see us, Amber. I promise you."

She needed no convincing. Slipping off her jeans and her t-shirt, she walked to the jungle's edge and placed them neatly on top of Justin's clothes. She hesitated and then added her panties to the pile. Instantly, a swirling breeze eddy rushed in and licked her palest parts.

I would never do this.

Erotic to say yes to never.

She was supremely conscious of her nakedness. Her hair tickled her back. Stopping, she tied it up in a bun, trying to look casual in the fastening.

Justin stood silent.

Very softly he said, "You are the most beautiful thing I've ever seen."

Bending, she grabbed the loop on the bow of her kayak.

"You pick it up like this," she said.

They could see the island from the shoreline, a small, dark hummock. It took fifteen minutes to paddle there. The wind was backing off. It still produced a small bathtub chop on the water.

Amber had thought she might be afraid of paddling on the open water at night, but it was like paddling through a dream. Their paddles made a soft, rhythmic splashing. Her breaths fell in step. The breeze blew faltering gusts in their faces. If she closed her eyes, it felt like someone gently caressing her breasts. Her nakedness contoured to the kayak seat. She smelled her own musky excitement. Her breaths began to run ahead of her strokes.

The island took more definitive shape. It was little more than a ring of sand, a lone cluster of palms at the center. Something bulky sat beside the palms. It became two boulders.

She could feel the water running along the sides of the kayaking. Bumping beneath it too.

"The wind will be at our backs on the paddle in," Justin said.

She was almost afraid to look over at him. If she did, she might wake up.

"Too bad," she said.

He laughed.

"That's my girl," he said.

The smooth boulders retained daylight's warmth. Propped against them, they drank half the bottle of champagne, intentionally spilling it so they could watch the foam run down their naked fronts. Half a bottle was all the waiting they could manage. Still it provided a happy combination, making her pleasantly woozy, yet more alert to sensation.

Once they thrust the champagne aside, Justin fell back to patience. His kisses lingered, moving to linger again. Mimicking the fitful breeze, they assumed urgency, then melted away, then became urgent again. Beneath and away from the kisses and the tracing fingertips she felt a spreading warmth not unlike the water that had looped about her thighs as she pushed the kayak into the water.

As they moved, sand scratched against her back. The palms made a brushing, castanet clicking. A lover's lullaby. When she opened her eyes and looked up into the sky, she half saw that the clouds had lowered.

A warm thick rain began to fall.

Afterward they sat against the boulders again, finishing the champagne and looking out at the water. The rain had stopped. The sand had made its way to uncomfortable places. She looked forward to washing it off. The thought made her smile. *Even in a dream, fastidious.*

"I love this dream," she said.

"It's yours anytime."

"Always the giver. It's really good champagne."

"Drinking it naked helps."

"When you're president, we'll know champagne."

"Being president would drive me to drink." He ran his palm lightly over the sand. "I prefer this."

She had meant it as a joke, but she regretted it immediately. She felt like she had just shaken loose part of the dream.

"I like this better too," she said. "Let's stay here and drink coconut milk."

"We can put a message in the bottle. Do not disturb."

She wanted the moment back. He returned it to her.

"I love your hair," he said. "The way it falls around you. And me. I love the way your eyes are dark and I can still see what you feel. I love the kindness you show other people. I love how, when I look at you, I feel like I'll never need a gift."

"Do you always say the right thing?"

"Mostly though, I love chocolate-fudge Pop-Tarts in the morning."

She swatted him.

"I don't know how an adult can eat that junk. Sometimes you're such a child."

"I don't think that's a bad thing."

The kayaks lolled at the water's edge. The tiny waves made a tiny hissing.

"My favorite place," he said.

"Thank you for sharing."

"It was easy."

"It was?"

"My favorite place is next to you."

After they shipped the kayaks and Justin re-hid the paddles, they took turns toweling each other off.

They stood naked, looking out to sea and dreaming their own dreams.

Amber yawned.

"I might be over my jet lag."

Justin smiled at the water.

"I thought this might do it."

In the darkness, something landed on his shoulder. She nearly shouted --
insects gave her the willies, and in less than a few hours she had discovered
the gargantuan insects of the tropics gave her worse -- but she caught the
cry in her throat.

"Oh," she said.

Going up on her toes, she looked at it closely. Bulbous eyes looked back,
unreadable as marbles. In the dark, the neon green wings still shone.

"We're back in Chicago," she said.

"I hope the docent isn't on his way."

Justin placed a finger on his shoulder. The dragonfly produced a brief
whirring, and crawled on to his finger.

He held it out between them.

"Am I supposed to get on one knee and kiss that?" she asked.

"Maybe we both should."

The dragonfly made a slow turn on Justin's knuckle. It did look like a jewel.

"They almost seem too beautiful to be from this world," she said.

"*You* were about to squash it."

"I was. Considering it."

The dragonfly lifted from Justin's finger and hummed off into the jungle.

"They can't read minds, can they?" she asked.

Justin didn't answer. He stared into the dark jungle as if following contrails
of color.

"No words from Winnie the Pooh?" she asked softly.

"It's good to know there is something better than us."

He sounded so sad she deflated for a moment.

Turning to her, Justin smiled.

"They can mate in mid-air," he said. "We should try that."

Two mornings later they had a kayak charter. Marty had only booked eight clients so that Amber and Justin would have a kayak.

Amber and Justin melded in as if they had been working the trip for months. They greeted the customers as they came on board and helped them stow their gear. Justin made self-deprecating remarks about his kayaking abilities, and Amber befriended a nervous twelve-year-old girl from Omaha who had never seen the ocean before.

When they slipped the kayaks into the water, Amber sat as easy and erect as a yogi.

"Great," said Marty. "Another natural."

"She looks like she was just in the water yesterday," Justin said.

Amber flashed a quick smile.

"Not quite," she said.

Fury again led the entourage under the arch. Out on Blacktip Lake everyone again eyed the luffing fins nervously until Justin, watching a two-foot juvenile wriggle along the side of his kayak, declared, "We're gonna' need bigger boats." Amber escorted twelve-year-old Tammi Jo about the lake, the two of them, equally wide-eyed, making discoveries together. Fury, a staunch proponent of staying on schedule, left his watch in the dry bag.

After Blackfish Lake, they paddled to the same beach for coconut milk and meat. Amber gave her half to Tammi Jo, who by now had decided that Amber was going to be maid of honor at her wedding. Fury watched Justin walk away from the group and place his coconut slice on a rock.

Back at the dock the customers left reluctantly, as if they knew days like this were as rare as a paddle with blacktip sharks.

When everyone had gone, Fury and Justin unlashed the kayaks, carrying them by twos to the storage room behind the dive center. After they deposited the last two kayaks on their respective shelves, they stood in the cement floored room, enjoying the cool and the smell of neoprene emanating from the line of hangered wetsuits.

"You don't like coconut?" Fury asked.

"A man is rich in proportion to the number of things which he can afford to let alone," said Justin.

Most of all, Fury liked how the boy flushed and quickly added, "Not my words. Henry David Thoreau."

Fury straightened a slipping wetsuit.

"I am familiar with the passage," he said, pretending to occupy himself with a zipper. "My father read "Walden" to us when he was passing. People thought it a strange way to occupy his last days. I thought it was strange too, until I realized it is one of the world's greatest books. Mr. Thoreau saw many important things. He helped change the world and make it a better place. My father did the same for me. He remained a fine father until the end."

He had never told this story to anyone. But this pale boy had won him over at the first hug. It still surprised him. He had never had a close friend. He was different. People had always treated him so.

"I'm sorry about your father, Fury."

He liked the sound of his name on the boy's lips.

"We both know these things can't be helped," Fury said.

"Yes. We do."

"Your mother sounded like a remarkable woman."

Justin looked in the direction of a distant dripping. In the quiet it rapped like a hammer strike.

"She was."

Fury was shocked to hear his tongue continue on without him.

"My mother was an alcoholic. She left us when I was four. My father raised the entire zoo of us. He would give us pennies when we recited a poem to him. Any poem. When they got older, some of my brothers made fun of my father behind his back. He heard them, I know. The people on our island mocked him too, for reading poetry and writers like Mr. Thoreau. I worshipped him. When he wasn't looking, I slipped into his room and gave him his pennies back."

That was enough. More than enough. Was there nothing he wouldn't divulge?

"On the day my mother left, she told me thirteen was bad luck."

The dripping was deafening. Fury wanted to run to it, and keep on running.

"I believe she saved the best for last," Justin said.

Through the window, deep orange clouds perched atop the jungle.

"Yes, well I believe far more people have seen "Jaws" than read Mr. Thoreau," Fury said. "'We're gonna' need bigger boats.' That was some funny shit."

"You don't have to sleep here," Justin said.

Fury stood very still.

The boy looked at him without pity or judgment.

"I came back here to find a life vest. I didn't find one," Justin nodded in the direction of the dripping, "but on the last row of racks in the back I found a sleeping bag stuffed in a box. There was a sketch pad too. I didn't look at the sketches, but the artist had written his name on the front."

"I send the money home."

Justin nodded.

"A man is rich in proportion to the number of things which he can afford to let alone," he said, and left.

Thursday was their day off.

Tuesday, after dinner, Justin found Marty alone on the bridge. He made the request Marty had dreaded ever since Justin set foot on the tarmac.

"I'd like to go out to Long Drop Off."

The sun was setting. Already half submerged in the sea, it splayed red and orange across the sky. The colors sifted down to streak the still harbor waters.

No amount of beauty could stave off the icy seep of dread.

He almost wished the boy was gone.

He wasn't.

Justin gave a small cough.

"We could leave Wednesday evening," he said. "Spend the night out there, so we're there first thing in the morning."

"The reef is still closed to boats," Marty said. "If they catch us, they will fine us."

He knew it was pointless.

"Does a fine matter?" asked Justin gently.

Marty wasted no more breath.

"Wednesday night it is," he said.

"Thank you."

Now that it was upon him, Marty just wanted it done. He knew the answer to this question too, but he asked in the futile hope that the answer would be different from the only one possible.

"Will you be diving?"

Justin smiled his odd knowing smile.

"I know this isn't easy for you, Marty. I'm sorry."

"Do apologies matter?"

The smile grew wider.

"Every day I see why my mother married you."

Shadows crept across the console. Marty felt the weight of the cloth in his hand. He had come up to wipe down the console. A triviality in a world of trivialities, performed while the world shifted beneath their feet.

The sound of running water rose from the galley.

"Does Amber know?"

"She knows some things. She really is wiser than me, but I don't want to give her too much, too fast. I'm thinking you understand."

The boy was still smiling, as if this was all part of the plan. Maybe it was. Although a plan seemed impossible.

The smile wavered, a flame in a once still room.

A tea kettle whistled.

Marty thought he knew why the boy rubbed his eyes.

"Marty, she's the second most amazing woman I've ever met, but I don't know what's going to happen when I tell her. I want to tell her in digestible pieces, but as you know, eventually that's not possible. I don't want to lose her. I need her help. I need your help."

The sun was gone. The cloud edges clung greedily to the last of the orange, already going duller. In two minutes the clouds would lose their battle. In the tropics night arrived like a roundhouse hook.

"You really think she needs to know?"

"Eventually we all need to know."

As easy as that, their roles reversed. Marty had known the time would come. Now it was here. He accepted it willingly. Gratefully. He was the owner of a pinhole dive operation on a dust speck island, co-captain of a match head boat on the sweeping sea. This boy, now smiling at the horizon as if anticipating an encounter with a kindly uncle, this boy was something vastly different.

A breeze rose with nightfall.

"Do you still dream?" Marty asked.

"Yes." The smile disappeared. "Now more than ever. Time's running out, Marty. It's why I came. You knew that."

"She's there? Out at Long Drop Off?"

"I think so."

"And the others?"

"I don't know."

"Do they communicate with you?"

There were bags under his eyes.

"I'm not sure. But I don't think so. I think everything I see and feel comes from her. But it's impossible for me to tell."

For the final time, Marty took the helm.

"Shouldn't that be of some concern? Maybe they don't have her capabilities. Maybe they're more," he searched for the word he knew was right, "primitive."

Justin thought of the eggs. Ivory white with a dusting of gold, they had rested on the cavern ledge like some otherworldly artwork in a flooded museum. Just looking at them had made the world feel right.

Water whispers.

But water can also scream.

He spoke quickly, before fear entered his voice.

"I don't know what they are. But I hope to find out soon."

Marty suddenly felt old. Old and helpless.

"How did I get into this?" he said, attempting a smile.

"I believe you were bullied."

Justin lifted the dangling rag from Marty's hand. Picking up the Windex bottle, he sprayed the Plexiglass windshield.

"We need to see where we're going," he said.

Justin came up on deck just before dawn. Marty was waiting. He hadn't slept. He had made his bed quietly and come up in the dark. He knew the boy would dive at first light.

Time is running out.

Justin gave him a sheepish grin.

"Good morning, Marty. Sorry you couldn't sleep."

"We know where the fault lies," Marty said, but he couldn't muster a smile. "Amber?"

"She's having no problem sleeping. I didn't tell her about this. It's too much. Not yet."

This Marty understood.

He stepped aside, letting Justin pass.

Sitting on the swim step, legs dangling in the water, Justin smiled up at him.

"She truly is beautiful."

This, too, Marty understood. Amber had been forgotten.

Tentacles thicker than a man's torso. A beak like a scythe. Marty had also seen her apex handiwork.

"Justin."

"It's okay."

Justin set the mask on his face. He looked out across the water. In the now graying light, the ocean surface was bruised purple. The ocean rose and fell easily, not in time to his breaths. He had dreamed last night. He knew she was here.

Do you think this is wise?

His mother had asked that.

He didn't know.

He pushed up and off the swim step.

The water was surprisingly cool. Chill shot through him and goosebumps flowered. When the bubbles cleared, he saw the reef forty feet below, dirty gray in the half-dark. Eyes adjusting, he began to pick out the details he knew by heart. On the eastern side of the reef, the fields of lettuce coral, through which moved rivers of fish. On the western side, the single enormous coral bommie, rising up like a triumphant fist. Ringing the edges, the deeps were more black than blue.

It was exactly as he remembered it, every detail cemented now by hundreds of dreams. But this was no dream.

He could taste his fear.

The fish were gone.

He finned away from the boat, heart thumping in his ears. Treading water on the surface, he focused on easy, measured breaths. Through his face place he could see Marty, up on the bridge now for a better vantage.

It wouldn't matter.

Did any of this matter?

He thought of Amber sleeping, snug and dry, in her bunk. Two worlds, not at all separate.

Below him, 20,000 feet of water pulsed and swayed.

Breathe easy. Breathe easy again.

He knew she was rising up.

Softly, so softly he reflexively cocked his head, his mother spoke.

The dreams you have. They're not always just dreams, are they?

He threw his legs overhead and finned down.

She rose, bigger than the reef itself.

A single tentacle, corpse pale, reached out for him.

CAPE HATTERAS, NORTH CAROLINA.

The free diving world was a small one. Word of Paul Wiley and Lacey Goodenall's brush with the pointer reached Jimmy Maas in a day. Maas did not know the woman personally, though he knew her reputation as a scientist and a diver. He did know Paul Wiley.

The first e-mail was brief.

Lucky you. Now you've had a once in a lifetime encounter.

Sprawled on the living room couch, Maas thought for a moment, then typed out another single line.

And no tattoo required.

He clicked send.

Maas placed the laptop on the coffee table and stood. Technology served its purpose but so did arsenic. He went into the kitchen and fixed himself lunch. He took the tuna sandwich – Italian dressing instead of mayonnaise – out to the weather-beaten porch and ate in the sun. The ocean sparkled. White clouds paraded like fat sheep. Except for the swarm of tourists on the beach, it was a fine summer day on the Outer Banks. Better still, he could feel the humidity building. In an hour or two it would erupt. The local weather station was predicting a whiz-bang of a storm. Sizzling lightning and booming thunder had stirred something in him since he was a boy. The thought of everyone running for cover gave him pleasure too.

But right now it was just shit hot, muggy like a sponge with a little flame thrower thrown in. He reached for his ice tea but it wasn't there. Had he fixed one? Christ, he couldn't remember. He remembered sticking his head in the fridge, the cool like a stroking, reaching for the pitcher of lemon-heavy iced tea he always kept at the ready – in the back, far left, just in front of the milk -- but then he had started thinking about Paul Wiley and now he couldn't recall if he'd poured the goddamn tea or not.

He went back inside, padding barefoot through the immaculate living room and beneath the ceiling fan that at the moment was accomplishing zero good. He had never considered air conditioning. His neighbors' windows were tinted and shut. His living room was filled with the smell of the sea.

He located the glass beside the fridge, just beneath the framed poster that said "The Beach. The Only Time Salt Lowers Your Blood Pressure." The poster had been a gift from a long-gone girlfriend. He saw that he'd forgotten the bowl of pistachios too. He glowered at them as if they had betrayed him. Attention to detail mattered. Several times it had saved his life.

Carrying the ice tea and pistachios out to the porch, he glanced down at the computer. There was a message on the screen. Likely Paul Wiley. The man must sit on top of his computer on the lifeguard stand. But, of course, Paul Wiley didn't sit the beach any more. He was old, and so he was now in charge. Probably spent his time in an office, putting off paperwork and searching for craft beer on the internet. Maas smiled. The man loved his beer.

Maas paused at the screen door. He could see his sandwich on the picnic table, warming appreciably in the sun. It was good tuna, sushi-grade; he had speared the yellowtail himself. These days he speared tuna sparingly and ate it more sparingly still. This lunch splurge was his single birthday present.

He wanted to walk out into the sun. He wanted to eat his sandwich, and feel the growing promise of the storm. But Paul Wiley was a friend of thirty years. Stepping out on to the porch, Maas snatched up his plate and brought it inside.

Sitting on the couch, he read Paul's response.

Won't lie to you mate. Shook me up good. Full disclosure, came close to shitting myself. Thought I was going to be a chew toy like Murray. I don't relish finding my head in a white shark's mouth. I dislike tattoos equally.

Maas clicked back.

Heard the girl saved you both.

Heard right, mate. Placed her hand on me puckering bum and shoved me right into the boat.

Right where you like it.

Maas concentrated on the crunch of sprouts and the fleshy joy of tuna. Happy Birthday to me.

He thought for a moment. He didn't like things dangling, and there was only one cure for that. He typed again.

Heard the impact damaged her shoulder. How is she?

Three months before she can pig hunt. So the first doctor said. So she found a new doctor. This one says two months. I believe she'll sack him too. Small town. She'll soon run out of doctors. Doesn't matter. Pretty sure she puts more faith in pigs.

Maas laughed and the laugh died in his throat.

James, don't know if you heard. Terrible attack the next day. Fourteen year old boy. Pointer took his legs. Dead before they got him to the beach. I'm betting it was the same shark.

Maas was suddenly sorry for his glib remarks. But facts were facts.

He typed back.

We all know the ocean has its joys and risks.

He took another bite of sandwich. He thought Paul might have logged off. He knew the conversation had gone on too long for his own taste.

He leaned back against the couch.

Far out over the Atlantic, thunder rumbled.

Maas looked back at the screen.

I'm starting to wonder if one far outweighs the other.

Jimmy Maas finished his sandwich on the porch, watching the cumulus clouds billow into the heavens and reaching a decision. He booked the flight. Surprise. An unexpected birthday present from me to me. He hadn't had a real birthday since he was a kid. He remembered the long table, every inch rightly covered with a happy checkered paper roll, his clamoring friends spilling things and yanking on the confetti poppers his mother had carefully aligned at each place. His mother had been even more obsessive about neatness than her son would be, but for both of them his birthday was the year's one riotous exception. He had especially loved the poppers and their mess of happy colored strands.

Now no one knew it was his birthday. He didn't like a fuss. His mother and father were dead, conveniently leaving one child behind.

Thunder rolled like lethargic cannon fire.

He let the memory linger for a moment longer and then he put the poppers away.

That night, Jimmy Maas composed a second e-mail. This time he chose his words carefully. When he finished, he turned off the computer and took a St. Pauli Girl Lager from the fridge. It was still his birthday somewhere in the world. Hopping over the porch balcony he walked along the beach, watching the last of the lightning wink and fork over the dark water. For once the meteorologists were right. It had been a whopper of a storm.

When he finished the beer he placed the girl carefully in the sand so she could keep an eye on him and he went for a swim, the dark water clasping him like a friend.

Jimmy Maas didn't dream. Or at least he hadn't remembered a dream in his entire life. But he remembered everything else. Sprawled in his boxers across the double bed, salt dry on his skin, he again felt the oven heat of the tropical sun and heard the harbor water's sighings as it rose and dipped against the barnacled pilings.

Cedar Mahoney stood before him. She had been a beautiful woman. It was the curse of every man to be distracted by such things, in all but the most desperate moments. Sometimes even then.

She, on the other hand, had spoken to him with fierce, focused earnestness.

I think we communicate in some way. I think it reads my thoughts. I think, to a small degree, I feel what it feels. I don't think it's dangerous. At least not to most of us. I think it's selective in what it kills.

He had seen with his own eyes what it had done to the swordfish.

And then it had killed the children. Children he had known.

And he had known he would never let any of this go.

THE. SEA.

In a fashion, I am afraid too. Actually it is more like anxiety, and so perhaps worse than clear-cut fear. You might see it as a mother's worry as she rocks her infant and stares into a blank future. What feeling it is, it doesn't matter. Whatever it is, it reverberates through me as I rise past the reef and reach for him.

His arm extends and, for a brief moment, I remember the boy I saved; lighter than anyone I have ever encountered as I lifted him toward the sun, my own heart running rapid with the discovery and the renewed possibility of an ending other than ruin.

The boy floats in the water column, his frail form a fingernail sliver. Just before we touch, he recoils slightly, for we are all hardwired for survival, and I am predator and he is very much prey. Truth is, I feel his blood coursing; I inhale the scent of muscle and fatty marblings. It is sore temptation. The bitterest irony, should I give in. My turn to destroy hope.

For the second time, we touch.

Connected in the most intimate fashion, I show him the things he needs to know.

I try to make him understand.

KOROR, PALAU.

Justin had expected the e-mail from Jimmy Maas. Hoped for it sooner. He had been about to reach out to him. He couldn't do this alone. Whatever this was. And Jimmy Maas was a rarity. A man of the sea, yes. But more important still, someone who would understand the hard decisions that might have to be made. Decisions, possibly impossible to live with. Decisions only the very clear-sighted might justify.

Justin typed back.

The sooner the better. Thank you.

He knew Jimmy Maas appreciated brevity.

There was a pause.

I was thinking about your mother.

Justin had no reply for this. He knew Jimmy didn't expect one.

Justin's phone buzzed again at two in the morning. Amber sighed, rolling away from the noise. Sitting up, Justin plucked the phone off the shelf beside the porthole.

Cupping the phone to hide the light, he read the text.

Is there more than one?

Justin smiled. Jimmy Maas was already thinking, though not about time differences.

Justin tapped.

There are four now. And the mother.

Is that good?

Justin typed the only honest answer.

Too early to tell.

There was nothing more from North Carolina.

In the morning there was an e-mail.

Sorry about waking you up. Patience isn't my strong suit.

Justin typed, *One reason I need you.*

He didn't send the message until he was sure Maas was up.

That night before dinner, Marty decided to go into town for supplies. In Koror dinner time was a good time to shop. Palauans took their meals seriously.

Justin, Amber and Mongkol sat on milk crates in front of the dive center. As Marty approached he saw they appeared to be talking. Mongkol appeared to be talking. Marty could see the man's hands moving with an actual degree of animation. The sweet smell of cloves tumbled along the dock.

Marty stopped when he reached them. He worked hard to look nonchalant.

"Good," he said. "A little rest and relaxation after a day well done."

Mongkol had stopped talking. Looking down, he flicked a bit of ash from his expansive chest. His t-shirt read "4 out of 3 people have trouble with fractions."

"Hi Marty," said Amber. "We're plotting your overthrow."

"Ah. For starters, I suppose Mongkol would like to smoke on board."

"Fortunately, his isn't the only vote," Amber said.

"I've been told I'm capable of handling a mutiny."

Amber swung her head to and fro.

"Fraid not. You're too soft-hearted. That's a good thing."

"He's got a black belt in soft-heartedness," Justin said.

"And so, a lethal combination," Amber said.

Justin nodded approval.

"I told you she was wicked smart," he said. "Not the sort of person you want plotting a mutiny."

"Fair warning taken, Mr. Christian."

"Fair warning offered, Captain Bligh."

Marty couldn't help himself.

"What were you talking about?"

"Music," said Justin easily. "It turns out we all like a lot of the same things."

"So I've heard. I now know aneurysm has two meanings, although I believe they are linked."

Justin and Amber smiled. Mongkol offered no facial tic.

"Music to some ears," said Justin. "Where are you heading?"

"Into town to pick up a few supplies."

"I'll come along."

Justin started to rise. Marty put a hand on his shoulder. Maybe things would have been different if he hadn't. The little things, they are like dominos unspooling until they crash into a brick wall.

"Stay here. I'm only getting a few things. I'll call in your offer when it's actual work."

Amber hummed a tune Marty didn't recognize, smiling to herself and lightly tapping out a beat on the edge of the crate. In the soft evening light, the girl looked almost ethereal. Better still, she radiated a joie de vivre that made him want to dance to whatever it was she was tapping. She had the same effect on the customers. He was happy for Justin. Now that he was here in Palau, Justin was a constant reminder. A minute didn't pass where Marty didn't remember this boy had lost his mother. Amber made Marty a little sad too.

"Hey now," Amber said. "I know you have a better smile."

Marty returned himself to the present.

"You should know, and you're the reason," he said. "I can't remember if I've told you what a pleasure it is to have you here. I don't think our customers have ever been happier."

So much color flooded the girl's face, Marty feared she might rupture.

The ensuing smile was beyond wattage.

"Thanks. It's a joy to be along. I don't know if I've ever been happier. I think this is my favorite place in the world."

Marty saw how Justin's hand went to her knee.

Good then. Time to move along.

"Well, good then," said Marty. "I won't expect a mutiny in the near future."

"No more misfits," said Mongkol.

Marty did his best not to jump. Hearing the man speak was like having cold water dumped down your back. He suppressed the laugh tickling his vocal chords.

"There's still me," Marty said.

Mongkol took a long inhale, followed by an equally long exhale.

"We have all seen you dive," he said.

Mongkol gave a single yip. Justin fell off his crate, and began rolling around on the dock. Amber looked unsure, and then she was laughing too.

"Sorry," she said, choking the word out.

"No apology required," said Marty. "Four out of three people agree."

Walking to the car, he relished the bounce in his step. Sliding behind the wheel, he turned the ignition, the truck knocking to a start. He reached for the stick shift, and his hand stopped. A wall of jungle filled the windshield, enormous fronds and bright flowers spilling everywhere. It was quite literally tropical paradise, but Marty didn't see it.

He sat very still in the seat.

It was the first time he had laughed since Cedar's death.

He knew the poem now by heart. Cedar had given it to him two days before she died.

In the gravel cul-de-sac, she spoke again in his ear.

Henry Scott Holland. He must have been like you, Marty. A beautiful man.

Marty spoke softly, drowned out by the rattling engine.

Death is nothing at all.

I have only slipped away to the next room.

I am I and you are you.

Whatever we were to each other,

That, we still are.

Cedar had been unsure of Heaven, but the poet and Professor of Divinity had not.

Nothing is past; nothing is lost. One brief moment and all will be as it was before only better, infinitely happier and forever we will all be one together with Christ.

Marty recited the poem to its end. Through the windshield he saw one of the White Squall employees step out the back, dump the trash and stand staring at him, bucket swinging in his hand.

Driving away, he glanced down to the dock. The three of them sat on the crates, singing.

Marty spoke to Cedar again.

"He is you and you are him. He will make us all proud."

Marty knew the three men in the grocery store. Two of them were Miss Patsy's nephews. Often he saw them sprawled across the left-leaning steps leading up to Miss Patsy's porch, drinking beer and staring blearily out at the street. Ensconced in her porch swing, Miss Patsy often ignored them. But she kept them in beer. Family was family. The third man was not a relative of Miss Patsy's, but at six-foot three, most of it tattooed muscle, Leonard Chima was impossible to miss. He, too, was often part of the step sitting. When he was, the other two men had to sit in the grass.

The three men stood beside the rows of beer. When Marty came around the corner, they were pulling cans from a twelve-pack and stuffing them down their pants.

"There must be easier ways to stay cool," Marty said.

He had come up behind them. The closest one, skinny with a scraggly goatee and a shiny head haphazardly shaved, whirled about. His threatening look fell away when he saw Marty.

Clapping his hands together, Nounpotu said, "Fuck me. Buzz Aldrin. You gave me a little squirt."

Nounpotu was the smartest of the three. When he was a boy, Marty had read Nounpotu a story about Buzz Aldrin. Nounpotu had taken a keen interest in the astronaut, particularly his career as a jet fighter pilot during the Korean War. Later he had taken a liking to the man's first name. Roughly translated, Nounpotu meant "child of a navigator." His father had been a respected fisherman. Nounpotu had steered his own ship off course.

Being smart, Nounpotu did not look entirely relieved.

"How you been, pilot man?"

Marty wondered if Nounpotu had forgotten his name. He looked ravaged and almost ill. His body disappeared inside his clothes. A scrawny man could still have a fleshy throat.

"I've been good, Nounpotu. I'm running Cedar Mahoney's dive boat now. As you probably know."

Nounpotu gave a chipped toothed smile.

"I knew before you knew."

"Your aunt is a very wise woman."

"So she tells us."

Marty could see the other two awaiting Nounpotu's cue. Leonard was still as an animal. The other man, even skinnier than Nounpotu, moved his feet about as if trying to rub his way down through the tile floor.

The aisle reeked of alcohol, body odor and marijuana. Marty tried to remember the name of the skinny man. He was about to give up when it came to him. Samson. He wondered if it had been a cruel joke.

"Heard that boat was for sale," said Nounpotu suddenly. "Thought maybe

I'd buy it."

"I'm glad you didn't," said Marty.

Nounpotu lowered his voice.

"You understand, man."

"Not really, Nounpotu."

Leonard Chima stiffened. His eyes were redder than the sunset painting the street outside. When he stepped forward, a beer can slid along his calf like a burrowing mole. It snagged momentarily in the cuff of his baggy jeans, then rolled out and struck the tile floor with a clack. It kept rolling, as if it had decided to meet someone outside.

Leonard let it roll.

"Don't be stupid, asshole," Leonard said.

"Back the fuck off, Leonard," Nounpotu hissed. He looked to Marty with pleading eyes. Marty knew it wasn't for his safety.

"We're friends," said Nounpotu.

"We have been."

Marty thought he saw the faintest flicker of hurt.

Nounpotu's lips tightened.

"Not anymore?"

"You were a bright boy. I'm sorry for what you've done."

This time the flicker was an undeniable spark.

"High and mighty pilot cunt," Leonard growled. He took a step forward. "Your face breaks as easy as anyone's."

Nounpotu spoke to him like an exasperated parent.

"Stop it."

Leonard Chima stopped stepping.

"He's going to tell Mr. Dahl," Leonard said.

Nounpotu turned back to Marty.

"Are you?"

He was trying to look threatening, but all Marty saw was the eager boy sitting on his lap.

Marty pulled out his wallet. He handed Nounpotu a twenty.

"Just the twelve-pack," he said. "Use the rest to get something to eat."

Marty bought more supplies than he planned. Every time he turned down an aisle, he saw something they needed. It was always that way. He couldn't believe how expenses stacked up. Cedar had never talked about it. He wished she had.

He finished shopping as quickly as he could. He was tired. His good mood was long gone.

Reading a magazine against the cash register, between watermelon seeds Mr. Dahl said, "You know dem' boys?"

"A little."

Mr. Dahl gave Marty the same look he gave everyone who came through his line. Many people stole from him.

"Thought you might. Bad seed. On their way to no good. Jail or worse."

Marty placed the bags in the grocery cart. His back was stiff. He wondered if he was too old for all of this.

At the door he turned back to Mr. Dahl.

"Do you remember what they bought?"

The man deposited a phlegmy glob into a halved aluminum can beside the register.

"Same thing they always do. Beer and more beer."

Out in the truck, Marty sat looking out at the run down store. Nounpotu was maybe six years older than Justin. Starting the truck, he tried to forget the animated boy on the porch, but he couldn't.

THE SEA.

I worry about the boy.

Gandhi, Kennedy, your Christ himself. They are like magnets, attracting your best and your worst.

It could all end in a lightning strike of blind hatred, ignorance, arrogance or plain unfortunate happenstance. The new horsemen of the Apocalypse.

So many things, none of us can control.

KOROR, PALAU.

Amber and Justin helped Marty carry the packages on to the boat. Mongkol was on board, firming up two of the tank holders. He ignored them, but he was impossible to ignore. Either the clove cigarettes or the steady breeze had masked the odor earlier on the dock, but now breeze and clove were gone. Mongkol exuded a ripeness almost beyond description. Justin thought of Jonathan and smiled. Jonathan had smelled like something lost in the back of the fridge, or possibly like Mongkol.

Mongkol did not come out on the trips. If there was trouble on the water, Ernan could care for the mechanics. But Mongkol did help with the loading and unloading and, during those proceedings, customers were often about.

Carrying a heavy box of sliced deli meats, Marty paused near Mongkol, though not too near.

"Four out of three people think you should wash that shirt."

Whether Mongkol heard him was anyone's guess. Marty didn't wait for a response.

The next morning when Marty came up on deck, stepping into a warm, lovely dawn, the shirt, neatly close-pinned to a guy wire, fluttered slightly in the southeast breeze. Marty leaned in as close as he dared. He leaned in closer. He was rewarded twice with the pleasant scent of Tide.

At six am Mongkol came aboard shirtless. Stepping past Marty, he unfastened the shirt and pulled it over his head. Wordlessly he handed Marty the clothespins and stepped back off the boat.

"Your pants will be ready this afternoon," Marty said to the man's departing back.

Down in the galley, eating breakfast with Justin and Amber, Marty said, "I wish to thank whoever is responsible for the new and improved Mongkol."

Justin had made cinnamon oatmeal. Two Chicago winters had seen him master delicious cinnamon oatmeal.

Justin and Amber paused in their quiet spooning.

Justin's green eyes shifted slightly the left.

Marty said, "Thank you, Amber."

Justin said, "He was starting to remind me a little of Jonathan. Minus the leathery flap of wings."

Amber regarded Justin with drowsy reproach.

"You're cruel," she said.

"I loved Jonathan. Jonathan was his own bat."

Sleepy, Amber looked even more doe-eyed.

"You think you can squirm your way out of everything?" she asked.

"Hopefully."

The Wendell Holmes rocked gently. Sunlight wandered through the porthole making ripples on the ceiling above their heads.

Amber shrugged and turned back to her oatmeal.

"How can I be mad at anyone in a place like this?" she asked. "I want to stay here forever."

Amber returned to spooning. Justin did not. He stared out the porthole. His face was sad.

Marty remembered when Justin had told his mother exactly that.

Now the choice was beyond him.

That afternoon when they returned to the dock, Mongkol was waiting.

He handed Marty a three word list, scratched on the back of a lottery receipt.

Taking the stub Marty said, "If you'd won, would you have stayed on?"

Mongkol smiled a sphinx smile.

It took Marty less than a minute to find caulking and engine oil on Koror Marine's orderly shelves. Stepping back outside, Marty looked at his watch. It was only five o'clock. The afternoon was lovely, squeaky clean and unseasonably temperate. A downpour twenty minutes earlier had scrubbed the air. In its aftermath, instead of steam, it left tantalizing cool. The dust on the street was still sleeping.

Marty put the bag in the cab of the truck and walked. Preoccupied, he forgot the lovely afternoon. He forgot where his feet were carrying him. He was dimly aware of the jar of his footfalls, and the occasional pothole of muddy water, but mostly he just walked through his thoughts.

A voice called out to him.

"Buzz Aldrin."

This time Marty smiled.

"How are you today, Miss Patsy?"

"Better now that I'm getting an eyeful of you." Miss Patsy leaned forward so that the chains on the swing groaned. "Such a pretty boy. You can come closer. Increasingly, I am a very slow spider."

Marty walked up the rutted path to the steps.

Miss Patsy was wearing a sweater over her muumuu. Someone else's sweater. It did its best to accommodate her breasts and then gave up at her midsection.

She gave the sweater a downward tug.

"The weather is changing everywhere."

"We should be skiing," Marty said.

"One can only imagine the forward momentum."

"You still move with grace."

"As does your tongue. Tell me, how does a man your age stay so handsome?"

"I suppose I should be happy with a mixed review."

"It is the best you can hope for at your age."

"True. Thank you."

Miss Patsy waved a dismissive paw.

"I only say what other women lack the nerve to speak."

My God, the man was handsome. She was barely listening to her own banter. What she wouldn't give for a romp with him. But her romping days were over. With age comes wisdom. What a load of shit. Mostly, thought Miss Patsy, age brought everything you didn't want. It was like being served lima beans.

She sipped her drink. It made her feel a little better.

Lowering the plastic cup until it was lost in her lap, she said, ""I did not call you over to proposition you. I wish to thank you."

Miss Patsy liked to watch people puzzle things out. It was one of the great joys in knowing things.

Marty Haruo was annoyingly quick-witted.

"I didn't recognize Nounpotu at first."

"Those who know him these days would have recognized him because he was stealing."

"He told you?"

"He likes to drink his beer here in my shade. After a time, he tells me everything he knows. He is the same little boy. But now what he says is usually of little interest. Sometimes the passage of years brings sadness."

Behind them a horn blared, a rare thing in Koror. They turned to see the driver of the rental car waving a fist at a man riding his bicycle down the middle of the street. The upright man on the bicycle gave no sign of acknowledgment.

"Even our coolest days drive them to madness," said Miss Patsy. "Buying him the beer was wrong, but kind."

"I'm sorry. I remember him as a bright and sweet boy."

A happy look flitted about Miss Patsy's oval face and then it ran off.

"You and I are among the few who do," he said. "He has forgotten. So much promise, wasted."

Miss Patsy's free hand rested on her thigh. She had planned on hefting the muumuu a little, giving the handsome pilot a glimpse of calf. Her calves, still shapely, were her best feature. But her hand rested listless. Suddenly she wasn't in the mood for flirting.

"He is flying," she said, "but not how he imagined it."

She liked how the quiet man offered her nephew no excuses.

"I hear your business is thriving," she said.

"We are doing better than I expected. I attribute it to my crew and the beauty of our waters."

"It is true, our home is like no other." She had been gathering up her nerve, but now she realized she couldn't do it. She raised her glass and looked down into its bottom. Why was it always empty? With her free hand, she shooed Marty Haruo away. "Get on with your head in the clouds ambling. And no more beer for my nephew, please."

The man on her stoop nodded, but he did not leave.

"I'm afraid," he said.

Miss Patsy's heart leapt straight up and tried to crash its way out of her chest. *How could he know?*

"Not of spiders," said Marty, "but bewitching sirens."

Miss Patsy felt herself collapsing, but she remembered to smile. She had weathered bigger shocks.

"Always the charmer," she said.

Watching Marty Haruo walk away she realized that she liked him a great deal, but not for his white teeth and his firm butt. After all these years she still saw him clearly, Nounpotu on his lap, patiently explaining how Buzz Aldrin had worked so hard to become a famous astronaut.

She looked out at the evening, but she did not see the busy street. She had not called him over to reminisce, or to admonish him about the beer. On those long ago afternoons, she had seen how Marty Haruo listened to her nephew's stories about his imaginary space explorations, tales as big as space itself, winding on and on and growing wilder and wilder. He seemed like the only person who might listen to her tale without dismissing her as mad.

She knew that many viewed her as a fat, addled old busy body who saw no farther into the future than her next meal. *Strange thunderclouds rollin' in off the horizon.* Even in her own mind, it sometimes sounded like a load of shit.

But the truth was she did see, and she was seeing more and more. Her night dreams were filled with heartbreaking and impossible things. Things that made her think she really was crazy. Things that made her fill her cup too often.

Heaving herself up with a grunt, she waddled into the kitchen and poured herself another vodka.

THE SEA.

The woman, she does have a gift. I do not send the dreams to her. She is not a mover of stones. She has made her bed. People will not listen to her.

But as I send the dreams out to those who can orchestrate change, she snatches them up as readily as a child catching the sugary scent of fresh baked pie on the breeze. This metaphor, I stole it from a writer. I don't know what it means. But you do. You can taste it, feel it, remember it.

Because, for the moment, you are still here.

THE EASTERN NORTH PACIFIC.

For five days she revels in an oasis. Here, 500 miles west of Central America, there is a tremendous upwelling; waters from the ocean deeps raising sustenance. Beneath drizzly skies, she gorges upon incomprehensible masses of krill. There is plenty. Eden.

Perhaps the drizzly skies make her difficult to see. More likely, the oceans' spread absorbs even our planet's grandest being.

Her final spout of spray and vapor, before the blood appears, draws light from somewhere, producing a brief rainbow.

She weighs almost 60 tons. This offers no defense. The container vessel's towering black bow strikes her broadside, precisely in her middle.

First come the lacerations, great snowy furlings as the prow cuts quick and deep through skin and blubber. Vertebrae are crushed. Ribs splinter; foot-long segments assume new positionings, cutting as they rearrange. Framework compromised, she folds from the middle. For a time she is, quite literally, wrapped about the bow. One great dark eye bangs a somber beat against the container ship until it sees no more. The other looks out to blue water, ribboned with red vapor trails. Your kind could swim inside the arterial vessels of the blue whale. Imagine the outpourings.

The cranium fractures last.

The captain of the container vessel does not know. On a vessel proceeding at 40 knots, no one notices a half knot drop in speed. Amidst air-conditioned hum and the Doors' "L.A. Woman," the captain tells a bawdy joke. Everyone on the bridge laughs because they have to spend months at a time together.

At last she slides off the bow. She scrapes along the port side. As a finally parting gift, the propellers lop off a fluke.

She floats, alive, on the surface. The sharks and birds arrive to feed.

When there is not enough of her to retain her place on the surface, she seesaws down into the depths. This takes time.

Back and forth, back and forth.

Rock-a-bye baby.

A dark lullaby.

THE SEA.

Despite the work of all who heartily feasted at the surface, when she settles on the ocean floor she is still a windfall. You can almost hear the scuttlers and pickers and blind gropers of the black deeps applaud. These final resting places, you call them "whale falls." It has a certain poetic chime.

The reality is blunter. All her flesh will be ingested within a few weeks. Her bones, sustaining bacteria and mouthless, eyeless animals you call zombie worms, will rest on the bottom for 60 to 100 years.

Pale-colored blocks, dwindling down incrementally in the darkness.

Don't miss the lesson.

The zombie worms, only recently did your scientists notice how they are spreading, somehow traveling great distances across the seafloor, making their way from one carcass to another. How they travel is not important. Why they go is what matters. They are driven by hunger and insatiable need. As your scientists also recently discovered, females of the species Osedax japonica produce eggs constantly; these eggs, in turn, are fertilized by harems of males. Near reproductive mayhem.

The zombie worms, they are not the most immediate danger to you. They are smoke on a distant ridge.

But they are a telling example of adaptation.

And there are other hungry innovators much closer at hand.

KOROR, PALAU.

They were in this together. He and Marty and Amber and, for that matter, the rest of mankind. But mankind would have to wait. It was Amber he wanted to tell now.

Marty had cooked braised snapper for dinner. After dinner, Justin scooped green tea ice cream for Marty and Amber and sent them up to the bow while he cleaned up.

When he came up on deck, Marty stood at the railing and Amber was sprawled in a deck chair. They were both laughing. Marty was actually bent over the railing, as if looking for something he had dropped.

They both stopped.

Amber looked sheepish.

"A small laugh at your expense," she said.

"A small laugh?" Justin eased into Marty's chair, extending his legs carefully so as not to kick Amber's empty bowl. "I believe you're still wiping away tears."

"It has a sad ending?" She looked to Marty for help. Marty was too busy wiping his own eyes. "It's a funny story," she said. "You'd laugh too, even if you are the punch line."

"Try me."

"Try him," said Marty. "Although my stomach hurts so much I don't know if I can go through it again."

Amber raised the spoon in her hand, a teacher collecting the class's attention.

"Once upon a time there was a young man who had superb taste in women. This young man, there was something special about him. It was hard to put your finger on it, but you might say he seemed composed in every situation. It was strange, and sometimes maybe even a bit off-putting. This young man," she smiled a glowing smile at Justin, "he liked the young woman even more than he knew, and who could blame him? One day, the young woman brought her parents to the young man's apartment to meet him for the first time…"

"I guess we could stop here," Justin said.

"Ohhhh nooooooo… As I was saying, the young man was meeting the parents for the first time." She offered Justin a conciliatory glance. "In the young man's defense, they did arrive twenty minutes early. The young man had just stepped from the shower, but men are quick, if not particularly sharp, and so he arrived to answer the door in impressively short order." It was a slow grin, growing more wicked. "Maybe the young man took a moment to assess himself before he opened the door, but this would have required a full length mirror, and, in light of the outcome, it's doubtful. The young man opens the door to the parents. It is impressive. Immediately, the woman of his dreams can see he has cleaned up his apartment, banished his roommates, and even had someone else make hors d'oeuvres that look nothing like macaroni and cheese. She also sees that the young man is wearing a new pair of khaki pants. A very nice fit. Later, after the embarrassment is never quite over, she will find out that the young man had actually worn the pants the day before to remove some of the stiffness."

Marty was starting to giggle, a funny sound coming from a man who looked so distinguished.

"Lord, give me strength," said Marty.

"I could just give you a push," Justin said.

"Don't be mean spirited," Amber said. She was waving the spoon now, making small circles in the night, as if rousing the masses to new heights. "This young man, he foresees *almost* every eventuality. They stand at the door, all on their best behavior, and then the mother looks down at the young man's shoe. 'What is that??' she asks politely. Everyone looks down. This object rests on his shoe like an oversize hanky. Before anyone can draw their next breath, everyone knows what it is. It seems that when the

191

young man yanked on yesterday's pants today, he neglected to remove yesterday's briefs stuffed in the leg."

Amber ran through the last sentence at full speed, finishing just as she choked. Marty made a noise that sounded something like a goose's honk, and bent over the railing again, his breaths coming in rapid fire wheezes.

Justin waited for them to both stop crying.

"Maybe I was a little nervous," he said.

Amber managed to compose herself.

"I was touched you were," she said with a hint of apology. "It wouldn't be so funny if you weren't so annoyingly composed all the time. I mean you weren't even nervous when you met the President of the United States."

"You're not his daughter."

It might have been the only thing that could have saved Marty from asphyxiating.

Straightening, he wiped his eyes.

"What did you say?" he asked.

"He met the President."

"*We* met the President," said Justin. "At a fundraiser. I ran an arm through both pant legs before I got dressed."

"It's the rare man who learns from his mistakes," Amber said.

Marty looked at the both of them as if he had never seen them before.

"You met the President of the United States? And when were you going to tell me?"

Justin lifted his hands in plea.

"Now?" he said. "Honestly Marty, it wasn't anything other than a quick thrill. It was brief. Briefer than brief."

"Brief," Amber whispered, starting to giggle again.

Laughter was the farthest thing from Marty's mind.

"Where did you meet him?"

"At a fundraiser in Chicago. A couple of professors arranged the meeting. I have a class with one of them. Public Opinion. He wears flip flops to class. He loves to bonefish. We've talked a little about fishing. We have a lot in common. Professor Blackstone. I really like his class."

Marty didn't have to ask Professor Blackstone to know why he arranged the introduction.

"What happened?"

He hadn't meant to sound so abrupt. Justin was watching him curiously. Amber had stopped giggling. The spoon dangled loose in her hand.

"Almost nothing," said Justin.

"Tell me about the almost part."

"Sure. Okay. Let's see. They had us wait around until after the fundraiser was over. They were literally folding up the chairs. The President came down from the stage. We all shook hands. We exchanged a few words, some polite niceties. A lot fewer words than this." Justin looked down at the arm of his chair. He spoke a little faster. "He said he'd heard good things about me, that we shared a love for the oceans; that he'd just been to Kauai and come back with a wicked sunburn. That was it. He was in a hurry. He was on his way to something else. It was fun, but it was nothing. A handshake, a few brief words and then he moved on."

Not if he is smart.

In that moment Marty felt an almost crippling love for Justin. The boy knew many things, but this he was too blind to see.

Standing beneath the dome of stars, Marty felt a curious sense of relief. It had no basis, but there it was.

Perhaps a step. Perhaps a very important step.

Justin turned to Amber and took the next step.

"My turn for a story," he said. "You have to promise to patiently hear me through to the end."

"You didn't."

"This story is different."

Amber couldn't sleep. Reaching up to the shelf beside the porthole, she took down the framed photograph. Justin had replaced the original handmade frame with a simple wooden one.

"You were such a cute little boy," she said. "I don't know what happened."

"Thank you."

"So much innocence. And such a pigeon chest. You must have poked holes in all your shirts. How old were you?"

"Maybe seven."

Sometimes both the waking and the dreams seemed like a dream. Now that he had told her he felt relieved, and mildly lost. And tired in his bones. Outside he could hear night's symphony of sounds; steady insect drone and the whisper of water, punctuated now and again by a single bird's staccato song. The sounds had been his childhood lullaby, but it was no lullaby he was living now.

Amber tilted the picture slightly so it caught more light.

"The shell is beautiful," she said. "What is it?"

"Conch. Back before we decimated it."

Justin looked at himself, conch shell pressed to his ear, happy light in his eyes, listening to the whisperings. *Mommy, the sea is talking to me.*

And so it had begun. It had been straightforward then. A game, really. Like childhood. But he wasn't a child anymore, and the time for games was long past.

Amber spoke softly.

"Did you know you were actually hearing a voice?"

He considered it yet again.

"Yes and no," he said. "A part of me thought it was imaginary. A part of me wished it was imaginary. It scared me a little. But mostly it made me feel good."

"You didn't tell your mother?"

"No. I think I knew it would just plain scare her. She was all alone here with me. It was enough already, without thinking that her son was hearing voices."

Leaning over, she kissed his cheek.

"A pretty wise decision for a seven-year-old," she said.

"Children have good instincts."

"Some do. But now you're crazy as a loon." Reaching up, Amber put the photo back on the shelf. "I really should catch the next plane."

"I'd take you, but crazy people shouldn't get behind the wheel and Marty hates to be woken up."

Amber settled back against her pillow.

"I could transfer schools. Finish at Harvard. I always liked crimson. I could meet someone new. Maybe marry into old money."

"You'd get in. And you can marry anyone you want."

"Would I need a restraining order?"

"Definitely. I wouldn't give up."

She rolled over to face him.

"That's because you're the luckiest man in the world."

"I know."

He tried to kiss her, but she put a finger on his lips.

"No," she said. "You *don't* know. I trusted you the instant I met you. I believed in you within the week. I would have trusted you with my life. Now I do trust you with my life. It was weird. It made no sense. It still makes no sense. I hear myself saying it and I think I'm the one that's crazy. But what you understand is sometimes different from what you feel. That's good enough for me."

The bird sang.

"This is the part where you kiss me," she said.

He did.

"You should still get that restraining order," he said.

They lay still, listening to each other's breathing.

"Do you think there's hope?" she asked.

"I can't think anything else."

The Wendell Holmes rocked. She still tasted the green tea ice cream. It had been a normal night, and then it hadn't. She thought of the ocean. All that unknown. It didn't frighten her so much as it made her think. But it did frighten her. She remembered a book she had read as a girl about pirates. The book had had a fold out treasure map in the middle, emblazoned with sailing ships and mysterious sounding islands. She had spent a long time staring at the map's ragged edges.

Beyond here lie monsters.

She trusted him with her life, but that didn't stop the oozing of queasy fear.

"Justin?"

He was asleep.

She understood now. She watched him, waiting. Time passed.

Like clockwork, the twitching and murmuring began. She had seen it many times before. Before, it had concerned her, nudging at her maternal instincts, causing her to stroke his hair and return soft murmurs of her own.

Now it chilled her.

She wondered if this murmuring flesh and blood boy was enough.

That night Miss Patsy had another terrible dream. In the dream children lay in yellow-brown water dying. They died slowly, their eyes stunned and wide. Like beached fish.

That afternoon on the porch, a puffy-eyed Miss Patsy turned to Miss Claren and said, "I am glad I did not have children. They are too much heartache."

Miss Claren was occupied with thoughts of the shed, but it was such a strange statement it drew her away from her wet day dreaming.

Miss Claren regarded her enormous friend with curiosity.

"Why do you say that?" she asked.

Miss Patsy sipped her drink and said nothing. Wood cooling the roughened soles of her feet, Miss Claren drank her beer and watched three children playing in a neighboring yard. All three tugged on a plastic jump rope. The rope snapped. One of the girls began to cry.

"We cannot share," said Miss Patsy.

Miss Claren knew she still wanted children. But the hangdog pity and sadness on Miss Patsy's jowly face temporarily dimmed her furious desire.

THE SEA.

I did save his life, lifting his unconscious form to the surface, bumping him gently against the hull of the vessel so that he would regain consciousness and save himself. But in this I was not motivated by sentimentality. It is true, as I have evolved I have developed something akin to what you call emotions. I felt a bond with his mother. When the cancer killed her it left me with an emptiness that could have been hunger, but might have been loss. I do not know. I am still puzzling these matters out. Even you, the most emotionally endowed and buffeted species of all, are often unable to understand your feelings. It plagues you, from first conscious thought to last. The anguish of your poets and silent rooms.

But I will tell you, plain and true, it was not sentimentality that saw me save him.

I am never blind to my supreme motivation.

Survival.

If I have to kill him, I will do that too.

Now, you read these words in comfort. Survival is merely a word on this page.

But the day may come when you meet its black-eyed stare.

THE STRAITS OF MALACCA.

The refugees from Bangladesh and Myanmar have been at sea for three months. They have cigarette burns on their arms, infected knife cuts lacing their thighs, savage bruises on their ribs, backs and shoulders. The unluckier ones have had fingers and toes hacked off. These wounds have been inflicted by the sadistic smugglers. Other wounds, they are not inflicted by the smugglers. The refugees stab each other with long knives to steal one another's food. A man's eye is torn from the socket fighting over a handful of rice. The black-eyed stare of survival.

Many bodies have been tossed overboard, but several hundred people still remain. It is so crowded, only a few can lay down to sleep. Or die.

This vessel, it is weighted in the water with humanity and cruelty. Sometimes indistinguishable.

This evening on the Straits of Malacca is heavenly. It is still as a pond's deeps. The cloudless sky is many shades of red and orange with a leavening of pink. The colors splash on to the mirror waters. They throw heavenly glory back to the sky.

Only the smugglers enjoy the beauty. They are fed and satisfied. One has just raped a 14-year-old girl. It is not the first time this man has raped this girl. Three months at sea is a long time for some men.

The man smokes. He is happy, though his desire is again rising. For your kind, power is an aphrodisiac. He decides he will find the girl again tonight.

He is mistaken.

He flicks the cigarette over the railing. He leans out, idly watching the Spanish mackerel dart to the surface. He is about to turn away when a pale spreading appears below the surface. He closes his eyes for a second; it is a puzzling strategy when your life is threatened. The nautilus, they are shockingly quick. When the man next opens his eyes, he is underwater. But the suffocating he feels is not drowning. The pain is almost exquisite. Orgasmic. The last thing he sees are the Spanish mackerel, feeding again.

There is hardly an inch of free space on the vessel. The smuggler's departure does not go unnoticed. Already there is screaming. A few scream because they witnessed the man's end. Others scream because fear is contagious.

The four nautilus surface together. Pale tentacles extend, grasping the masts and railings gently. The vessel is carefully tilted; far enough so that all on deck are visible, but not so far that anyone slides into the sea. A dozen refugees jump overboard. One of them is old; he is led by the arm.

Those who remain on the boat go still. Not quiet, but still. Even the sunset sky holds its breath.

The smugglers and the refugees, they are all equal now, all of them prostrate, or as close as they can come on the teeming deck. Their faces press against wood that carries the smell of rot, fish and urine. Some bang their heads against the deck. There is fervent praying, panted chants carried off by no breeze. Allahu Akbar. God is great.

Delicately, the men are lifted from the deck. The smugglers' screams are no different from the screams of the victims they tormented. The Spanish mackerel feed.

When it is done, the vessel is gently righted.

Some of the refugees rise and come to the railing. A life of bone-crushing poverty forges hardness and sometimes suspends disbelief. They gaze mutely upon the shells lapped by the darkening waters. The spirals, echoing the curved arms of hurricanes and distant galaxies, throw back the last of the light.

This is the ship of pearl, which, poets feign, Sails the unshadowed main.

Most of these refugees, they will never speak of this. Speak or no, it doesn't matter.

These people, no one cares about them or what they say.

Beneath the first stars, the refugees captain the vessel.

THE SEA.

This calculated act, it is equally surprising to me. First regret. Now justice. My offspring, they are progressing with a rapidity that is astonishing to me.

But the refugees who leap into the water do not fare so well. They might have been rescued, but it is not to be. Among them, are a family. A husband. A wife. The wife's father. Those on the boat, reeling with confusion, terror and an odd elation, have not noted the missing. So many of you, beyond caring about your fellows.

Another boat will come along, they tread water not far from a shipping lane, but they will not be there when it does.

She takes the family. It is a game. She takes the husband and wife together. She does it quietly. They are pulled under before they can shout. Water stifles the rest.

The old man floats in his night without stars. When he calls for his daughter there is no answer beneath the stars, but a hopeful mind is a powerful thing. Straining, he believes he hears a voice. His daughter and her husband, they have already been lifted to safety. He laughs and reaches up to no one in particular.

She lifts him gently from the sea. For the briefest moment he thinks he is being raised to safety, but one is not rescued from beneath. Cold caresses him as if he is already a cadaver. Then pain and steamy warmth take their place.

She understands justice and regret, though she possesses none of the latter.

She has seen what you have done to the seas.

A helpless old man? Yes. But cast no stone. Anger has colored your judgment, influenced your less than magnanimous actions.

And her anger, I understand.

In this instance, I see her clearly.

BYRON BAY, AUSTRALIA.

Jimmy Maas landed at Ballina Byron Gateway Airport at 9:30pm. At ten-fifteen he was standing unannounced at Paul Wiley's door. A swarm of bugs brained themselves against the single bulb above the door. He could smell the sea. Jimmy stood on the stoop and inhaled. The muscles in his neck were loosening. It felt good. Airplanes were like coffins. He would have swum, if he could.

A rumpled Paul Wiley opened the door. First, his mouth dropped. Then his gaze fell to the dive bag in his friend's hand.

"Oh lord," he moaned.

Paul Wiley woke the next morning to the smell of coffee and frying sausage.

Rolling over, he squinted at the clock. Five-thirty.

"Awwww, bugger me."

When he padded into the kitchen barefoot and wild-haired, Maas saluted him with the spatula.

"You look a little thin," Maas said, falling back to turning the sausages.

"What are you doing?"

"Ignoring last night's rude greeting."

A carton of eggs and pancake flour rested on the counter beside the stove.

"I don't have to be at work until nine, James."

Maas smiled down at the sausages. Paul Wiley had called him James from day one. Paul was a descendant of the first Englishmen shipped to Australia to relieve England's overcrowded prisons. Perhaps formality helped him retain that connection to nobility.

Maas liked Paul Wiley. The man was who he was, a rarity these days.

"I didn't know you were a sleeper."

"Christ." Paul walked to the window and flipped open a slat of plantation shutter to be sure. "It's black as coal out, James. I wouldn't have gotten up if I was sure you weren't burning my place down."

"I won't start the eggs and pancakes until you're nicer."

"Awww, bugger me."

"And I will never do that."

Defeated, Paul plonked down at the linoleum table. Salt, pepper and a bottle of hot sauce already formed a perfect row.

Maas placed a cup of coffee in front of him.

"I assume you still drink it black."

"I do. And now I'll need to drink it all day."

"You were in bed at eleven. That's six hours. Old people need less sleep."

Paul sipped his coffee and watched his friend at the stove, cracking eggs in a bowl. The man never stood still. He never seemed to change either. He stood, straight and wide-shouldered. From the back he looked like an eighteen-year-old who had experienced a shock that had turned him gray. Paul felt a twinge of jealousy.

"You know, I work today," he said.

"Good. I'm glad you have something that gets you out of the house." Maas cracked another egg deftly. "You won't need to worry about me. I'll spend today wandering about town, finding out what I can about you." He gave the eggs a swift whisk beating. "We'll dive first thing tomorrow morning. The conditions look good."

Paul felt a deadening in his chest. Maybe he could assign himself overtime.

Maas brought two heaping plates of scrambled eggs and sausage to the table.

"And don't assign yourself overtime," he said, sliding one plate across the table.

Lacey Goodenall spotted him in the supermarket. He was lean, a bit sun spotted and taller than she thought. Photographs so often lie.

He appeared to be hypnotized by a mound of mangoes, but as she passed by he looked up.

"I know your specialty is marine science, but I'm guessing you know a little something about local produce too," he said.

She slowed, but she didn't stop.

"I thought you'd know something about mangoes given all your travels," she said.

"I can't seem to remember everything."

"From what I've read of you, you remember everything."

"Journalists stretch the truth. Or outright lie."

She stopped the cart. When she stepped up beside him, she smelled Irish Spring.

"How many do you want?"

"Six please."

She plucked them quickly from the mound and dropped them, without ceremony, in his basket.

"They don't bruise?"

"Perhaps you need to hire a personal shopper."

Maas laughed.

"Honestly, I have a difficult time letting anyone do anything," he said. "Except, it seems, picking ripe mangoes."

More than anything, she hated alpha males. All that confidence masking incompetence. She made it a point not to smile.

"I've heard you're a control freak," she said.

"Heard or read?"

"Heard. I'm discriminating about my reading. One article about you was enough."

"One too many," he said agreeably.

She watched him pick up the mangoes she had selected, examining them one by one. He didn't put the bruised one back, but he did select another perfectly ripe one.

Placing it gently in the basket he said, "I don't mind a bruise, but Paul's tastes might be slightly more refined."

"Believe me, they're not."

Lacey knew what was coming next. *Bugger me. Why didn't I duck down the soup and condiment aisle?*

"It's possible you saved his life."

She was glad he had the grace to at least speak quietly.

"It's possible you picked an overripe mango," she said.

"The consequences are different. Thank you."

Now his face looked like it did in all the pictures. Deadly serious and more than a touch earnest.

"He's my friend too," she said.

"I'm sorry about the boy."

She felt some of the tension go out of her.

"Yes. Thank you. No one should lose a child."

Oh fuck. Fuck fuck fuck. She was an idiot. A self-absorbed, self-righteous, self-inflated, self-destructive idiot. She was an alpha-female, covering up truckloads of incompetence.

Maas was pretending to look for something in the basket.

Sorry would only make it worse. Probably why he said, "I need to get some fruit into our friend. His fridge looks like a stockyard."

"He *is* an Australian male," Lacey said with a trace of kindness.

"One of his many strong suits."

"You don't have to put up with them," she said, but she smiled at him.

 "Well," Maas said, "I'd better pick up the rest of the things on my list. Diving tomorrow."

He departed so quickly she didn't even have time to say goodbye. She watched him walk away, taking long confident strides. She realized, with mild surprise, that they hadn't introduced themselves. She also realized she despised him a little less.

That night when Jimmy Maas raised the possibility, his friend said, "I dunno."

"It's your call," Maas said.

Paul Wiley picked up his beer and drank.

"I call bullshit," Paul said.

"I dunno," said Maas.

Maas sipped his beer and waited. He had witnessed this process before.

Paul unfolded from the couch with a looseness befitting a man half his age.

"You're relentlessly annoying," Paul said.

He walked into his bedroom, but he forgot to shut the door. Maas saw him pick the cell phone up off the cluttered dresser.

He spoke into the phone without preamble.

"Listen Lacey, James and I are diving tomorrow morning…"

Maas did not miss the forced casualness.

She was sitting cross-legged in the sand in front of lifesaving headquarters when they arrived.

Stepping out of the lorry, Paul Wiley said, "It's my fault we're late."

Lacey rose without putting her hands to the sand.

"I know it is," she said.

Paul looked mildly surprised.

"You're on time," he said.

"Yes."

She was already in her wetsuit. Paul hadn't told her, but she knew where they were going. It was a short boat ride. In deference to the already warm tropical morning, the wetsuit was folded to her waist. Fortunately she wore a rash guard over her bikini top. He had seen enough to haunt him already.

Maas came around the side of the lorry. He was in his wetsuit too. In deference to the already warm morning, he had pulled it down to his waist. He was not wearing a rash guard.

Lacey focused on the outstretched hand. She noticed, in scientific fashion, that the fingers were long.

"We haven't met. Jimmy Maas."

"Lacey Goodenall." *Why not?* she thought. "Personal shopper."

When people laughed, all their stuffy adultisms fell away.

"I brought a few of your perfectly ripe mangoes," Maas said.

"Wrong."

He was leaning back into the jeep to pluck his dive bag from the back seat. He turned to her. Not annoyed. Curious.

"You picked one of them," she said.

They were quiet on the ride out, hiding behind the outboard's bee hive buzz. On the floor of the zodiac things jounced and rattled.

The headland loomed, the sea beyond it indecipherable as always.

To his credit, when Paul shut off the engine Jimmy Maas did not try to make idle conversation.

The morning was bright, but to Lacey it still resonated threat. The odds of the shark being here right now were roughly the same as the odds of Jimmy Maas picking an overripe mango. She knew this in her mind, but it wasn't what she felt.

Her friend looked positively ashen.

"I don't want to do this," Paul said.

To her surprise, Maas looked at him kindly.

"You don't have to," Maas said.

Maas stood, carefully pulled his wetsuit up, sat, and pulled his fins on. He placed his mask on his face. He picked up his spear gun, the thick rubber bands dangling.

The mask pinched his nose, making his voice nasally.

"I would understand perfectly if you didn't go in. I don't know if I would."

Maybe it was the squeaky, nasal voice. Maybe she was more frightened than she realized.

She burst out laughing.

"Well I'm not falling for your bullshit," she said. "I'm not letting you have all the fish."

They dove for three hours. The sun came up, looking down on an ocean of happy blue. It was a big reef. Maas swam out far from the zodiac. Lacey and Paul did not. Nor did they take the first good shot, or the second, or the third. When Lacey finally speared a good-size Spanish mackerel and rose with it to the surface, she was acutely aware of the thin ribbon of blood, like a vein itself, and the vibrations of the struggling fish running through her arm.

Climbing over the side of the zodiac, she deposited the mackerel in the cooler and slid back into the water before she could think. Finning back down through the bright-white waters, she still saw shadows.

The following day dawned dark and stormy. Standing at the picture window, coffee in hand, Lacey looked out at the crisscrossed sea. It wasn't as strong as the earlier blow, but it precluded any free diving. She hated her relief.

She was still staring absently out the window when she saw Paul Wiley's jeep jouncing up the hill. The jeep came to a standstill. Jimmy Maas got out.

The long legs brought him to the door before she could get to the bedroom.

She opened the door before he could knock. For some reason she didn't want him to think he had surprised her.

"I hope this means I'm not too early?"

He was smiling, but on this morning his smile seemed a little forced, as if he'd practiced it on the drive up the hill. She wondered if he had.

She was conscious of her nakedness under the terry cloth robe. She cinched the tie around her waist. The movement reminded of her of her mother.

"I'm an early riser," she said. "I don't like to waste time. Paul's still sleeping?"

She knew he was working today. This falsehood added to her growing sense of annoyance and bother.

"He's working today."

"If you call shopping for beer on the internet, training on our good citizens' dime, and going for an occasional drive on the beach work."

This smile was more natural.

"I think we both agree he's carved out a pretty good life for himself. But as we both know, there's more to him than meets the eye. He's reading Ulysses."

"I didn't know it was a picture book," Lacey said, but it pleased her to see a man buck up for his friend. "He's a passable bloke at times. Coffee?"

"Yes. Please."

She brewed a full pot every morning and drank it through the day. Maas stood quietly while she poured his coffee. She knew he was looking around. He was an observer. She'd read that too. Favorite musician, John Mayall. Favorite author, Ethan Canin. Favorite meal, homemade spaghetti. Biggest tuna speared, a 495-pound blue fin. *That* was a miracle. It embarrassed her that she remembered so much of the article. She remembered the sad bits too, and her embarrassment came flooding back.

Handing him the coffee mug, she avoided his eyes.

"I don't stock cream or sugar. They'll kill you."

"I'd prefer to enjoy the day." He sipped the coffee. "Perfect as is."

"Good. Then you are welcome for coffee here again." *God, that sounded like a come on.* "That wasn't a come on."

Maas gave a perfunctory nod.

"Understood. I hope you won't think *this* is forward, but I wonder if you touch your left ear with your left hand when you're embarrassed. I think you did it at the grocery store. Just in case you take up poker."

It felt good to finally smile easily.

"We're both observers," she said.

"A blessing and a curse."

"A scientific necessity."

"In some circumstances."

She desperately wanted to sit. She felt as if she had become her mother, standing there, smoothing her bathrobe. She nodded to the picture window.

"What say we observe the ocean?" she asked.

"I'd like that."

Lacey pulled up two chairs, setting them side by side. Like a movie. He waited until she sat.

"My favorite movie," he said.

"It's why I bought this house. That and the garden."

"Some cutting edge form of xeriscape, I'm guessing."

"Yes. But the rain here is a problem."

Maas watched the marled sea.

She glanced at him out of the corner of her eye. He sat easily, as if he spent every morning having coffee in a strange woman's house.

"Have you read Ulysses?" he asked.

"No. Too dense for me."

"I tried. I couldn't do it either. It still makes me feel a little inadequate."

That, I'd relish seeing, bad Lacey thought.

Instead, good Lacey said, "I read somewhere where Joyce's wife once asked him why he didn't write something people could read."

"Thank you. Nora Barnacle," he added.

Now she looked at him fully.

"What?"

"Nora Barnacle. Joyce's wife."

"Tell me you're not making that up."

"I'm not making that up. She was born in Galway. Like most Irish, she was straightforward."

"I like her already. But that sort of literary criticism couldn't have been easy on their marriage."

He had a habit of nodding slowly, as if he was still considering the thought. She remembered a poster she once saw on a coffee shop wall. *The biggest communication problem is we do not listen to understand. We listen to reply.*

"I think they had a good marriage at first, but it wore on both of them," he said. "She thought he drank too much. She also often told him she wished he'd been a musician instead of a writer. In his youth, Joyce was a beautiful singer."

"I had no idea. I'm starting to wonder if you're a Joyce scholar."

Maas smiled slowly too, as if considering if the joke was worthwhile.

"No, but a friend of mine is. He's the one who convinced me to try Ulysses. He's also the one told me it was okay to quit. I read Dubliners, so as not to disappoint him entirely."

"What did you learn from Dubliners?"

"That his short stories are easier to read."

They fell silent. It was a comfortable silence. The morning sea danced for them.

Lacey turned to Maas.

"I don't have a garden, but I do have a lab."

In the lab Jimmy Maas was curious about everything, but touched nothing. She knew his free diving had seen him cross paths with some of the most famous marine biologists of the day and she knew he was meticulous in his own matters, but it was still nice that he kept his hands to himself. She didn't want to say it, though. She didn't want to chance another comment being misconstrued.

She showed him the two-headed fetus last.

He was very quiet.

"Axial bifurcation," he said.

He bent, looking directly into the tiny maws.

"A fisherman friend brought it to me. He said it was a bad omen."

She meant it to sound light.

The silence lengthened. She concluded he hadn't heard her.

"It makes me a little sad," he said, straightening.

'What?" she asked, mildly surprised.

"That some things aren't meant for this world."

That afternoon she didn't return to the lab. She slept. She never slept in the afternoon, but there it was. She had no explanation. The draining effect of the previous day's diving. The nervous energy she had expended trying to be entertaining. Trying. There was no doubt she had. If she was honest with herself, she had tried really hard.

Maybe she slept to ignore this.

That night Maas couldn't sleep. He hadn't forgotten James Joyce. The author always lurked at the edges of his mind. But talking about him had again brought Joyce, and his own always present pain, front and center again.

Maas lay in the too-small guest room bed, looking at the seascape paintings hung about the walls as if someone had played a game of musical chairs. Stop. Hang it here. Stop, hang it there. The paintings, all oils, were all works of Byron Bay artists. Some were very, very good. Some were less so. In the half-light they all looked the same.

It was true. He had enjoyed Dubliners and greatly admired Joyce's skill with words, right up until the last story. He had known the story was coming. Truth was, Nora Barnacle had gripped him far more than her husband. How, before she met Joyce, she had fallen in love with a teenager named Michael Feeny. Almost as soon as young Nora experienced the piercings of first love, Michael Feeney died of typhoid. The human heart being ever receptive, Nora fell in love again. Michael Bodkin died. A friend – the term, thought Maas, has broad connotations – dubbed her "man-killer." James Joyce knew of his wife's star-crossed path. The final story in Dubliners was based on what Joyce knew. For once, Joyce had been spare with words. The story was titled "The Dead." Maas had fought his way through it only because he had quit Joyce once before.

He looked over his toes at a painting of a rowboat being tossed at sea. It was ridiculous. He didn't believe a person could be an albatross, just as he didn't believe anyone's love could be the kiss of death.

But it didn't dispel the thought either.

Shutting your eyes made nothing go away. It was a child's game that didn't even work for children.

Jimmy Maas lay awake until just before dawn and then he got up and made coffee.

Two days later, at precisely 6pm, someone stood outside Lacey Goodenall's door, apparently trying to kick it in.

When she jerked the door open, Paul Wiley's foot dangled in mid-air. Behind him, Jimmy Maas looked away, mildly sheepish.

Paul held two brimming grocery bags.

"Didn't have a free hand," he said.

Maas held an Igloo cooler.

"What about your friend?" Lacey asked. "He doesn't know how to use his free hand?"

"Oh, he does," said Paul Wiley.

She wanted to smack his head, but she didn't want to acknowledge the locker room joke.

Paul leered, helping her along.

Behind him, Jimmy Maas gave the footpath serious consultation.

"James and I brought dinner," said Paul. "When you let us in, we'll be able to cook it for you."

"Why should I let you in? That smile makes you look like a perv."

"All the more reason to let me in," said Paul, stepping past.

Maas still stood just off the stoop.

It irritated her. It was silly, his waiting. Had he already forgotten about their morning coffee?

Before she could stop herself bad Lacey said, "What are you standing there for?"

"An invitation."

In that instant she realized it wasn't irritation that piqued her. It was hurt.

She swept into a low bow so she could look at the ground.

"Come in James Maas, you finishing school graduate."

It was a superb dinner. She already knew Paul was a marvelous cook. Jimmy proved to be on the same level. It should have come as no surprise. Fussy men make fussy cooks. Still, it seemed to Lacey that all the surprises had knocked her internal gyroscope off.

It might have been the wine too. They drank and told stories, and laughed and fell somber, and drank and laughed and fell somber again. At some point Maas put on John Mayall. She didn't see him go to the stereo, but she knew it was him. Paul's favorite group was AC/DC.

They had brought a checkered table cloth and matching red and white candles. Lacey had been to Paris once in her twenties. She had loved Paris. It was spontaneous and whimsical and impulsive. It was everything she wasn't.

No one had turned on any lights. The candles flickered, shadows casting dreams that might have been.

She knew the wine had gone to her head, but she didn't care.

"I feel like I'm at a Paris bistro."

"I hope the service is better," Maas said.

Lacey laughed.

"You're not nearly as self-inflated as I thought you'd be," she said.

Maas raised his wine glass.

"Well then, this seems like a good time," he said.

Lacey and Paul raised their own glasses and waited.

Lacey saw that Jimmy Maas had his serious face on.

"I'm not much for toasts," he said softly, "but your performance merits one. Here's to two of the bravest people I know."

"Here, here," said Paul Wiley. "To us. The heroes."

Maybe it was the wine, but Lacey's mind floated to the sun-splashed reef. It was a pleasing visual, as pleasing as the vision of Paris. And then shadows drifted over them both. Light and dark. Always.

When her hand dropped to the table, the wine leapt and spilled over the side.

She looked at the red stain already spreading on the tablecloth.

"Someone should call the waiter," Paul said. "Or the bouncer."

Maas was watching her. She knew she was flushing. She reached for her ear. *God damn it.*

She pushed back her chair and stood.

"I've had enough," she said. "In fact, too much."

Maas rose.

"We'll clean up," he said.

"No you won't."

"Good," said Paul. "Time to leave then."

Lacey was aware she had her chin out. She hated that stance. As far as she knew, she'd done it since birth. When she was ten, a friend of her mother's had dubbed it her "she thinks she rules the world look, and if she doesn't, she's going to make it so." With a touch of the poetic, the same woman had called her "a rough-edged princess."

Paul was already weaving for the door. Lacey noticed that his right flip flop was broken and haphazardly repaired with electrical tape. Probably just before they came over. Part of her mind silently mocked her. *Always the observer.*

The other part spoke out loud.

Turning to Jimmy she said, "I'd like it if you stayed."

Maas said nothing. Stepping up beside her, he took her hand. Not so absently she felt the fingers.

Paul Wiley turned at the door.

He didn't leer. He smiled affably at both of them.

"Fine decision," he said.

Maas said, "Wait in the jeep while I call a cab."

They undressed each other meticulously.

He wore his serious face.

They stood very close. He had yet to kiss her. She could feel his body heat.

Again, she had had enough waiting.

"Come in," she said.

She woke to sticky sweat and the smell of coffee.

He came into the bedroom holding two mugs. He had pulled on his jeans. He had a nice chest, but she knew that already.

"I like this better than you coming up the drive," she said, sitting up.

"Now you'll have to take me home."

"Maybe I will. Maybe I won't."

He just stood there smiling.

She felt herself breathing faster. It was a feeling she had not felt since Paris. The boy there had been dark-haired, painfully shy and poetically French. He had brought her coffee too, but in tiny cups. Over the years, her lover's face had faded to a creation of her own. But she had never forgotten the inlaid gold on the tiny cups, a crest of perfect waves circling the rim. Memory was the strangest thing.

He hadn't rushed last night. He didn't rush now.

She was acutely aware of the curve of her breasts. It was not the morning cool that saw her nipples harden.

She wanted to jump out of bed and swat the coffees out of his hands. She knew he wasn't interested in coffee. She observed his jeans.

"It appears you *are* self-inflated," she said.

She closed her eyes as he slipped back into bed.

His lips touched hers gently. They descended with equal grace to her breasts.

She felt his fingers, light against her thigh.

She parted her legs.

His fingers were just the right length.

He left five days later, staying three days longer than the French boy. She didn't take the French boy pig hunting either.

Paul Wiley was already in the jeep.

She wasn't going to the airport.

They were both awkward, as if each knew something the other didn't.

"Thank you," she said.

"I'll be back."

"They always come back."

But, of course, they didn't.

THE SEA.

You are the new cataclysmic asteroid. Your hand is unfathomably heavy. Your scientists guess that, by the end of this decade, one-third of all reef-building corals, a third of sharks and rays, a quarter of all mammals, a fifth of all reptiles, and a sixth of all birds will be firmly on their way to oblivion. That would be 30 to 50 percent of all life on Earth.

Do you think they are happy about it?

On the sidewalks of suburban New Jersey, a man is chased and bitten by a coyote while walking his dog. In a neighboring town a man is attacked by a coyote while working in his yard. Your experts say such attacks are extremely rare.

This is true.

But the truth changes.

SOMEWHERE ON THE COSTA RICA COAST.

It is quite easy. The worms rise into the current. They ride not so much like undulating questions marks but like airborne flower seeds. Zombie worms is an imaginative name, but your Latin derivative is more accurate. Osedax. Latin for "bone-eating."

You didn't even discover your zombie worms until the beginning of this century. That first species, you found them living within the bones of a decaying gray whale at 10,000 feet. Deep-sea worms, you proclaimed. Three years later, you discovered a second species of Osedax living at 400 feet. Then another and another and another. Shallower and shallower.

Now you are finding them everywhere.

Do they subsist strictly on whale bones or is their appetite more far-ranging? Your scientists aren't quite sure yet.

The old man sits in waist deep water at the mouth of the river. The current is gentle, but sometimes he topples over. He enjoys the toppling. He lays on his side, head immersed in a dark green song. Listening to the river's happy burbling, he counts out the seconds in his head -- how long he can hold his breath? -- and then he pushes himself up, surfacing with a great whooshing inhale. It is a game, like the games he used to play as a boy. He remembers those games as if he just finished playing them, but the woman who eventually fetches him from the river, he is not sure who she is. But she helps him up gently, and she laughs when he holds his arms out at his sides and spouts water from his mouth like a fountain. Her voice is pleasant and she promises to bring him back to the river tomorrow.

But he will not be back. He has played his last game. Two worms, roughly an inch long, are lodged in his ear. It is a good place to start. The bones there are small and fragile. Osedax have no teeth. This particular species, one you have yet to discover, secretes a strong acid, allowing it to bore into bone and acquire the nutrients it needs. For the player of games, it starts as an ear ache. It proceeds quickly, becoming more like an ice pick probing into the skull. Medical help is distant from this village. There is nowhere to go. The daughter holds her thrashing father as they both scream and weep. Eventually, one of them stops.

Another item, infinitely fascinating and, perhaps, revealing. Male Osedax, you never see them. For their entire life they exist as microscopic dwarfs inside the lumen of the gelatinous tube that surrounds their chosen female. One female can house hundreds of these males in her tube. In unscientific terms, it is like a harem on amphetamines.

All those busy harems.

Do they subsist strictly on whale bones?

I think we can answer that now.

It is not revenge. This is too much to assume, given such a primitive creature. It is simply survival. But it is no less final.

I am sorry about the old man. It is slow, terrible and sad. I don't condone it, but it cannot be avoided. Or maybe it could have been. The whale that fed these Osedax before the old man took its place, it was the whale your container vessel killed.

Zombie worms.

The dead don't walk. They're just dead.

KOROR, PALAU.

Jimmy Maas decided that Palau's airport had changed for neither better nor worse. Customs passed quickly, they didn't seem to care if you had a passport or a live chicken, and the cabbies still dozed against the curb until something passed by with ample breasts.

It remained one of his favorite airports.

He checked into the tidy pension, paid his respects to Mr. Villalobos, the distinguished white-goateed owner, unpacked his things and distributed them in the single chest of drawers, re-tucked the mosquito netting and then found his way to the main street and hailed a cab. The backs of his thighs stuck to the vinyl. The breeze looping through the cab was heavy with the fecund smell of jungle and approaching rain. He realized how much he had missed the place.

Happiness and sorrow shared space in his heart.

The harbor hadn't changed either, though someone had painted a handsome new sign above the always open door (there was no door) of the White Squall. Maas spent a few minutes admiring the depiction; a whale boat on the losing end of an encounter with a great white whale. The whaleboat stood almost on its stern, like a harpoon itself. Men and lines looped through the air. The whale's fluke was readying to descend again. The artist had substantial talent. Oddly, all the whalers, those still clinging to the boat and those pin-wheeling through the air, had red hair.

There was no one behind the counter of the dive shop, but he heard the clanking of tanks in the back. He waited, enjoying the sound of the clanking and the whirring of the fan perched on the counter.

He had again decided to arrive unannounced. He told himself it was because he didn't like fanfare, but he didn't believe himself entirely.

The man who exited the back room possessed a plethora of tattoos, an intelligent look and bright red hair. Jimmy suspected he might have found the artist.

The man was consuming an energy bar in large bites. It was gone before he reached the counter.

With a last swallow he said, "May I help you?"

"Good evening. I'd like to go diving in the morning."

A lifetime of tallness had taught Jimmy Maas that short people reacted to height with either mild subservience or an offense of belligerence. The man peering up over the counter exhibited neither.

He simply said, "And we would very much like you to come. But it is also supposed to rain like hell tomorrow."

It was so honest, Maas laughed.

"Maybe you'd better check with the rest of your crew before you give me blanket approval, and then persuade me not to come," he said.

The man regarded him in circumspect fashion.

"You've been out with us before."

Again, pain fluttered in his heart.

"I have."

The man nodded perfunctorily.

"It really is supposed to rain like hell tomorrow," he said, leafing through some paperwork he pulled off the counter. "A hard rain affects the visibility on some of our reefs. Not as much as rain affects other reefs in other places, but still a measurable effect. But I suspect you know this."

"I'm familiar with a few of your reefs, though not as many as I'd like."

The man continued to thumb through paperwork, as if he was deciding something.

"I did not know her, Mr. Maas."

"I did. I was lucky for it."

"I believe you." Fury stopped the paperwork façade. "I am an admirer and a free diver too."

Maas said, "Wise on one front."

"I could take you to the boat now. They would be very glad to see you."

"No thank you. I'll wait until morning. I have some errands to run. But I wanted to make sure I was on the manifest."

Picking up the clipboard beside the fan, the red-haired man made a scratching notation and then grinned.

"Rest assured, you'll have a spot on our boat, Mr. Holmes."

Justin woke the next morning to voices; one so soft it was barely discernible, the other so loud it was a surprise. Amber slept like the dead, but the second voice was loud enough to wake her.

She threw an arm over her eyes.

"Oh my god. What time is it?"

Justin glanced at his watch.

"Five fifteen."

Amber groaned.

"He sounds like he's in our cabin." Amber still had her eyes shut. "Please tell me he's not in our cabin."

"He could be, but I think there's a better chance he's out on the dock."

Justin swung his feet to the floor.

Amber regarded him from an elbow.

"You're getting up?"

"Don't you want to find out who can get Mongkol to talk?"

When the boy came up from below, Maas saw he had changed. Physically, he wasn't much different. Maybe two inches taller, the shoulders a touch broader, a bit more muscle everywhere. But something else made Maas pause for an instant. He couldn't put his finger on it except to say the green eyes were even brighter, and he held himself with an easy grace.

Not sixteen anymore.

But he turned sixteen in an instant.

Justin gave a short frog-like hop as if someone had just stuck him with a pin.

"Jimmy!"

Three strides and he was at the stern. Another hop and Justin crushed Jimmy Maas in a hug.

The boy was definitely stronger.

Justin didn't release him.

"You're crushing the air out of me," Maas said finally.

Justin let go with a laugh.

"Like that will ever happen."

"Full of hot air," said Maas.

The boy looked at Mongkol affectionately.

"Apparently the same can be said of our mechanic."

Mongkol pointed an accusatory wrench at Maas.

"He asked why I no longer fish."

"You've been known to duck a question. Not to mention every other kind of exchange." He wanted to know himself. "What did you tell him?"

"What he knew," said Mongkol, walking away down the dock.

Maas and Justin stood grinning at each other.

"Well," said Maas. "You certainly inspire unconditional loyalty from your crew."

"It's not my crew. Someone more capable is in charge. Not that Mongkol answers to him either."

They watched Mongkol turn into the dive shop. Justin remembered the air compressor was having problems.

"He walked down here with you?"

"I'm guessing he didn't want a complete stranger coming aboard at this hour."

"Did you tell him you weren't a complete stranger?"

"I told him I was no stranger than most."

"Around here there's plenty of competition."

There was something else about the smiling boy. Standing in the quiet, brine-hung morning, it nagged him, and then it came to him. He looked even more like his mother.

Maas vainly tried to sweep away another pang.

He looked up at the silent boat.

"I hope somebody in your operation got around to fixing coffee," he said.

Maas had the coffee brewing and was pulling a bag of bagels from the cupboard when Marty came into the galley.

"Good morning, captain."

Marty hugged him without a word. Marty held on for a beat longer too.

When they parted, Maas said, "I'm sorry."

"I'd say it's okay, but it isn't," Marty said.

"Remember how happy she was when we were all here?" Justin said, pouring the last orange juice. "I know she's happy about this."

Both men looked at the boy as if he was their son.

"Do you always say the right thing?" Marty asked softly.

A cabin door closed.

"No," said Justin. "And here comes my witness."

The girl was beautiful, but more important to Maas, her handshake was firm and her eyes held his.

"Amber, this is Jimmy Maas," Justin said.

Maas fell in love with the sly smile.

"I *know* who this is, silly boy. You practically built a shrine to him. You know, you're his hero."

"Most heroes disappoint," Maas said.

Justin did not look embarrassed.

"Not mine," he said.

The three men stood quiet while more water rushed under the bridge.

Amber clapped her hands.

"*Most* of our clients traditionally arrive in about forty minutes, so we'd better eat."

In honor of Maas, Marty picked a reef they rarely visited. A group of Germans had hired the entire boat. They were lifelong friends and excellent divers. The forecasted rain had blown east without a trace. The sun burned down from a cloudless sky, turning the waters to sparkling fairyland. Because the reef was off the beaten dive charter track, it was filled with life.

On the first dive, Justin and Fury went in with scuba gear, monitoring the Germans as they finned about the reef. Having ascertained the Germans' capabilities, on the second dive Justin and Fury free dove with Amber and Maas. The Germans spent the first five minutes exploring the reef, and the rest of the dive watching the free divers move as if they were born to water.

After the Germans left and everything had been washed down and readied for the next morning, Maas and Justin stood together on the bridge. Marty was up at the White Squall, negotiating for ice. Sam Creighton was always trying to raise the price.

Maas and Justin could see Marty waving his hands in the dimness beneath the thatched awning.

"Likely not the hard-nosed negotiator your mother was," Maas said.

Maybe because of the day's glory and the late afternoon's beauty they each felt only a twinge of sadness.

"No," said Justin. "Winning them over quietly."

Marty stopped waving his hands. The two men laughed and then Sam Creighton slapped Marty's back.

"Quietly and quickly," said Maas.

"Mom would be proud of him." A cloth bag poked out from the compartment beneath the console. Justin picked it up and studiously pushed Ernan's sunglasses all the way in. "Proud of him, but not surprised."

Maas changed the subject.

"I like the new sign. Your friend Fury painted it."

The boy stood a little taller.

"He's unbelievably talented," Justin said. "He told you?"

"He didn't have to."

"It's possible there was a discount on red paint."

"Possible, but not likely," said Maas. "But I am curious. Other than white, is there any connection between the sign and the establishment?"

"Nope. Fury marches to his own drummer. He also fancies Moby Dick. Actually, he fancies Ahab. He greatly admires his single-mindedness."

"Some would call it madness."

"Fury wouldn't." Justin smiled a slow accusing smile. "I don't think you would either."

"What? You're minoring in psychology?"

"Just interested in people." The smell of diesel fuel drifted across the water. Somewhere, a bilge pump did its sloshing work. "Especially the ones that are mad. Or single-minded."

The boy was making him squirm. And enjoying it. Maas changed the subject again.

"Your friend Fury is also one hell of a diver."

"He is. It's possible he was showing off a little. It's possible I was showing off a little. Now that you know I have a shrine to you, I can be honest."

"It was a joy to watch," said Maas.

He meant it, but it also had the hoped for effect. Justin flushed and walked to the rear of the bridge.

Maas followed him.

Below them, Amber was stretched out on one of the stern benches reading a book. She wore baggy sweats. She dove without a wetsuit. By the end of the day, the ocean had sapped away her warmth.

Maas spoke softly.

"Did you teach her to free dive?"

"Technically, yes. One lesson she didn't need. She's a natural. It's also possible she was showing off today too."

Amber put the book down in her lap. Maas waited for her to look up at them, but she didn't.

"She won't see us or hear us," said Justin. "She's lost in her own world. Sometimes, when she gets to a part she really likes, she puts the book down and thinks about it."

"An admirable trait."

"Yea. As my Boston roommate says, 'She's wicked smart.' She hardly has to study. It makes me a little jealous."

"We've had good reason to be jealous of women," Maas said.

"We have."

Beyond the breakwater, over the sea, darkening clouds massed on the horizon.

"Apparently today's rain may come tomorrow," Maas said.

"Please stay for dinner."

"Only if you let me contribute."

"We have everything we need."

With their dark bottoms, the clouds seemed improbably white. Alongside the diesel, Maas smelled plumeria and lush damp. He smiled, thinking of Lacey and her junk yard garden.

Maas thought, *At this exact moment, we do.*

The thought was as sudden as it was unexpected. He had never been happier.

"I don't like to show up empty-handed," he said, "but on this perfect day I'll make the rare exception."

The book was still on Amber lap. She was taller than Issy; her hair not blond, but midnight black. But Maas already saw more than a few similarities.

"I like her," he said. "She's herself."

"Thank you. I can't believe how lucky I am."

Maas liked how Justin's face lit up like a kid who had just won a prize at the carnival. Did kids still go to carnivals?

"You seem to have a knack for finding women to keep you on an even keel."

"We all need direction," Justin said.

Marty didn't join them for dinner. He drove off, proclaiming a need to work on the plane. Amber did join them, but she kept nodding off at the table. Maas had ordered fish chowder from the White Squall as his contribution.

Amber's head was low to her soup and proceeding lower.

Reaching over, Justin gently put a hand on her arm.

"Amber. I can't let you drown at the table."

"Uh-huh."

When Justin guided her to their cabin and tucked her in, she didn't object.

"Better company tomorrow," she murmured, already asleep.

Returning to the galley, Justin said, "A big day for her. She doesn't usually do that much diving. Or wake up that early."

Maas could look sheepish.

"I'm sorry. I'm a creature of habit."

"I don't think mom beat you to the coffee maker once."

"No one does."

Justin came around and took Maas' plate. Maas started to object, but Justin gave a dismissive wave.

"You've spent enough time on boats to know this is a one man operation." Justin went to the fridge and pulled out a lemonade pitcher and two cold mugs. "My version of dessert on the deck. Amber hasn't started our baking lessons yet."

"A good heart, teaching you to cook."

"And there was me, thinking the exact same thing." Justin handed Marty the mugs and the pitcher with a wink. "But teaching me to cook is also wicked smart."

It took Justin twenty minutes to clean up. Trying to be quiet made it take longer. Their cabin was fifteen feet from the galley. Before he went up on deck he leaned against the cabin door, listening to Amber's even breaths. He thought of his mother again. It was strange sleeping with Amber on the Wendell Holmes. They were adults, but it still felt like a violation. He wondered how his mother would have handled it, and then he realized she would never make another decision for him again.

He leaned against the door with his eyes closed.

Maas was draped between two deck chairs, his long body bowed like a rope bridge. He was so still that Justin thought he had fallen asleep too.

Maas dropped his feet to the deck and shimmied himself firmly into the one chair.

"I could get used to this fast," he said. Reaching down, he picked up his mug, raising the lemonade in a toast. "I'm usually early to bed, but for this exceptional day I'm making yet another exception. Thanks for the perfect cap to the perfect day. It was the best macaroni and cheese I've ever had."

"Thanks," said Justin, taking the vacant deck chair. "I've had some practice." Heat lightning flickered above the jungle canopy. "You know you can stay in Marty's cabin tonight if you want. He's not coming back. When he goes to the airstrip, he spends the night in his office. He's got a cot there."

"A kind offer I cannot accept. Mr. Villalobos will sit up all night waiting for me. I don't want that on my conscience. I also called for a cab to pick me up at eleven, and I had a hell of time reaching that cabbie once."

The boy's disappointment was obvious and pleasing.

"Did Marty really have to work on the plane?" Maas asked.

"Maybe. He went out to the airstrip two days ago. Sometimes he just likes to be alone. He's the sort of person who absorbs sadness. I think he needs to be alone to release it before it drowns him."

What was he? Nineteen?

The lightning create brief powdery glows above the dark jungle. The ensuing darkness seemed blacker. Everything was ephemeral.

"Chicago looks like it suits you."

"It does," said Justin.

The boy's smile made Maas' heart ache. Justin was three years younger than Trevor. The hole was always there. Every waking moment. He was glad he didn't dream.

"Honestly, it's a pretty big surprise," Justin said. "I love my classes and it's an amazing city. I don't even mind the winter. I even like the wind. It makes you feel alive, and it makes you feel a whole lot better than that when you get out of it." He gave a slight, embarrassed shrug. "It's kind of funny now, to remember how badly I didn't want to go. I saw it as the end of everything."

Life is full of surprises. Maas didn't say it. The boy already knew this.

They were quiet, listening to the outgoing tide's lappings. Bob Marley sang from a sailboat moored at the jungle's edge. Buffalo Soldier. Someone danced to the music. The lit end of a cigarette bobbed in the night.

Justin smiled.

"Mom never really liked reggae. Too much of the same plinking, she said. At school you hear it at all the parties. I'm kind of lukewarm to it too."

Maas looked into his mug.

"There's a lot of your mother in you. I admired her tremendously. She was captain of her own fate."

"She was."

Sadness looks worse in a young face.

And then the boy blindsided him.

"I dove with the Nautilus. The mother. It's why I came here."

Jimmy Maas was rarely loose of his mooring, but he groped for the ropes now.

I don't think it's dangerous. At least not to most of us. I think it's selective in what it kills.

Cedar had been wrong.

He put down the mug before he dropped it. He nearly dropped it, putting it down.

"When?"

"Before you told me you were coming." Justin looked away to the lightning. "I'm sorry, Jimmy. I didn't know what to do. I knew if I told you, you'd worry. Now that I've told you, I know that you'll worry that I'll do it again."

"You will."

"Yes."

"And you're telling me now because?"

"I need your help."

"I don't know what I can do."

"I don't know either."

Maas considered the darkness.

"You dove at Long Drop Off?"

Justin nodded.

"I went out with Amber and Marty. Amber was sleeping. She still doesn't know. Marty stayed on the boat," Justin added unnecessarily.

"You knew it would be there?"

She. Now there were others.

"I was pretty sure. Though we both know there are no guarantees down there."

Bob Marley was singing No Woman, No Cry.

"You're also as brave or as foolish as your mother. I'm still trying to make up my mind which."

"That's why I need your help. I need a skeptic."

"In this, you've exhibited a trace of wisdom."

If the boy heard him, he gave no sign. He was looking out past the ragged outline of the breakwater to the night beyond. The smile grew on his face.

"When I was growing up, she always gave me books that meant something. They were always good stories, but they always had some underlying message. It took me a long time to figure that part out. She never said anything. She just gave me the books. She made me read every night. There were plenty of times I would rather have just picked up a comic book or fooled around on the computer, and a few nights when I did, but, honestly, most of the time I read because she was my Mom." Justin gave a soft laugh. "Still, we had some knock down, drag out fights. But once I figured out the message thing, it became kind of fun, like trying to figure out a puzzle. Sometimes the meaning was obvious. Sometimes it took some work. After a while I started to feel as if the books were like letters written directly to me. I know that sounds weirdly self-important, but it's exactly how it felt." He shrugged. "It's also possible I am self-absorbed and she was just trying to be a good Mom. Which she was. I never asked her about the messages. I wish I had, but I didn't."

"She just would have told you what you already knew," Maas said.

"Do you really think so?"

"I know so."

"I think you're right. But sometimes you just aren't sure of things, you know?"

It wasn't a question. He was still looking out at the breakwater. Maas watched him, a boy on a small boat in a small backwater. So far removed from world events. So vital to everything.

His finger circled the rim of the mug, again and again.

"I'm scared, Jimmy. Really scared."

Maas knew Justin wasn't looking for reassurance. He couldn't give it.

The finger stopped circling.

"Do you want to know what I saw?"

Jimmy Maas, a man who had always met life head on, paused to convince himself.

"Maybe."

Beneath the lightning dabbed heavens, Justin described the terrible visions he had seen when hand and tentacle touched. Blazing fires, parched landscapes, cesspool seas, raging storms, mats of bacteria like great sloughings of flesh. One by one he marched through the visions, now seeing and not seeing, unconsciously gripping the arms of the deck chair so that, when he finished, his fingers ached.

Justin told Jimmy Maas everything she had shown him, all the messages but one. The cruelest thing he kept to himself.

When it was done, Maas said nothing. There was nothing to say. It was the same when he had picked up the phone and heard the strange, sober voice. *I'm terribly sorry. I have bad news. Your wife and your son are dead.* The voice had hurried on, going over necessary details, while a steady ticking grew in his consciousness. They had been riding in a cab in Manhattan. Trevor was a high school senior. They were touring colleges. The garbage truck had gone right through the light. "What about the cab driver?" he had asked, but he wasn't sure he cared. He was more interested in the ticking. Finally, he placed it. The pencil in his own hand, tapping out the interminable seconds that remained in the rest of the night and the rest of his life.

He couldn't wallow in the past now.

He brought himself back.

A small boy sat across from him, alone and confused.

"Am I crazy, Jimmy?"

"No. I wish you were."

"What do you think?"

"I think we should be scared."

"But we can't be."

The green eyes watched him. It was more than a spark. It was like watching lightning fork inside the green eyes.

"Do you dream, Jimmy?"

Maas did not miss the hope.

"No. My sleep is as blank as the spots off the edges of the map."

"There are a lot of those."

The green eyes wandered the harbor. The still water. The sailboats and the hanging jungle flowers, all the bright colors gone to gray. It was a long, slow wandering.

When the eyes returned to his face, they had changed again. Something Maas couldn't quite place. Then he realized the lightning no longer flickered. It had taken hold.

"I'd rather be here," Justin said. "Just be a dive boat captain. Spend my days and nights just like today. Tucked away. It would be nice. But we have to be heroes."

The wandering was a goodbye.

Maas watched light dance on Justin's face. It was moon and starlight, he told himself. Reflection off the water. Nothing more.

"Do we have a chance?" Maas asked.

He was just a boy. But in the starlight Maas saw now what had risen into his eyes.

"We're not finished yet."

Maas drank the lemonade down.

"Do you have anything stronger?" he asked.

That night at the pension, Jimmy Maas couldn't sleep. He picked up the book, but he didn't open it right away. His eyes wandered the room. Virtually everything in it was rattan. The lone chair, its back spread like throne, the coffee table, the bed in which he lay, even the statue of Christ on the cross, affixed above the door to the bathroom. Mr. Villalobos had outfitted his pension via a liquidation sale at the now defunct Rattan Shack.

Overhead, a rattan ceiling fan sliced at the steamy night.

Maas opened the book. The room disappeared.

After the poem had cast its initial spell, he had done some research. He had learned that Oliver Wendell Holmes had written "The Last Leaf" to honor a man named Thomas Melvill; at first glance a queer old fellow who had lived far past his time. But people are much like poems. Sometimes they reveal their hidden beauty when you look between their seams.

With "The Last Leaf," Oliver Wendell Holmes had written a lovely tribute to Melvill, and, perhaps, something more. In a letter to a friend, Holmes wrote that Melvill reminded him of "a withered leaf which has held to its stem through the storms of autumn and winter, and finds itself still clinging to its bough while the new growths of spring are bursting their buds and spreading their foliage all around it."

The first time Maas had read those words, he had seen them simply as a poet's perfect description of old age. But now, with countless readings, the words seemed to whisper something different, a meaning he couldn't quite yet grasp. Words he now saw as something more.

Taking up the book, he read the poem he had come to love. Maybe he loved it because he himself was approaching winter. Maybe he loved it because he had loved the woman who gave him the poet. He realized this now.

He finished the poem and put the book aside.

Hope in a boy's eyes.

Hope comforting a man who knew too much.

He fell asleep and he did not dream.

MADRAS CROCODILE BANK. TAMIL NADU, INDIA.

The egret, she approaches cautiously, stick legs making hesitant strides, instincts caught in a crossfire. Her nest, up above her in this very tree, requires perpetual shoring. The crocodile, with the stick somehow balanced on its snout, offers opportunity. For the egret, the great mass of scaly beast has also long offered protection from tree-climbing predators. Knight and champion.

The stick, it is strong. Ideal for the nest.

The egret leans in and the crocodile lunges.

Snap. Gone. Just like that.

Nifty trick.

A cautionary tale on two fronts.

Tool use by a purportedly no-witted reptile.

Your champion can also be your end.

WASHINGTON, DISTRICT OF COLUMBIA.

So many strange things crossed his desk, there were times he found himself looking around for hidden cameras. And, of course, there were hidden cameras.

But in a world of strange briefs, this one distinguished itself like a penguin beside a Florida highway. It fascinated him, and, honestly, provided a jolt of adrenalin too, which might have been a first for a brief. He knew something of the sea. Intelligence was looking into it, but Intelligence wasn't quite used to getting wet, and so was not at all sure what to make of it. They had, intelligently he thought, contacted one of the world's premier marine biologists, an expert on cephalopods. The man was flying in from California in two days. He had told them he couldn't come sooner. His oldest daughter had a soccer game. Russell Shaughnessy could have pushed him to come sooner, but, regarding such circumstances, Russell Shaughnessy didn't push. He liked Tom Browning already.

At the moment, he only had the brief spread beneath his hands and three somber looking public servants sitting across from his desk.

He skimmed the brief again. He hated briefs. So much left out, just the facts ma'am, as if he were a child who couldn't digest anything substantial. But this brief still contained plenty that was attention-getting. The first person to hear of the incident, outside of the refugees on the boat, had been an aide worker for something called the International Organization for Migration. She had worked at the refugee camp in Langsa, Sumatra for six months. It was a remote place. She had written her own report sitting on a dirt floor furrowed with rows of large black ants.

Russell Shaughnessy looked up from the brief. The immaculate Oval Office looked back. The Malacca Strait. He never got used to it. These places so far from what he had known growing up in middle class Chicago. Back then, Bangladesh and Myanmar would have been the moon. But over the years he had traveled and done his homework and then some; reading and thinking about this implausibly diverse world as his family slept in increasingly larger bedrooms. As he rose through the political ranks, his grasp on the world grew.

But words were not experience. In cases like this, his grasp was grasp-less.

He was aware of the refugee crisis in Bangladesh and Myanmar; broken-spirited countries whose broken-spirited people were trying to escape crushing poverty. Reading those reports nearly broke his spirit.

But during the first reading, this report had simply made him sit up straight (the expression always made him think of his mother; again, he gave a silent thanks to her now) and blink repeatedly, a habit he had formed as a small boy when confronted with things he couldn't manage. Bullies. Flirting girls. Walking in on his parents one Sunday morning.

They watched him and waited; the Secretary of State, the vice president and the dark-eyebrowed man from the Office of the Director of National Intelligence.

"It's impossible to grasp," Russell said.

They all nodded silently. It was so predictable, he almost laughed. It was a measure of his discomfort.

He held up the paper, as if they hadn't seen it before.

"It says it's been corroborated by at least forty people," he said.

"And that's been corroborated too, Mr. President. It makes it hard to write off as wild storytelling."

"I agree, Maggie," he said. "Almost impossible."

He liked and trusted his Vice President. He had known her since their early Congressional days. She had always been a straight shooter. Other than the obvious drawbacks, he never worried about his own assassination. She would fill in more than ably.

He turned to her now.

"What would you have us do?"

"What we're doing," Maggie Cassiday said. "Bring in people who know about things like this. If there are people who know about things like this."

Maybe Jules Verne, he thought, but he kept it to himself.

"Anyone care to wager how many cephalopod experts have visited the Oval Office?" he asked.

The Secretary of State and the man from ODNI performed obligatory smiles, but the Vice President gave her friend what she hoped was a buck-up smile. This was far beyond them.

"For the first time, I'm a betting woman," she said.

"So for now I'm betting we keep this between just the four of us?" Russell said.

The man from ODNI had such a soft voice, maybe from telling so many secrets, that Russell had to lean halfway across the sprawling desk.

"Five. The aid worker signed a confidentiality agreement."

"Was she the only one the refugees spoke to?"

"Yes."

"Why?"

"She's been in the camp for six months. In that time, it seems she has earned the trust of many of the refugees there. She also learned the language. Helpful, since many things can get lost in translation."

He never ceased to be amazed. How did they learn these things so quickly? And how could they be so cocksure about them?

"We ran a background check on the aid worker?" he asked.

He had gotten pretty good at reading body language. This man's posture, ever so briefly, registered offense.

"Yes sir."

"No offense. Just a necessary question."

"No offense taken, sir."

Sometimes Intelligence were the worst liars.

He had a meeting in ten minutes. He could postpone it, but if he had learned anything in his two years as President it was that meetings didn't go away. They were like weeds. When he retired he wasn't going to meet with anybody but his wife and his children.

"Is there anything else I should know at this moment?"

"No sir," Maggie said. "We just wanted to know what you wanted us to do."

"What you asked me to do," he said.

"Good then," said Maggie, rising. "Glad to see you're trainable."

After they left, he read the report carefully one last time, looking for help he might have missed. He found none. It was hard to believe, but the ocean was a very big place. Things were lost until they were found.

Leaning back in his chair he gazed past the couches – always on their best behavior, everyone always left the pillows tidily arranged – to the fireplace and the painting of George Washington over the mantel. Washington looked supremely confident and presidential, but a painter the likes of Rembrandt Peale could make the Three Stooges look decisive. Without doubt, there were times when George foundered, wholly baffled and lost.

Standing, Russell took his jacket off the back of his chair. Folding the single sheet of paper crisply, he slipped it into the envelope and slipped the envelope into his suit breast pocket.

Patting the pocket, he spoke to George.

"Imagine if you had seen *that* crossing the Delaware."

Walking through the carpeted hallways, surrounded by muffle – no matter how many times he did it, it always struck him as the strangest commute -- he wondered if anyone had paid attention to the name of the fishing vessel that rescued the first batch of refugees. They hadn't translated it in the report, but in his early days with the Peace Corp he had spent six months in Sumatra. He had always had a knack for languages.

Rahmat Baru. God's New Mercies.

That night he slept fitfully. This was not unusual for a president, but the dreams were.

He woke thinking of the boy he had met in Chicago. This was most unusual of all.

At breakfast he admired his six-year-old daughter's latest drawing. It was a picture of their mountain cabin in the Poconos. The cabin was dwarfed by an enormous, somewhat bulbous pine tree and a great globe of happy yellow sun. It was easy to tell Cece it was beautiful, because it was.

After breakfast, he had a staffer make a call to Chicago.

Ten minutes later, the boy's name was on his desk. He thought briefly about calling his friend Daniel Brannon and asking how the boy was doing with his studies, but what was the point? When you were the president there always had to be a point. There was no time for anything else.

He typed the boy's information into his personal phone. He sat, phone listless in the palm of his hand. He had an excellent memory for faces and trivial facts. This had served him well as a politician. The boy had mentioned time spent in some Pacific paradise. He couldn't quite remember the name, but he had remembered wishing he could dive there.

He wondered idly if it was anywhere near the Malacca Strait.

That night he dreamed again. The yellow sun from his daughter's drawing was high in the sky. It began to weep. In the dream he searched frantically for his daughter. Only she could correct it. But she was nowhere to be found.

The yellow tears fell. They hit the yellow-brown water with an odd pocking noise that was not the sound of a teardrop striking water. Dead fish carpeted the surface, staring vacant-eyed at the raining sun.

Panic rose off the water. It poured into his heart.

He might have whimpered.

He felt his wife stroke his hair.

"Russ? What's the matter, baby?"

He pretended to be asleep. It was too much.

He woke thinking of the boy. Palau. The Federated States of Micronesia. He snatched his phone off the end table and called up a world map. Palau wasn't close to The Malacca Strait. But it wasn't far either. Another man might have sloughed it off, but Russell Shaughnessy had reached this juncture by not being another man. Instinct had seen him to this place. He wasn't going to turn his back on it now.

When Cece called from the next room, the world disappeared. For some reason, on this morning the chime of her bright voice made his heart truly skip with joy. He rose and went to her. With a vague sense of unease, it struck him that he was almost running.

THE SEA.

I plant certain seeds. My offspring, they plant seeds too. Some will bloom. Others will lay fallow. There is no telling. None of us should ever forget that life, at its foundation, is a mystery.

By no means do we orchestrate everything. There are those who act without prodding. Those who simply see the world unraveling about them. This is encouraging. These people, they direct you toward resurrection.

This rare leader of men, he sees on his own. But with a man like this, additional prodding can't hurt. He can move many stones. It is like putting your money on a sure thing. Only there is no sure thing. Other than change.

The outcome of my personal efforts are not predictable. I drove the man Hitler to madness. In madness, he misinterpreted his dreams.

Here I am, there I am. In Oliver Wendell Holmes' poem. In Jules Verne's novel. Nor am I always front and center. Yes, Andrew Wyeth titled his painting "Chambered Nautilus," and yes, a chambered nautilus rests on a table at the foot of the canopied bed. But look closer still and you will see that the composition and proportions of the canopied bed and the window behind it mirror those of a nautilus. Just a little added fun. Mr. Wyeth, he was unaware that his hand, at times, moved apart from him. Mr. Verne was a different matter. More than once, he turned to his wife. "I hear a voice whispering inside my head!" This is not meant to be immodest. I am not trying to take credit for works largely those of the artist. I am merely trying to get you to look closely at the world around you; the seemingly obvious that is not so. And perhaps sense something larger than yourself. And maybe listen to the whispers in your own mind.

Yes. Very good. The little artist's rendering is another prod, a not-at-all innocuous addendum to her father's dream.

The future is rushing toward you.

At the moment, it doesn't look pretty.

KOROR, PALAU.

It had been another fine day on the water. They had taken out a group of college girls from Berkeley. Fury and Justin had put on quite a free diving show; Fury because he had taken a fancy to an aerospace engineer and fellow redhead, Justin because diving beautifully was simply what he did. Even Jimmy Maas had watched them with a touch of awe. Both moved through the water like world class dancers, and, like world class dancers, there were no extraneous movements. It was ballet of ruthless efficiency and, at a casual glance, effortless. Almost as if the sea itself clasped them and carried them down. Fury, in an attempt to impress the redhead, had gone deep. Justin, because he was nineteen, had followed. They had dissolved into the dark blue for a long time. Sixty feet below the surface, Amber, serving as a dive guide alongside Maas, had shot Maas a look of concern. He had given her the okay sign, though he was a little uneasy. And then they had risen out of the blue, streaming silver bubbles, long fins swaying languorously; Fury first, and then, Maas had timed it, Justin thirty seconds later.

At lunch the two redheads had sat close, laughing and sharing sushi.

Now Fury paused in his tank unloading to watch the girls walk off down the dock, laughing and chattering, the redhead at the center. It seemed to Fury the other girls orbited her like dying planets.

Justin stepped up beside the forlorn man.

"She's smart," Justin said.

"She is graduating from Berkeley in California."

"I meant to take an interest in you. You know, it would have been a lot easier just asking her for her number instead of taking us to 100 feet."

"One hundred and ten. You only went to 100."

"I recognize limits."

"Not that I can see."

"You lost a few brain cells today. If I were you, I'd do that sparingly."

Fury ignored him. The bus from the Pan Pacific Hotel was parked beside the White Squall. The rest of the girls clambered into the bus. The redhead stood with her head cocked up in the direction of the White Squall's signage. Turning toward them, she pumped both fists overhead.

"That seems like a glowing review," Justin said.

Fury made no comment. They both watched as the girl turned on the bus steps for a last wild wave, and then disappeared into tinted darkness.

The bus rumbled up the short hill, belching diesel.

Fury's face actually drooped. He had stopped waving, but his hand was still raised hopefully.

"You could see her tomorrow after we get back," Justin said. "I think it would be a good idea for a member of our staff to stop by the hotel and resupply our promotional pamphlets, maybe even butter up the manager. I could go, but I promised Amber we'd go to dinner. Ernan has plans, and I'm not sure if Mongkol is up to it. I've heard the whole hotel comes down for the Polynesian happy hour at six. I'm thinking that might be a good time to find the manager."

Fury looked at him without enthusiasm.

"Their flight leaves tomorrow evening."

"Did you ask her for her e-mail?"

"No."

"It's on the liability form. Remember, Ahab never quit."

Fury the smitten was inconsolable.

"Ahab was somebody," he said. "Even my mother had no interest in me."

Marty Haruo also had a woman on his mind.

When they finished readying the boat for the next day, Marty turned to Maas.

"You're working as hard as anyone," Marty said. "I'd like to pay you."

Maas waved a hand at their surroundings.

"You are."

Marty looked at this man Cedar had respected.

"I have a question for you, but I can't ask you here, Jimmy. I also won't ask you if I can't be sure you can keep a secret."

"Jimmy Maas isn't even my real name."

"Perfect. Let's go for a drive."

Marty drove for fifteen minutes before Maas said, "I thought the landing strip was on the western side of the island."

"It is."

"If I was driving, I'd at least be following the sun."

"I'm no Boy Scout. For starters, I'm not trustworthy. Truth is, my plane sits at the airstrip woefully neglected."

Maas looked at the man driving beside him.

Marty Haruo gripped the steering wheel and stared out the truck's windshield. He looked both happy and sad.

"Confessing feels good. I've been to the airstrip once since I started running our business. Because it still is *our* business." Marty turned from the windshield to smile at him. "You don't want to know where we're going?"

"I'll find out soon enough. The island isn't that big."

"A practical approach."

When Marty pulled the truck into the small clearing fifteen minutes later, Maas already knew Marty had been here many times. Each dirt road had led to a successively smaller one, like some kind of foliaged shrinking maze. The final road was little more than a dirt path. Maas had to roll up his window to keep branches and fronds from poking out his eyes. The clearing had appeared like a bull's eye.

Marty cut the engine. There was dust and ticking. They were ringed by towering trees. Angling down through the canopy from some other bright world, the sun spread only hazy light on the jungle floor.

They got out of the truck, standing amidst a throwback world of ponderous fern, leaf, vine and creeper. Maas had the distinct feeling the jungle was about to pounce, devouring this last holdout of bareness and them with it.

"I love this place," said Marty.

The afternoon's stifling humidity had waned to pleasant fireside warmth.

The bagpipes were in the trunk.

Settling the pipes comfortably in the crook of an arm, Marty regarded Maas with the same happy-sad look.

"What they call a captive audience," Marty said.

Marty gave a few preliminary honks – a warmup, or a tuning or both, Maas couldn't even guess – and then he started playing.

He played for five minutes, cheeks swelling and deflating, fingers working methodically. Other than his fingers and his cheeks, and the luffing of his chest, his body remained stock still. Notes rose skyward, soaring through the canopy. Two hearts followed them.

When Marty stopped playing, he stood, staring into the jungle. Maas had the distinct impression he was returning to the world. Or coming to the surface.

The brave, bittersweet sounds still seemed to ring in the canopy.

They had elevated the world.

"It's called Scotland the Brave," Marty said, a trifle apologetically. "It's probably the most recognizable bagpipe song there is. At least under normal circumstances. It's better, accompanied by drums."

"Jesus, Marty. It was beautiful. Incredibly beautiful."

"I've been practicing a fair bit. I've got a long way to go, but playing came a little easier than I thought."

The two men stood in the foggy light.

"It makes me feel good," Marty said. "It reminds me of her, but I also love the music. It's like drifting away, and arriving at the things that matter. I know it sounds strange."

"No it doesn't."

"I miss her," Marty said. "It's no better."

Did Marty really have to work on the plane? It was the question he had asked Justin. *Maybe. Sometimes he just likes to be alone.*

It was an unsettling thought. Not fear, just a questioning of many things he had once held to be true.

"Has Justin ever heard you play?" he asked.

"You're the first."

"Well, their complete and utter loss."

"Thank you. It's not about performance, but thank you anyhow. I also taught myself Amazing Grace." Marty gave a rueful smile. "I don't do originals."

A tremendous crashing rose in the jungle, somewhere off to their right. It was hard to tell exactly how far away it was, but there was little doubt it was coming their way.

"Does Palau have bears?" Maas asked, half in jest.

"No. It might be an irate Scot."

Leonard Chima burst into the clearing so suddenly Marty didn't even have time to lower the bagpipes. Leonard Chima was equally surprised. The three men stared dumbfounded at each other and then Samson crashed into the clearing too.

The skinny man stumbled slightly, came to a standstill and joined in the staring too.

Samson recovered the quickest.

"What the fuck?" Samson's high pitched voice rose an octave. "Bagpipes?"

Nounpotu was not with them. Marty knew instantly this was not good news. The smaller man had a hoe and two shovels over his shoulder. This was not good news either.

Leonard Chima had gathered his wits. He had also followed Marty's eyes.

"Fucking pilot cunt. Two Scottish fags alone in the forest. You forgot your dresses."

His eyes were redder than any sunset.

Maas stood quiet. For this, Marty was relieved.

"Kilts are too itchy for this heat," Marty said.

Leonard laughed amiably.

"Wool is not part of our fabric," he said.

For a mistaken moment, Marty thought everything was going to be alright.

Leonard's laugh died as if it had been choked.

He pulled the fishing knife from his waistband.

"Braveheart was a fucking badass," Leonard said. "Chopping people's heads off."

As he had in the grocery aisle, Samson looked mildly confused. He stared at Leonard, and then he dropped his gardening tools and produced a fishing knife too. He starting making an odd whining noise, like a dog straining at a chain.

"Where's Nounpotu?" Marty asked easily, though the time for easiness had passed.

"Fool is working," Leonard said. "Digging fucking ditches in this hot-as-fuck dump for twenty dollars a day. Thanks to you, we'll outearn him in ten seconds. Give me your wallets." He pointed the knife at Marty. "We need more beer money, fucking pilot cunt."

Samson balanced rapidly on one foot and then the other. He made short stabbing motions with his knife.

"Someone could come, Leonard."

Leonard did not look at the fidgeting man.

"Yea? You're the first fags we've seen all day in our jungle," he said. He turned to Maas. "I can smell rich fucking cunts, and you're choking me with rich fucking cunt. It's our lucky day, Samson. I can't wait to see Nounpotu's face. Maybe I'll let him have one beer. Maybe I'll ask him to suck my cock first. Or have Miss Claren do it."

He had been having his way with Miss Claren for a long time. After drinking on the porch, he would take her out to the shed and have his way with her. In the half dusk of the shed, Miss Claren would stuff her lifted skirt into her mouth and groan with pleasure. Sometimes he would help her along by nearly choking her.

The memory of his dominance aroused him further.

He waved the knife at Maas.

"You like this fishing knife? You know what it's for?"

"Fish."

Leonard Chima regarded Maas intently. A predator knew a predator.

He did not smile.

"Don't fuck with me. Give me your fucking wallet before I run this down your spine, maybe take you home and eat you."

"Fry him up." Samson giggled. "Faggot fillets.

"You at the bottom of the food chain, rich cunt," said Leonard. It surprised him, this cleverness. He didn't know where it came from. It felt good. Even better than Miss Claren's pleas and groans.

He was going to say something even smarter, but fucking pilot cunt interrupted him.

"You can have our wallets."

"That's a good girlfriend," said Leonard.

Marty tossed his wallet at Leonard's feet.

Without taking his eyes of Maas, Leonard bent and snatched up Marty's wallet.

"Smart pilot cunt."

Maybe it was the cunts that bothered him. His mother had always hated the word. Maybe, in this instant, Maas had reached his fill of life's bullies and cowards.

He didn't lose his senses. It was the skinny man who worried him, twitching like a landed fish.

Maas addressed Leonard Chima, but he watched the skinny man.

"You don't think this is a mistake?" he said evenly.

Leonard regarded him curiously and then he guffawed.

"Yea. Yours. What? You fucking Bruce Lee? Now comes the part where you chop us up with your bare hands? Wa! Wa! Wa! Lying in heaps on the ground! No, it is no mistake. It is brilliant fucking luck."

"It's a small island."

Leonard's smile departed.

"Where you from?" he asked, though something in the lean man's face made him leave out the word cunt.

"North Carolina."

"Ah. North Fucking Carolina. The United States of Amereeeeeeca. Not from here. You don't fucking know us." He waved the knife at the clearing. "You see other tourists here? Maybe a helpful policeman? It is our word against yours, and our people deciding." Amidst the Edenic beauty, the smile seemed crueler. "If you go to the police, it won't help. It will make things worse for you. Much worse. I don't know any cunts in North Carolina. But I know lots of cunts here."

The skinny man had jitterbugged close to Marty. The knife in his hand moved with a mind of its own.

Maas felt fear's iron touch along his spine. As if Leonard were already fileting.

"I'm sorry," Maas said. He reached slowly for the wallet in the back pocket of his shorts. "You're right."

"The fuck I am," said Leonard.

Leonard Chima stepped forward before Maas could toss his wallet. Maas had let his attention wander from the big man. Small mistakes become big mistakes before we blink. Maas felt the wallet lift from his hand, just as he felt Leonard's right hand deliver an abrupt punch to his solar plexus.

"Fuck you, North Carolina."

Maas heard Marty shout. The two men were running. Maas didn't bother giving chase. It was a bit of a puzzle.

Something made his knees weaken.

He was grateful to Marty for grabbing him before he fell.

"Thank you."

Marty was breathing fast, helping him to the truck. He tried to make his feet work so Marty didn't have to drag him. Maas wondered idly where the two men had gone. There was nothing but jungle.

When Marty eased him into the front seat, the pain flared.

Marty's frightened face filled his field of vision.

"The hospital is twenty minutes away."

"Good."

The wet was coming on; the pain with it.

He counted out his breaths, making sure they were long and even.

Marty had his shirt off. He folded it quickly and handed it to Maas.

"Here," Marty. "Direct pressure."

"Good."

"Good?"

"You know what you're doing."

Marty run around the truck. The chassis sank as Marty slid behind the wheel.

"You're forgetting one thing," said Maas.

Maas saw the face fighting back panic.

"Bagpipes," Maas said.

When Marty fell back behind the wheel again, Maas nodded to him.

"I'm just glad I'm not ruining a good kilt."

Head against the door frame, Maas felt the rutted road. He liked the slight rattling it made against his temple. *The sun is shining and we're on the right side of the sod.* It had been one of his father's favorite expressions.

Somehow the sky had grown dark.

He saw the first star.

He wondered if Lacey was seeing it too.

BYRON BAY, AUSTRALIA

Paul Wiley came over before Lacey left.

She didn't answer the door, but she always left the door open.

He found her in the bedroom, packing.

She looked up. She had been crying. She made no attempt to hide it.

"Come in," she said.

"I can take you to the airport."

"I called a cab."

"Why would you do that?"

"Because I need to get to the airport."

He knew her cab company. He called to cancel and then he leaned against the door jamb and watched her finish packing. She packed her bags with the meticulousness she applied in her lab. Color-coded plastic baggies went into specific corners. When she finished, the inside of the suitcase looked like a pie chart.

"It looks like a pie chart," he said.

She crumpled up an orange windbreaker and stuffed it roughly behind the suitcase netting. She tossed a toothbrush in after it.

"The biggest slice measures the percentage of people who can't keep their noses out of anyone's business."

"They're called friends."

They had talked on the phone the night before. It was probably the longest conversation they had ever had. He had considered going too, but in the end he had decided that Lacey's recent change in relationship status made one visitor the perfect number. He was just glad his friend was alright.

She was packing a few last items. If packing could be a term for something that looked more like boxing. She stuffed them into the suitcase with near fury.

If he let it go, they'd have a more pleasant ride to the airport.

"You're angry," he said. "Angry people do foolish things. Don't do anything foolish. He's okay."

"Fuck off, Mommy."

Lacey smiled, but it was crooked.

It was a silent ride to the airport. Paul Wiley accepted it.

At the curb, she leaned across the seat and kissed his cheek.

"Thank you. I'm sorry," she said, and she was gone.

She had requested a window seat. She liked to look down at the sea. As the flight attendants stuffed oversize bags into undersize compartments and two babies wailed a duet, the well-heeled man settling in beside her said, "Business or pleasure?"

"You minding your own business is all the pleasure I require."

Eventually she rested her head against the window. She liked the slight rattling it made.

One eye on the endless spread of ocean, her mind turned to the package she had mailed to Justin. A photo would have served virtually the same purpose, but after some debate she had made the decision on her own. She had asked Justin not to open the package, only to put it on ice and tell no one. Jimmy had told her a little about the boy. Only a few things, but they had made an impression. She hadn't told Jimmy about the package, but she had offhandedly asked him if Justin was the sort who could keep secrets.

From across the Pacific, Jimmy Maas had issued a short pained laugh.

She woke when the plane bumped down on the tarmac.

KOROR, PALAU.

Despite his protests, the doctors kept Jimmy Maas in the hospital. The fishing knife's thin blade had slipped between vital organs, but the doctors were still concerned about infection.

When she walked into the hospital room he looked up and smiled.

It was shock to see him pale.

"Maybe *you* can tell me why I'm still here?"

"Because no one else wants you underfoot," she said, and then she started to cry. It was so unexpected and embarrassing, she cried harder.

The man in the bed motioned her over.

He held her hand until she was done.

When she finished crying, she took her hand away.

"The expense of last minute plane tickets upsets me," she said, kissing his stubbled cheek. "The airline would have discounted the ticket if you'd died."

Four days after Lacey arrived, Marty, Lacey and Justin moved Maas back to the pension. When they arrived at the pension Maas apologized, stretched out on the bed and fell asleep.

The single room had a patio, just big enough for two chairs, a round rattan table the size of a basketball and three people. Lacey and Marty sat. Justin stood at the railing, looking out at the jungle.

Now that Maas was going to be fine, Lacey was angry again. She had been angry when she stepped off the plane. Then she had been frightened by his appearance and the strength of her feelings. Now she was very angry again.

"There's no recourse?" she asked. "Two marijuana farmers stab someone in the stomach, and it's finished?"

The boy said nothing. Jimmy had talked so much about him, she had been curious. Justin had been courteous since her arrival, but quiet and withdrawn. He was not the boy Jimmy had described. She liked Marty instantly. She could see he was worried about the boy's behavior. To her scientific eye, Marty was an open book. The boy was a different story.

Marty spoke, but she watched the boy. She didn't know why, but she found his silence reassuring.

"Yes, both are crimes," Marty said. "And no, there is no recourse. At least not without the tremendous application of resources and even more trouble for everyone. Just for starters, they have a thousand family members and twice as many alibis. Here, the truth is like taffy."

She'd been sitting for two minutes. The plastic straps of the chair already stuck to her back.

This man Marty was bright.

"You know what I want," she said.

"I think I do."

"You do."

"Lacey, you can't have it."

It was a smile of true kindness. She knew why this woman Cedar fell in love.

She looked past the boy, out to the jungle. She liked that you couldn't see into it.

"Well then," she said. "That's that."

The man's face blossomed with such a gawp-faced look of surprise, she almost laughed.

"You're willing to let it go?" he asked.

"Yes. What, pray tell, did James Maas tell you about me?"

"That you don't give in easily." Marty paused. "Maybe that you never give in."

"Well. Isn't he the silver-tongued charmer?"

"In this case," said Marty, "you're doing the right thing."

Lacey was only half listening. She watched the boy's flared back and wondered about him yet again. He had showed her the package shortly after she had arrived. It rested in the hold, on ice and still securely wrapped, as she had asked. But she had the feeling he knew what was in it. It was more than a feeling. It was almost a certainty. Maybe he didn't know exactly, but close enough. And how could that be?

Now he turned. He possessed a masculine beauty. *Like Michelangelo's David,* she thought.

Again she was struck not by his beauty, though that was the effective mask, but his equanimity.

She knew he had made a decision.

It was almost as if the jungle fell quiet to listen.

"It's hard," he said to no one in particular. "Doing the right thing."

He looked at her without judgment.

She stared back and thought, *Fuck that.*

They used some of the money to buy weed and beer. Good weed. Not the ragshit they grew. There was still plenty of money left over too. They drank and smoked in the jungle. Miss Patsy drew the line at weed. She would also ask where they got the money. When it came to questions, Miss Patsy was one relentless bitch. Leonard regretted that he wouldn't be able to give Claren a good fucking. It was always better high, but that was that.

So they sat in the jungle and got stoned. It was amazing dope. Sprawled against a vine-wrapped tree, Leonard Chima felt as if an anvil rested in his lap.

Nounpotu was with them, though he had done nothing to secure the largesse. Leonard Chima was a magnanimous man.

"Fine bud," Leonard said, blowing a funnel up through a spider web. He watched the spider bob its way across the web. Koalas got stoned. Dogs too. Did spiders?

It *was* fine bud, Nounpotu thought dimly. His mind had wandered off down its own corridor, locking itself behind a door he couldn't open. His legs were stumps. He wondered if maybe it had been laced with PCP.

"Bank of Cunt," Leonard said.

Nounpotu had been truly upset when they first told him. He was less upset now. But he was still a little upset.

"You shouldn't have stabbed him."

"North Carolina."

"What?"

"He is from fucking North Carolina." Leonard looked at Nounpotu with mild interest. "What you care so much about a tourist for?"

"He is my uncle's friend."

"Check your dick. That natty haired bitch is not your fucking uncle. He doesn't even like you."

This made Nounpotu quiet and sad.

Leonard watched the spider work its way toward a struggling fly.

"I should have stabbed him a couple times."

"You're lucky he's okay," Nounpotu said.

They all knew this was true. Murder was not so easily swept aside.

Still, the comment offended Leonard's sensibilities. He was Braveheart.

"Maybe I'll have another go. Let him know who is king of the jungle."

Nounpotu's mouth was already opening. To cut him off, Leonard nodded at Samson.

"This boy, good thing he was wearing his Depends. You know man, you sound like Mickey Mouse when you're scared."

Splayed out shirtless in the dirt, Samson had attained a buzz that rendered him beyond insult. It was like floating in a humid dream.

"Mickey Mouse is fucking scary," he mumbled.

Leonard thought about this. Samson thought about this.

After a time Nounpotu said, "That tree won't live much longer."

He wasn't even sure why he said it.

Leonard turned his head so his cheekbone pressed against the mildewed bark of the tree. It was moist now, but he knew the moisture was being squeezed away like juice from an orange. Inches from his eye, a vine looped. It looked like a hairy snake.

They all knew the strangler fig.

"Start out as a harmless creeper," Nounpotu proclaimed. In his ears, he sounded like a preacher. "No one pays any attention. Then it becomes the assassin tree. Then nothing stops it."

Samson shifted slightly in the dirt. He stared up at the sky, drained of thought.

Leonard thought, *King of the Jungle.*

Leonard Chima became aware of the oppressive heat. There was one beer left. It had rolled away, wedging against a mossy limb. Red ants circled the rim.

Leonard walked over and unwedged it.

"Hey man, that's the last beer," whined Nounpotu. "It's fucking hot. Share some."

"Nope," said Leonard, popping the top and striding off into the jungle.

"Hey," he heard someone say, but they were already behind him.

He was as surprised as they were. He didn't know why he was walking. The weed made him fucking tired, but he walked. He drank the beer as he walked. The uneven ground saw him spill some down his front, but he hardly felt it. He didn't feel so great. He was hot. Truly fucking hot. Born and raised in an oven, he had never felt this kind of heat. It felt as if someone had wedged a burning match head into every one of his pores. Stumbling along the jungle path, fat fronds slapping and scratching his face, he was dimly aware of ants and spiders and skittering things. He felt his own jarring tread. A butterfly fluttered soundlessly in a web.

No line between us.

It sounded like a voice in his head. It may have been the first lucid thought he had had in his twenty-seven years.

It was so fucking hot he almost forgot his fear of the water. He half slid, half fell down the steep embankment. He knew now he had been following the hint of cool. It rose off the water, cupping his face like a loving mother. He didn't like the fucking ocean. It scared the fucking shit out of him. It was dark, and filled with things he couldn't see. But this lake, it was the lightest blue. Like a child's marble. He could see the corals on the bottom.

He could feel the cool. It reached up to him, shrieking of relief.

Leonard Chima plunged into Blacktip Lake. It was like heaven. Oh, it felt better than anything he had ever felt before, better than his mother's kisses, better than the ball cupping hummers Claren gave him in the tool shed, better than the hand jobs he gave himself when she wasn't there.

Oh yes.

He was a clumsy swimmer. He thrashed jerkily out toward the middle of the lake. It looked cooler there. The water was milky but still clear. He was glad for this. He could see the coral on the bottom and all the happy little fish.

The first fin looked like a leaf. It wasn't much bigger than the end of his thumb. When he realized what it was he laughed and gave it a hard swat, and it darted away. King of the Fucking Jungle. As he swam he saw more of them. The fins looked like black butterflies with their wings folded, resting on the surface. But they weren't resting. They were sliding in his direction. He remembered that he was afraid of what he couldn't see. He put his face under water. His eyes stung. He kept them open. It looked like a black thundercloud rolling toward him.

He lifted his head to his own screams. People were shouting too. A man on a kayak was paddling toward him. The man on the kayak wasn't shouting. He was just paddling smoothly.

The first bites were like bee stings. Leonard Chima was so terrified a part of him only wanted to sink into the black cloud and disappear forever. But he was a survivor, and the man on the kayak was moving closer. Leonard beat at the water. The black cloud did not care. It simply moved from where he struck and pressed in elsewhere, a furious swirling of sandpaper scrapings and incisive bites.

Something struck his head hard. It cleared his mind for an instant. Looking up, Leonard saw that the man on the kayak had reached him. He was withdrawing the paddle with a queer knowing smile.

Leonard saw the man was only a skinny boy. This was a sore disappointment. Beneath the water, the black swirling continued. He was crying now, bawling like a wet-diapered baby. There were other kayaks close by, bright colors, their occupants shouting and slapping the water with their paddles. The boy's kayak was yellow, like his hair. The boy's paddle rested easily across his lap. The boy looked down at him with bright eyes. He knew the boy.

The boy leaned over very slowly and grabbed the waist of Leonard's shorts. It was a wedgie to remember.

Leonard felt the hard plastic ribbing beneath him. He felt the slowly growing warmth of the sun. He lay in the kayak, still bawling like a baby. His legs dangled in the water, the recipients of countless bee stings. But Leonard was more concerned about his heart banging against his chest. He wondered if he would die of a heart attack.

The boy's face was so calm. Like a mother's.

The boy bent and, like a mother, whispered to him only.

That night Leonard dreamed. It was a strange dream, filled with fire. There was a man floating on the water, sitting on a toilet seat.

It was the strangest dream. It made him very, very sad. He knew it was beyond him.

But he could change. He had been given a second chance.

He woke sweating. The water-stained ceiling became the boy's face staring down at him. Again Leonard Chima heard the boy's soft words.

Remember. You will always be part of the food chain.

Marty had invited the entire crew for dinner; Ernan, Fury, Mongkol, Amber and Lacey sat crowded around the cleared table. Only Jimmy Maas was missing. On Lacey's orders, he had stayed at the pension. The wound was bleeding more than it should. Movement only aggravated it.

Justin scraped plates at the sink. Fury had made the task easy.

It had been a subdued dinner. They had tried to talk about anything else, until now.

"There will be no keeping this just between us," said Fury.

He looked to Ernan.

"Most of the island knows," nodded Ernan. "The rest will know by morning."

Marty said, "I received a call from the Minister of Tourism right before dinner. He wanted to know what we should do. I told him no one had an answer."

The Minister of Tourism was Miss Patsy's second cousin. No doubt, he had been informed right away.

"How is Leonard Chima?" asked Fury, though no one really cared.

"Unusually quiet," said Marty. "They treated him at the hospital, and released him to his own care. I talked with the doctor. He said it was mostly just abrasions and small wounds that would quickly heal. He said there were a few larger wounds they had to stitch. He said Leonard just laid on the table, still as a corpse. He thought it might have been an overreaction to the pain killers. But he said, overall, he is fine. The biggest concern is infection."

Mongkol said, "Leonard is infection."

Marty shook his head at the big man.

"I won't have that kind of talk."

Mongkol did not look chastised. He did not look anything.

Fury said, "Whatever he is, he was very lucky we were there."

"We won't go there again," said Marty.

"Your decision, Captain, but I don't think it will happen again," said Fury. "I have never seen anything like it. I have never heard of anything like it. I have never imagined anything like it."

The table fell silent.

Everyone but Justin looked to Lacey.

She hoped she sounded convincing.

"I have absolutely no explanation," she said.

It couldn't be.

But it likely was. Two nights after Maas left the hospital, she had shown Marty, Amber and Justin the bull shark fetus, carefully unwrapping the package on the counter in the galley. Everyone had stood silent.

Finally Marty had asked, "Could something like this survive?"

"No," she had said, and she had been certain. "It's impossible."

Justin had found her later, alone on the deck.

On this night, he again waited until she was alone.

They stood side by side holding the railing and looking out across the harbor. Justin held the railing out of habit. Lacey held it to keep upright. When Justin pulled the big man from the water, her kayak had been the closest. Justin's words were the barest whisper, but the breeze had ferried them to Lacey.

Now, the two of them alone again, Justin told her what he had told her once before.

"Many things are possible," he said.

She looked down at the dark water, like a closed door.

Part of her wished she had never come.

She kept her eyes on the water.

"You did that," she said.

"Yes."

"How?"

"I'm not exactly sure. I think being angry made it easier."

She saw now how his hands kneaded the railing.

When she looked at him, he was a mother's son.

"Was it wrong, what I did?" he asked.

She was a good scientist. A careful scientist. A grounded scientist. Her entire adult life had been dedicated to grounded science. But there came a time when good scientists realized that some things were beyond current science.

She regarded him without judgment.

"It's hard doing the right thing," she said.

THE SEA.

It works quite simply. Think of it as a suggestive whisper in the ear. Or perhaps an encouraging nudge.

Some respond more readily than others.

But this is a first.

The boy, he did this. This is quite a surprise.

It seems we are not the only ones changing.

He spared the man.

I know the boy, but given your species' predilections this was a surprise too.

Vengeance resides at your core. It is the glowing ember that sees to it that the cycle of violence never ends.

Even he is not beyond this.

WASHINGTON, DISTRICT OF COLUMBIA.

The scientist was nervous. Maybe because he was a Republican. He knew they had run a background check.

Russell Shaughnessy honestly didn't care how people voted, as long as enough people voted him into office, but for some reason his staffers felt it necessary to inform him of the political leanings of his visitors. As if he might, in the final moments of a meeting regarding a global financial meltdown, apply himself to changing the visitor's vote.

He reminded himself of this man's name. Tom Browning.

He preferred informality, but a president couldn't always be informal.

"We sincerely appreciate you coming all this way, Mr. Browning." Slight smile for disarming effect. "It wasn't something we could discuss over the phone."

"I understand."

Tom Browning wore a tweed jacket that looked as if it was last worn at his high school graduation. He was sun burnt with work-hardened hands. Powerful fingers wormed around each other. The leather briefcase at his feet had seen its equal share of time and weather.

"I envy you your time in the outdoors. My job tends to keep me under roofs."

"My wife worries about skin cancer."

"It's good to have a wife that worries."

Tom Browning still sat up straight as a truant schoolboy, but he smiled slightly.

"Yes. Yes it is."

Tom Browning sat on one of the two couches that faced each other over the long coffee table. Maggie sat beside him. This was not coincidence. They had agreed that the proximity of a woman might make him more comfortable. The man with the dark eyebrows sat on the opposite couch. *Mike Neal*, said the helpful voice that always spoke in Russell's head, though in this case a reminder wasn't necessary. He and Mike Neal were becoming more than acquaintances.

The three of them had talked before Tom Browning was ushered in. During that brief discussion Russell had developed an added appreciation for Mike Neal.

Russell said, "We don't have much time, so I should get to the point. You read the report. What are your thoughts?"

Ninety-five percent of the ocean's depths are unexplored.

Instead Tom Browning said simply, "Honestly, it's hard to believe."

"Well then. It seems we're all on the same page. Please, tell us what we should know."

"Well, the first thing you should know is that nautilus are not my specialty. In fact, they're not many scientists' specialty. Very few scientists study the nautilus, which I suppose is rather surprising when you think about how remarkable they are. They're a living fossil whose ancestors go back a half billion years. Late Cambrian period, as you may know. Before the bony fishes. Before the dinosaurs. They were actually one of the dominant species of the time."

The work hardened hands had stopped knotting. One tapped a knee.

"There were thousands of different species of nautilus in the oceans then. But now they've dwindled to a handful. They live on the slopes of deep coral reefs in the southwestern Pacific. They migrate up at night to feed. If it weren't for nautilus jewelry, most people would never see them." Tom Browning paused, hesitant to voice anything that sounded like scolding. "It's illegal to harvest them."

"They're being wiped out," said Russell Shaughnessy.

Tom Browning gave the President an appreciative look.

"Yes they are," he said.

"I did a little homework. I couldn't find much. But I did find that."

"Again, not your fault," said Tom Browning. "As I said, there's a tremendous lack of knowledge, and that includes knowledge regarding their overall numbers and geographic range. On behalf of the scientific community, I should probably offer a blanket apology for our lack of understanding."

"Unnecessary. I'll never understand politics."

This smile was broad.

"I might have to change my vote."

"Differences are what make our country great. That, and our ability to adjust to a new paradigms."

Tom Browning's smile disappeared.

"As a species, we aren't very good at adjusting," he said. "We expect others to do it."

And some of them are.

The elephant stood in the quiet room.

"Mr. Browning, is it possible that these things that attacked this vessel are nautilus?"

It was the question everyone knew would be asked. Still they watched Tom Browning formulate his response, as if he were just thinking about it now.

"As a scientist, I have to say the word nautilus and this kind of," Tom Browning paused, "attack don't belong in the same sentence. It's true they are voracious predators, but on a very small scale. But it's also true that in the Cambrian period they grew much bigger. And were commensurately more ferocious."

"How much bigger?"

"Not as big as what these people purportedly saw. But big. Shells the size of trash can lids. Tentacles like thick ropes. Powerful tentacles."

"Ninety of them."

"That's right."

"True sea monsters?"

"You could say that, but I'm not sure if I'd corroborate it."

Russell Shaughnessy wasn't sure if he detected a slight smile.

"Mr. President, ninety-five percent of the ocean's depths are unexplored," Tom Browning said. "We don't know everything. We actually don't know much of anything."

Tom Browning's creased face exuded apology. The man spent a lot of time on boats. Not Princess Cruises.

"Many of the refugees were fishermen," said Russell. "They were convinced of what they saw."

Tom Browning nodded.

"I've never doubted the word of a fisherman, unless they had reason to lie to me, in which case they did a fine job of it," he said. "I was a commercial fisherman before I turned to science. Fishing paid better. Or it did."

"You seem to maintain a sense of humor in the face of all this."

"It's easier than crying."

"Have you ever been to Palau, Mr. Browning?"

Everyone in the room looked at the President curiously.

"No," said Tom Browning. "It's high on my wish list, though. An ocean lover's paradise."

"I've heard good things," Russell said.

Tom Browning's computer rested in the briefcase at his feet. More than likely, it was totally unrelated. It would only complicated matters. He didn't want to look like a fool either. The hyper-imaginative scientist, snatching up the ball of rationality and gleefully running off with it. But ego often turned you down the wrong path.

Looking around this room he'd never dreamed he'd see, he made his decision.

"With your permission, I have something I'd like to show you," he said.

Mike Neal pulled the curtains. Tom Browning settled the computer on the president's desk. The four of them watched the video three times.

When they finished, Russell sat back in his chair.

"What does this mean?" Maggie asked.

Tom Browning's hands hung limp.

"Likely one of two things. They're exhibiting behaviors we've simply never observed before. Or they're evolving and the behaviors are new."

"Becoming smarter?" said Maggie.

"In their fashion, yes. Whatever it takes to survive."

Russell Shaughnessy spoke in a soft voice without looking up.

"You don't believe it's the former," he said.

Tom Browning had come this far.

"No sir, I don't."

Russell picked up his water glass carefully. It wouldn't do to spill it on the next meeting's brief. He sipped without tasting, and set the glass down with equal care.

"You're a father," he said.

"Yes. Two daughters. I'm very lucky."

"I feel the same way. What do you think of their future?"

These people could make things happen. It wasn't his future Tom Browning cared about. He buried the last of his formality and reluctance.

"We're in very serious trouble. Quite possibly irreversible trouble. We have far bigger problems than the one you brought me here for."

The first thing Russell did after the meeting was cancel the next meeting. The next thing he did was call Daniel Brannon.

Ten minutes later Daniel called back.

"Sorry," Daniel said. "I was in a meeting."

"That's my line."

The chuckle on the other end of the line made him feel a little better.

"What happened to us, Russ? How did we become such pompous bores?"

"It's a mystery to me."

This time Daniel Brannon's laughed tumbled across the miles. It was the same laugh Russell had known in their undergrad days.

"And that is precisely why I voted for you," Daniel said.

Russell made his request.

"And Danny?"

"Yes."

"Can you put aside any other meetings and get back to me fairly quickly?"

"Is that a Presidential decree?"

"A friend's request."

"Good then. Will do. I never did worry about you outgrowing your britches."

"That's one of the nicest things anybody has ever said about me."

"I'm an academic. I only speak the truth."

Neither man missed the beat of pause.

"I've tried to do the same," Russell said. "But sometimes the truth is best left unspoken."

Daniel Brannon called back in nine minutes and twenty seconds.

"Thanks, Danny. I wish I always saw that kind of response time."

"Certain members of my faculty still answer my calls. And even when I first met you, you wanted answers yesterday."

"Now my job requires it."

The joke made neither of them laugh. So long ago. It made them both a little sad and tired.

Russell wracked his brain and surprised himself by coming up with the name.

"How is Professor Blackstone?"

"Very impressive, Russ. He's good, thanks. He sends his regards. He voted for you too. That aside, I have to tell you that Bob Blackstone is one of our best teachers, perhaps the teacher that I personally respect the most. I would have been back to you sooner, but I let him talk a little bit on the phone. He's been at the University for a long time, seen pretty much every kind of student, and he's not prone to hyperbole. He told me again he'd never seen anything like this boy."

I've dreamt about him.

Friendship knows certain boundaries.

"You're not going to ask why I want his information?"

"It's University procedure, but in this case I know it would be pointless."

"Thank you, Danny. You've always been a good friend."

"We've both been lucky. My secretary wanted to know what it's like being friends with the President."

"Oh? And what did you tell her?"

"That it doesn't get me tickets to a Red Sox game."

Daniel Brannon had always been punctual. The e-mail showed up the instant Russell Shaughnessy hung up the phone.

He knew he should consult with someone, but frankly he was always consulting with someone and it was a molasses process. Sometimes he was surprised they got anything done. Plus, they'd probably try to talk him out of it. He had to admit, it was a little like something out of The Prince and the Pauper. He didn't give a shit. It was possible they were running out of time for meetings and proper channels.

He wrote the e-mail and, before the politician in him could stop him, he sent it.

Then he walked across the carpet and found Palau again on the map.

It wasn't close to The Malacca Strait. But it wasn't far either.

Returning to his desk he picked up the phone.

"Miss Dexter? What are the chances of us getting two tickets to a Red Sox game?"

THE SEA.

Yes. The puzzle pieces. They are slowly arranging. But no one can tell what they will look like in the end.

So goes life.

KOROR, PALAU.

When they spied the shirtless Leonard Chima striding fast down the dock, everyone on the boat went still.

Ernan recovered first. Dropping down the ladder from the bridge, he stepped up on to the dock, allowing Leonard Chima to brush wordlessly past him.

Marty had been hosing down the stern. Leonard leapt aboard. Much of his torso was covered with caked dirt. The impact of his landing sent the Wendell Holmes rocking and triggered a pell mell fracturing; clots of dirt fell from Leonard Chima in a cow dropping rain. They quickly turned to muddy rivulets on the deck, ably watered by the still-running hose in Marty's limp hand.

Three Japanese divers were still on board. Free divers, they had been politely quizzing Maas for almost an hour.

They froze on the bench, staring up at the vast expanse of soiled man.

Maas stood slowly.

One of Leonard's ham-size fists clasped a club.

The big man trembled.

"I am sorry, Mr. Haruo. So very sorry." He stared hard at the deck. "You cannot know how sorry I am."

The air left Marty in a gust. His laughter did the same. He nearly dropped the hose.

"And you have no idea how relieved I am," Marty said.

Leonard's eyes rose to Marty's chest, but not his face.

"I should have warned you I was coming." He held the club out to Maas.

"For you. From North Carolina."

Accepting the offering, Maas smiled up at the stone-faced man.

"It couldn't have been easy finding Bass Farm sausage."

The Japanese divers still stared at Leonard Chima as if he had sprouted wings.

"I bought it from my cousin. He orders sausage from all over the world. He inherited money from his grandmother in Germany and now his belly is swollen like a woman's. I am sorry for what I did to you. I cannot take back the harm, but I will pay you the money. It will take a little time."

"The harm is past," said Maas. "The money can wait."

Many of the marks were so small they were barely visible. Others were reddish scrapes, as if someone had hacked at the skin with a peeler. A handful were swollen and purple, as big as a child's fist. These largest bites sprouted suture remains.

Perhaps suspecting some strain of pestilential contagion, the Japanese divers pressed back against the bench.

Lifting a muscled arm, Leonard consulted his rib cage.

Slowly shaking his head he said, "They look like hickies. But they did not feel like hickies."

Leonard turned to Marty.

"The boy?"

Preoccupied with his own potential demise, Marty had forgotten about Justin. The last time Marty had seen him, Justin and Amber had been intertwined on the couch reading.

As if on cue, Justin came up from below, Amber just behind him.

"We fell asleep," said Justin. "Hi, Leonard."

Marty saw how Leonard Chima stiffened. Fear held sway on his face, but something else dwelt there too. Oddly, it resembled rapture.

Leonard spoke very softly.

"I could think of nothing for you."

Justin smiled at Leonard with genuine affection.

"I don't want anything."

"I knew that was what you would say."

"How is the new job?"

Leonard looked startled, then ashen.

Justin nodded to Amber.

"We went into town for a movie. We saw Nounpotu. We talked to him on his lunch break. Then we saw your foreman in the theater. He said he was at the movies in the middle of the afternoon because you dig ditches faster than three men. Thank you."

Now pure surprise coated Leonard Chima's face.

"You thank *me*?"

"Not everyone can change."

"Coming here was what I needed to do."

He spoke firmly. He believed himself. He felt courage in his heart.

Then he felt the wet pooling about his feet. He looked down. The muddy rivulets moved like living things.

He had to go.

He could change, but he could never forget.

After Leonard left, Justin took the hose from Marty's hand and continued hosing mud toward the stern.

Amber said, "He looked like he'd just popped out of the ground."

"I thought that's where I was going," said Marty.

"It took nerve to come," said Maas.

Justin had worked his way to the swim step.

"Tmetuchl Baules told us Public Works is laying two miles of new pipe," he said, giving the hose a few last swings. "He said they are three days ahead of schedule and now they won't need a trencher. He said he has never seen a man work with such focus."

Justin washed the last dirt off the swim step. It pooled on the surface for a few seconds before sinking out of sight.

Like ashes.

"We could all do with a little more of Leonard's conviction," Justin said.

His world was becoming one of multiple shared secrets. Marty, Jimmy Maas and Amber knew almost everything. Lacey knew the secret of the blacktips. A few things he had shared with no one.

That night at dinner, Marty, Jimmy, Amber and Lacey at the table, he evened the playing field somewhat, telling Lacey Goodenall everything he had told the others. Each time, bringing someone else along. Each time, a lifetime's firmament turned on its side. Or shattered.

It took time. Ever the steady scientist, Lacey, struggling now, listened and asked the occasional question. Maas made regular trips to the fridge to refresh Lacey's lemonade. She drank the glasses in robotic fashion.

Justin talked easily, as if he were relaying plans for a picnic they were going on the next day. The story contained its' dark and painful moments. When Justin came to them, he stared down at the fork idly turning in his hands. Goodbye to Able. Goodbye to the children on the sailboat. Possibly goodbye to Man.

When Justin finished, no one spoke.

Lacey stared at the lot of them.

"Christ almighty," she said. "My stomach hurts."

"At my last count, you were up to five glasses of lemonade," Justin said.

Turning to Maas she said, "Help me, Jimmy."

"I'd write the lot of us off as nut jobs," said Maas.

"I'd like to, but I've already seen too much."

She did not look at Justin.

He spoke to her anyhow.

"Thirty feet below the surface, their power ceases; their influence fades, and their dominion vanishes."

It might have been the biggest shock of all. It had to be the purest coincidence.

She spoke the man's name as if she had never pronounced it before.

"Jules Verne."

"See?" Justin beamed like a small boy, and Lacey almost forgot what he had done. "It's easy explaining things to a scientist."

It took all her composure to return his smile.

"Easy? Fine then. Here's my scientific conclusion. The lot of you aren't nut jobs. The lot of you are fucking mad as hatters. At least I wish you were."

"All science is a mixture of right and wrong," said Justin.

The Wendell Holmes tugged at her moorings. The refrigerator hummed. Each of them swam with their own thoughts.

Amber broke the silence. Pushing back in her chair, she reached for Lacey's plate.

"If I had a world of my own, everything would be nonsense," she said. "Nothing would be what it is, because everything would be what it isn't. And contrary wise, what is, it wouldn't be. And what it wouldn't be, it would."

Even Justin looked at her dumbfounded.

Amber laughed.

"The Mad Hatter," she said, turning for the galley.

That night Justin lay awake, Amber snoring softly beside him.

He knew each of them was frightened. It might as well have been painted on their faces. Strange things were happening and they didn't have the faintest idea what they should do. He didn't have much of an idea either. Fear circled through him too, crippling at every turn.

But now he had a beginning to his path. He hadn't told them about the e-mail. It would have detracted from what he knew he had to tell Lacey. Some gut instinct told him she was a critical cog in this plan not yet formulated, much less off the ground. Maybe as critical as the President.

He couldn't believe it himself. He had been shocked first by the e-mail, then by the honesty in the words. Carefully, he had crafted a response. He, too, had been wholly forthcoming. Russell Shaughnessy had assured him no one else would see their correspondence. Russell Shaughnessy now knew almost everything. He was a man who could make things happen. The most powerful of allies. It was a small risk to assume he was an ally, but the e-mail had convinced Justin enough. And there was no time for nuance and games. He knew this now, with absolute certainty.

Lying beside Amber, he worked to quiet his galloping heart and mind. He supposed he had been vaguely aware since those first whisperings as a child, but a child, like a message, is a work in progress, and an adult, like a child, is lost in other things.

Perhaps the realization was triggered by Russell Shaughnessy's e-mail, or his own unveilings at the dinner table.

The truth had arrived like a thunderclap in this quietly rocking berth.

The words moved across his mind as if printed on a chalk board.

Things fall apart; the centre cannot hold;
   Mere anarchy is loosed upon the world,
   The blood-dimmed tide is loosed, and everywhere
   The ceremony of innocence is drowned;
   The best lack all conviction, while the worst
   Are full of passionate intensity.

He was thirteen when his mother first gave him William Butler Yeats' poem. It had made no sense then. He hadn't understood the lesson. Perhaps his mother hadn't understood the lesson, or her actions. The black poem had only scared him and made his nightmares worse. But there it was. Beginning its wait. Patient, until now.

The Second Coming.

Yeats' crowning title.

The revelation scared him more than the poem ever had. He turned toward the white wall. Heaven was white, wasn't it? He needed help from somewhere, but he had never known what to believe, and if there was a God, He just presented another unfathomable dilemma. Justin heard his own breaths, growing more rapid.

Fear was like drowning. He had almost drowned once.

But he hadn't drowned.

He had been saved.

He concentrated on the rocking, the hull on the water. He gathered himself.

Fear served only itself.

Leonard Chima.

Conviction was what he needed.

THE SEA.

In the deeps the shark moves in the easy sinuous way sharks do. Unhurried and seemingly purposeless until haste and purpose are required. So many more tiny pores probing for the minutest disturbance in heartbeat, a muscle twitch. Like picking up single motes of dust.

She rises, gathering speed in eye-questioning bounds, so that at the end she is a cartilaginous arrow. Impact registers as one part concussion, one part rending, for both are accomplished in the same violent moment, battering ram and scythe applied in a single beautiful killing blow. For the victim, simultaneous instants — surprise, shock, searing pain — and then the nothing to which we will all return, though not all of us as a meal.

She is truly impressive, this recent take on a prehistoric success story.

Twice as deadly. Twice as hungry. Not at all encumbered by two heads.

Oh, you had best gather yourselves.

KOROR, PALAU.

Miss Patsy woke coated in filmy sweat. The vision clung to her in similar fashion. Rising from bed always took effort, but on this night she was so distracted she forgot her own mass. She was on her feet as if she were young and slender again, and her mother and father waited in the next room to soothe her. Once on her feet she remembered that her mother and father were dead. She required other consolation.

Stumbling rapidly through the darkness, one paw found the door jam, clasping it as if to pull it loose.

Miss Patsy heard her own panicked breaths. Panic only made things worse.

Again she was in darkness far deeper than this darkness around her, sensing with absolute certainty an absolute end. The pain had been beyond comprehension, and mercifully short-lived. Then she was only meat; hunks of fat and shorn vessels still loosing blood, disappearing into the masticating gullet, stroked and pressed by ribs and muscles. Those parts not ingested spiraled away into watery darkness, a fleshy calliope ride pointlessly spinning.

Miss Patsy slid down the door jamb to her knees.

From that position she prayed.

What frightened her most was far beyond the devouring.

These dreams, snatched from the ether, were more than just random nightmares.

They were messages.

Underlain, always, with the faintest drumbeat.

She looked toward the kitchen. Already, her knees ached.

It would be hell getting up.

Fear would do it.

THE SEA.

She feels my very heartbeat. Our very heartbeats. What this means, I don't know.

KOROR, PALAU.

After a day of ditch digging, Nounpotu and Leonard Chima still made it
their custom to repair to Miss Patsy's porch to unwind and watch the world
go by, Nounpotu drinking beer and Leonard drinking a six-pack of Fanta
Orange, for now even the big man's tastes had changed. Samson was no
longer invited. Leonard had banished him, and neither Samson nor
Nounpotu protested. The new Leonard Chima remained an imposing stack
of muscle.

Every living soul on the island was familiar now with Leonard's encounter
with the blacktips. Nounpotu himself thought it all very queer, possibly
even a hallucination to end all hallucinations brought on by the ungodly
weed. Except for the scars. The scars were real. Nounpotu had once read a
story about a man who cut himself. The man had been so crazy he hadn't
even known he was doing it. Maybe this was the way with Leonard.
Nounpotu debated this with diffuse interest, and then let it all go. He was
not a man to think things through.

Once, Leonard had let him touch the scars. Crusted risings like crescent
moons. The once-black sutures were brown now. Leonard could not afford
to pay for the doctor. He had removed the stitches himself, eventually
losing interest.

On this particular evening, just past seven, the porch, as it always did,
housed a modicum of cool, while out beyond the sloped decaying roof,
soggy heat still kicked its mule heels. This place was always hot as fuck. If
he hadn't fucked up his life so badly, maybe one day he would have rolled
in snow. Now snow might as well have been the moon.

The three of them watched the evening rush of cabs clatter past, worn
Nissans and Toyotas imported from Japan after their owners had no use for
them, air conditioners laboring, fan belts screaming, as they carried tourists
to dinner.

"I don't understand how you can drink that little girl's drink," said Miss

Patsy, from the porch swing behind them. "Mr. Dahl must laugh himself into the squirts when you come to the register."

Sprawled on the steps, Leonard only half-listened to the old lady. The steps had always listed to the left. This had always bothered him, but now it didn't bother him anymore. Now he simply saw that they afforded a good view of the street.

He knew if he didn't respond, Miss Patsy would repeat herself.

"He congratulates me on my wisdom. Beer costs more than soft drinks."

"Funny thing to be concerned with now that you've got your first legal job," Miss Patsy said.

"I made more money in my other life," Leonard said.

He heard the hint of pine in his voice, but in truth he didn't miss his old life at all. He had already relegated the past to the past.

"Leonard found God," said Nounpotu, with only a touch of mockery.

Leonard had already finished four Fantas, the empty bottles lined neatly at his feet.

"He's finding his way to diabetes next," Miss Patsy said.

Both men noticed that Miss Patsy drank substantially more these days. The additional alcohol made her more belligerent.

Leonard barely heard Nounpotu and the old lady. His days on this porch were numbered. Each evening their stupid, gossipy conversation bored him more. But the porch afforded a straight shot view of the bus stop, and so he sat with his back against the familiar rub of splintery post and wished for seven-thirty. At seven-thirty the van from the Palau Pacific Resort arrived, disgorging all the pretty girls who worked at Koror's fanciest hotel. Leonard had taken a liking to one of them, a Filipino beauty named Gwyn. He knew her name because one evening he had sat on the bus stop bench and, though he kept his head down, read her name tag as she got off. She had not looked at him. The old Leonard Chima would have swaggered up to her, but the new Leonard simply stole a look at her shapely calves.

Something more than his taste buds had irrevocably changed.

Leonard hadn't found God, but he had discovered something. He just didn't know what it was yet.

He consulted his new watch. It felt good to buy something with money he had earned honestly.

"Where did you steal that?"

He looked back at Miss Patsy. Miss Patsy was changing too. He wasn't sure what was happening to her, but he had always liked her so he smoothed his anger.

"I bought it at Ben Franklin, Miss Patsy."

Ben Franklin was one of the biggest stores in Koror. Leonard had stolen many things there.

"The watch band is white," Miss Patsy observed.

"It was cheaper."

"It makes you look like a pimp."

Briefly, the old Leonard Chima considered the benefits of being a pimp.

The lack of retort turned Miss Patsy more antagonistic.

"All that sugar has pickled your brain." She glanced toward the bus stop. "I know what you're waiting for. It is a waste of time."

Leonard flushed and Miss Patsy knew she had found her mark. A small bit of joy rose inside her.

"That girl Gwyn, she likes her men rough. You would have been perfect, but now you are not her type."

Leonard knew Miss Patsy was probably making this up, but it still worried him a little.

"You don't know everything," he said.

"I do know everything."

The joy dried in her mouth.

To escape her sadness she said, "Why don't you drink the rest of that liquid courage and walk over to that bus stop and ask her to marry you? You're a real prize now, with your ditch digging career and your sporty wardrobe."

Nounpotu belched.

"Come on Aunty," he said in a mildly placating manner. "Leonard is a hard worker."

"You only say that because he's doing your work too."

Nounpotu turned to Leonard and grinned.

"Fuck if she can't read minds."

Miss Patsy got up from the porch swing as quickly as her three hundred pounds would allow.

Neither man missed the abruptness of her exit.

Nounpotu waited until she was well inside before he whispered, "Elephants can just piss on the ground, but that elephant needs her privacy."

"You should leave her be," Leonard said.

"The fuck? She was just making nasty fun of you."

"She does that because she is sad."

"She is sad only because she is almost out of vodka."

Leonard didn't know what Miss Patsy put in her plastic cup, but he knew Nounpotu was right. He also knew he had been right to end things with Miss Claren. He had never intended to marry her. They had only rutted like animals, without feelings. Or so he had thought. Miss Claren had not come to the porch anymore, and now he missed her.

Leonard looked at the soldierly row of empty Fanta bottles. Maybe the sugar was driving him out of his mind.

When Miss Patsy banged back through the screen door with a full cup in her hand, Nounpotu knew Leonard was right about the sadness.

Miss Patsy plopped down, producing a great rattling of chains and a sigh.

She wiped the plastic cup across her forehead.

"The price of global warming," she said. "I heard you visited Marty Haruo."

It was small news, but Leonard realized the woman still gave him the creeps.

He tried to be careful.

"I owed him money. I went to pay him back."

He wondered if she knew about their thievery too. Maybe Nounpotu had told her. Virtually everyone knew about the blacktips, but, as far as he knew, there were many who did not know about the stabbing. The man Maas had come into the hospital quietly. No one had been at check in. The doctor had been from off island.

He glanced at Nounpotu.

Nounpotu sprawled, quiet, contemplating a fly on his wrist.

Miss Patsy only said, "Marty Haruo must have been surprised to see you," and focused on drinking.

Wiping the back of her hand across her mouth she said, "I never took you for a cry baby."

His performance at Blacktip Lake was already a threadbare topic, but Miss Patsy was not one to ignore a little wear and tear.

When it became obvious no defense was forthcoming, Miss Patsy added, "That boy Justin saved your ass."

"He did," said Leonard.

"And now God has saved him," Nounpotu declared.

It was like a skipping record.

Leonard decided this was his last evening on the stoop. From now on he would sit at the bus stop, until he worked up his nerve.

Miss Patsy assumed a look of unfeigned wonder that neither man saw.

"Something about that boy," she said.

Strange thunderclouds rollin' in off the horizon, Leonard thought, but he kept the thought to himself.

Miss Patsy spoke slowly to herself.

"Yes, something downright odd about that boy. I can't put my finger on it. It is one of the few things I don't know."

It was the first time she had considered this. She didn't think it bothered her.

The Pan Pacific Resort van appeared around the corner. It did not clatter or scream.

"Well looky there," said Miss Patsy. "Here comes the bride."

She hated herself for saying it, but she was not herself anymore.

That night Miss Patsy went for a walk. She didn't want to walk, but the alternative was sleep. As she walked, she looked in windows and tried to ignore the ache in her hips. She had read that in other places people kept their shades pulled and their doors shut. That was behavior without explanation. As she shuffled, her exertions echoing in her ears, Miss Patsy watched life through the windows. An old man, illuminated by a tattered lamp shade, asleep in an armchair. A couple eating silently at a table. Two women, sisters Miss Patsy knew, sharing a laugh.

Miss Patsy stopped in the warm darkness. The boy and the girl disappeared and reappeared in the window, their arms over their heads, no doubt swung there to give height to their leaps. Miss Patsy watched them bounce on whatever furniture lay beyond her sight. With each successive leap, they came closer and closer. She waited until their heads clacked, and then she shuffled away, leaving the children's wails and the shouting parents behind.

Miss Patsy was not much for praying, but when she reached a dark patch where the light of homes did not reach, she stopped and looked up at the crescent moon and folded her hands in front of her without knowing it.

She wished she hadn't seen the children. It was children who haunted her sleep. Her eyes were closed, but all she could see was the bouncing, laughing children, innocence rising and falling from heaven to earth.

But it wasn't heaven that loomed on their horizon.

Looking at the white moon, she prayed she was wrong.

MORETON BAY, AUSTRALIA.

Fishing was a lonely business. Often Peter Allen thought of Lacey Goodenall. She was beautiful, yes, but mostly he liked the way she was. He knew few women who pig hunted. He liked how her lab was pin neat. He kept his boat the same way; a place for the few things he had, and the few things he had in their place. For a time he had employed a crew of one, but always the men cleaned up after meals haphazardly and left their smokes lying about the cabin, so now he fished alone.

He liked how Lacey had cocked her head and called him a sly codger; because he was quiet, many mistook him for slow. He liked that "Twenty Thousand Leagues Under the Sea" was one of her favorite books. He had not missed how her face had softened when he told her how his mum had read the story to him in the bathtub. He also liked how her hair fell far down her back and her legs curved, smooth as a seashell, to her hips. Many times he had imagined those legs wrapped about him, a near strangling visual until he had done what he needed to do to loosen the vise. He was a focused man, but Lacey left him profoundly distracted.

But that was all she would ever do to him. Nemo meant nobody, and he was a nobody. Lacey would never favor a man like him. But nobody could take his fantasies.

At the moment he was imagining his face buried in the luxuriant tangle of hair. The result was he nearly knocked himself cold on the top of the hatchway. Stepping out into the squinty bright afternoon sunshine, the waters of Moreton Bay spackling happily, he told himself to pay attention, but the fantasy didn't listen.

He saw the mats floating on the surface as he prepared to drop the second net overboard, but he registered them absently. The hairy, weedy tufts, like floating scalps, had been there for so long now they had become part of the background. *Lyngbya majuscula* the scientists called it, but Peter Allen and his fellow fishermen just called the nasty shit fireweed. It had started showing up in Moreton Bay maybe ten years ago, and now it was apparently here to stay. If you mentioned *Lyngbya majuscule* to anyone on dry land, they just stared at you blankly, but the fishermen in Moreton Bay knew the evil stuff intimately. Contact provided them painful rashes on their hands and legs. The fumes stung their eyes. One fisherman failed to wash the weed's residue from his hands before he pissed off the side of the boat. His shouting had brought his crew running. They had found him stumbling about the deck brushing madly at his privates. For this he earned the nickname Flaming Willy.

Even now it made Peter Allen chuckle. Unless it was your pain, it was funny.

The net was baked stiff by the hot sun, and stuck together in places. Peter Allen separated the mesh carefully before hooking the net to the winch. Dangling in the sunshine, the net was still slightly tangled and gluey. Kissing his way up Lacey's legs, he absently gave the webbing a hard shaking.

The purplish residue was nearly invisible in the air. It hung there only briefly before Peter Allen inhaled it. Peter Allen didn't know it, but a week earlier at the University of Queensland's marine botany lab, fireweed samples placed in a drying oven gave off fumes that sent researchers coughing out into the street.

None of them had severe asthma.

Peter Allen made it to the radio, but by then his mayday was a rushed wheeze, like something escaping a balloon. No longer concerned with fastidiousness, he yanked open the drawers in the pilot house, turning them upside down, spilling logbooks, pens, clipped coupons and tic tack dispensers. Sweeping his hands through the detritus, he saw in his mind's eye his inhaler sitting on his bedside table.

When the Redcliffe Coast Guard arrived they found Peter Allen staring round-eyed up at the sun.

THE SEA.

Shark attacks send out global tremors, though when one of you is bitten by your fellow man (ten times more likely) the news is relegated to the fine print and the quirky.

Regarding true, freeze you in your tracks fear, you are looking in the wrong direction.

It's the little things that matter.

This weed, Lyngbya majuscula you call it, your scientists have identified it as a strain of cyanobacteria, an ancestor of modern day bacteria and algae that flourished 2.7 billion years ago. Your industrial runoff of nitrogen, carbon, iron and phosphorous compounds is both fertilizer and spark. Once again, the primitive bacteria and algae of the ancient oceans grow and thrive. You sleep; they spread. It is no slow eking. It is a conflagration. Fireweed can cover 100 square meters in a minute. Always thorough, you are catching all the fish that once kept these opportunistic bacteria in check.

Off the coast of Louisiana a spread of cottony white bacteria carpets miles of seafloor. In summer, bacteria blooms turn the Baltic Sea stinking and yellow brown. The bacteria suck up all the oxygen. Dead fish bob on the surface. They die like the fisherman.

This is neither lesson nor scare tactic. It is just fact. You are orchestrating a return to the primeval oceans over which the ever-adaptive bacteria lorded. A retreat of sorts. But a retreat can also be an advancement. Dawn of a different sort.

Lyngbya majuscula has many tricks. In the unlikely case you don't provide the nitrogen it needs, it simply extracts nitrogen from the air. When Lyngbya majuscula dies and decays it releases its own nitrogen and phosphorous into the water. And so the next generation feeds. An inspiring selflessness certain species would do well to emulate.

The fisherman dies alone.

He is nobody.

He is everybody.

KOROR, PALAU.

Lacey left the day she heard of Peter Allen's death.

"He has no family," she told Maas, emptying her drawer at the pension. "I doubt anyone has or will make arrangements. It's been two days. I don't want him put away by the state."

This was something she understood.

She kissed Maas gently.

"I also have work to do. A presentation in Sydney." She slipped her arms around his waist. "You know I can't stay in this paradise forever, flirting with you."

What she saw in his face made her love him all the more.

She shook her head.

"Coming wouldn't do any good, other than maybe doubling the size of Peter's funeral. Everyone here needs you more." She ran a hand along his thigh, finishing with a light squeeze. "In a manner of speaking."

Lacey made the funeral arrangements in transit. There was no time like the present, and no time was needed to notify anyone.

BYRON BAY, AUSTRALIA.

When she arrived at the Crescent Moon Funeral Home two mornings later, it was standing room only. Some two hundred men and women filled the long, narrow room with the pulpit and the simple urn up front. Every man was burnt by the sun. The women were the wives of fishermen, young and old and equally possessed of their husbands' hard-nosed resolve. There were children too. A few of them cried. No one silenced them.

When Lacey asked if anyone wished to speak, one man raised his hand. He was standing at the back of the room. As he shambled to the front, men reached out and patted his back. He did not acknowledge them. He kept his head down. He carried a fisherman's knit cap in one hand.

When he arrived at the podium, Lacey saw that the man had thick eyebrows that seemed to twitch on their own. She also noticed that the knuckles of the hand gripping the gray knit cap were white.

It was not from nervousness.

The man spoke to the crowd as if he knew every one of them, and Lacey realized he did.

"I'd like to thank you all for the honor of speaking on Peter Allen's behalf. We all know Peter would have wanted to keep it brief, and this was the best way to do it. I wish he had family to speak instead of me, but God decided otherwise, so he's got me."

There was a smattering of applause. The man stifled it with a half raised hand.

"This isn't about us," he said.

He placed the knit cap gently on the podium.

"Peter Allen was a fine fisherman and a finer bloke. He was my friend," the man looked out at the room as if sighting something on the horizon, "and he was your friend. For much of his life, he had no family, but he was family to us. To the outside world, Peter Allen was a loner and a bit strange. Antoine de Saint-Exupéry's little prince said, *"What makes the desert beautiful is that somewhere it hides a well."*

The man raised the gray knit cap. The eyebrows were jumping like mad.

"His Mum knitted this for me. I'm giving it back."

The man gently placed the cap on the urn and left the stage.

There was no applause. There was no movement at all. Even the children had stopped crying.

There was no reception. Everyone left wordlessly, and that was that.

KOROR, PALAU.

On their day off, Fury, Justin, Amber and Jimmy Maas went free diving. Fury borrowed Mongkol's panga. The reef where Fury wanted to take them wasn't far off, and the small panga would attract less attention than the Wendell Holmes.

"You don't have to give all your gifts away," Fury said, stuffing a dry bag under one of the panga's plywood benches. The sun was not quite up. They stood on the dock in the last darkness as Fury squared things away. He grinned up at them. "A golden egg, right under everyone's nose."

Justin eyed the panga warily.

"Now I know where all the world's duct tape goes to die," he said.

Fury gave the dry bag a last stuff.

"Now that Mongkol is employed, he only has time for stop-gap repairs." Fury nodded to Justin. "The cooler."

Justin had barely been able to lift the enormous cooler Fury had dragged out of the dive shop.

Lifting it again, he felt its weight dragging down his back and shoulders. He stepped carefully from the dock to the panga.

"You sure it won't go through the bottom?" he asked.

"You sure *we* won't go to the bottom?" Maas asked.

"Everyone on the manifest can swim," said Justin.

"Have fun at my expense now," said Fury, carefully positioning the cooler. "You will be glad it came along."

As they puttered out of the harbor, the sun made its regal rising, the sky a celebration of pink. Several fishermen, also in pangas, were already scattered across the water ahead of them, fingernail shadows on a milky sea.

Leaning drowsily against Justin, Amber murmured, "I'm still dreaming."

He could feel her warmth. He slipped his hand over hers.

"Amber in Wonderland," he whispered. "Nothing would be what it is, because everything would be what it isn't. And contrary wise, what is, it wouldn't be. And what it wouldn't be, it would."

"Do you remember everything?"

"Just the things you say."

"Hmmmmmm. I remember you're an incorrigibly sweet liar."

The sun sent its first light off the water. They could already feel its warmth.

Clearing the harbor, Fury opened up the throttle. Steering with the queerly long propeller shaft, he pointed them southwest, in the direction of Ngemelis Island. The panga skimmed across the slick water, winding through the maze of mushroom islands leading to the open sea. The outboard made angry coughs and noisy rattles. The panga's gunnels rode nauseatingly low to the water.

Maas sat on the forward bench with his back to them, his thin frame bowed to stay low in the wind.

Leaning close, Justin said, "I think he's praying. If we start to sink, there'll be no time for drawing straws. I vote we jettison Fury first. I'm betting that's lunch in the cooler."

"Mr. Mahoney. Are you afraid of a short swim?"

"Nope. I'm afraid of Mongkol if we don't bring his panga back."

The open sea held a slight swell. With each drop, the waterlogged floorboards clattered beneath their feet. Land sank away and the sea and sky grew. Closing his eyes, Justin felt the wash of salt and sun, like a cleansing balm.

He tried to concentrate on the pleasant washing, but his mind returned to his dreams again. Almost every night he dreamt of the blacktips. But it wasn't the dream that frightened him. It was the reality. He had directed his anger, but once it struck home it was like an arrow buried in the flank of a pain-maddened animal. He had had no control. As the blacktips surged about Leonard Chima, Justin had felt their rage. Their rage was not his. It was primal, unthinking, without hesitation or mercy; wholly focused on the end. He had no doubt what would have happened to Leonard had they not pulled him from the water. He wasn't sure what might have happened to them if they hadn't left quickly.

No one but Lacey knew about the blacktips, and he would tell no one this other thing. In this matter, he was lost. As a boy, he had directed the dragonflies. But only to a degree. Then, he had been glad for it; they were wild things. Now the thought haunted his sleep.

How Leonard Chima had ended up plunging into the lake as they drifted there, well he was pretty certain of that. He had been provided opportunity on a platter, and left with a choice. He had made his choice, and it had allowed a glimpse of mayhem and madness that still chilled him to the bone.

Today was a running away, but he already knew it would do no good.

He felt a warm hand on his arm.

"Justin? Hello? We're here."

He opened his eyes. Fury had cut the throttle to a puttering. He circled the reef. They could see it clearly, 70 feet below. The corals were sparse, but they weren't here for the corals. The reef sat atop a deep sea pinnacle that rose from the bottom 4,000 feet down. The night before in the galley Fury had gone into a near trance describing the profusion of Bluefin tuna, one in particular that he estimated to be 500 pounds.

Gazing down into the water, Fury relived his reverie.

"One hundred and ten feet... In the darkness it looked like a Volkswagen. It was so beautiful and powerful... We floated together in the water column, man and beast..." Fury killed the engine. In the sudden stillness, the heat came storming in. "This is a special place," he said.

"Thank you for bringing us here," Justin said.

Fury looked startled to see him.

"Yes," he said.

Fury lowered the anchor line, which fortunately appeared to be the one item bereft of duct tape. Pulling the dry bag from beneath the bench, he produced a tarp. First he rigged a makeshift lean-to. Maas helped Fury pull the cooler into its shade. Moving the cooler brought forth a heavenly sweet and salty smell.

"What is in here?"

Amber reached to look in, but Fury put his hand on the lid.

"No one touches the cooler until after we dive," said Fury.

"Fine," said Amber. "It's your party." Turning to Maas, she said, "You're quiet."

Lacey had left. Jimmy was leaving in four days. Justin and Amber were leaving for school in a week.

"Sad to leave this place," said Maas.

They all fell quiet at the thought.

"I guess whoever goes in last will be on the honor system," Maas said. Even as he smiled at Amber, he wondered if she could see his unease. "Or you could just stay in the boat. You're far and away the most trustworthy of the lot."

Amber peeled off a piece of duct tape, curling like a carrot shaving.

"I didn't risk my life to sit out in the sun," she said. "Nobody has to watch me," she added quietly. "I know the three of you want to go off in opposite directions. That's fine. I know what I'm doing."

Justin had already slipped into his wetsuit. Now he was quietly rigging his gun. Justin, Fury and Maas had each brought a spear gun, but not with Bluefin in mind. With global stocks plummeting, Palau's president Tommy Remengesau Junior had outlawed Bluefin catch in Palauan waters, which suited all three men fine.

Justin spit in his mask. Dipping it over the side, he rinsed it with water.

"Here's what I know," he said. "Keep up the way you're going, and one day you'll be the best diver here. And, thankfully, there are four points on a compass."

With that, he toppled back over the gunnel.

Maas looked at the other two.

"No shortage of silver on that boy's tongue," he said.

The reef and surrounding waters were prettier than Fury had promised. The corals were spare, but the reef top swarmed with life. Brightly colored Butterflyfish, Anthias, Blue Stripped Clownfish and Yellowtail Fusiliers swept about like fringes on a billowing skirt. A Hawksbill Turtle rose from the deeps, a languid, mossy bubble. Out in the blue, an enormous school of Jacks whirled like a silver hurricane. They saw no Bluefin and no one cared.

Again and again, Justin and Fury dove deep. Maas watched their fin tips dissolve into the purple. He made no attempt to follow the younger men, and he experienced a sense of relief each time they reappeared. He had never worried before. His uncharacteristic worry made him worry even more. He tried to focus on his own diving, but it didn't work. He found himself scanning the water. When, looking up from the reef he saw a flood of bubbles and Amber's yellow fins giving a last thrash to see her into the panga, he fairly applauded.

The sun rose, hovered at the top of its game, and began to descend. Maas had never been so tired, but he made sure he was last out of the water.

When Maas hauled himself into the panga, Amber and Fury already had a rib jutting from their mouth like a glistening cigar. Fury's fins weren't even off.

"Spare ribs, Southern style," said Fury, his rib bobbing off his lower lip. "Vinegary sauce, seasoned with mustard and brown sugar, lovingly applied while cooking."

Amber rolled her eyes.

"Ohhhhhh God, Jimmy. It was worth the wait." She looked adoringly at Fury. "These are the best ribs I've ever tasted."

Toweling off, Justin reached into the cooler and pulled out two ribs.

Plunking one in his mouth, he performed his own eye roll.

"Whoa. I suspect you'll believe you've died and gone to heaven," he said. "Or North Carolina."

Ducking out from under the lean-to, Justin, squinting in the sunlight, handed Maas his piece.

"I suspect I will," said Maas. He thought the words sounded easy. Good that Justin was already turning back for the shade of the lean-to. "See anything down there?"

Justin settled in next to Amber, stretching out his legs so that his feet were in the sun.

"If you mean Bluefin, not a one."

The boy's open face radiated nothing but truth and happiness.

Relief made Maas' smile almost real.

"Well then, perhaps Mr. Curtaine oversold the place. *Fifty feet down and the size of a toaster oven.*"

It was a surprisingly good imitation of Fury. Amber and Justin laughed.

Fury tossed a nearly bald rib over the side. There was flurry of splashing as a boil of fish picked it clean.

"You are not funny," he said. "They were here every time before. Maybe you make a bad imitation and bad luck."

Normally, the indignant man would have amused him.

"My apologies on both fronts," said Maas.

The ocean breathed about them. Milky smooth, its surface reflected the white clouds piling high into the sky. Maas sat in the sun, eating ribs. He was older, maybe that's why it took him longer to shake the chill. He looked at the three of them, reclining in the shade. Justin lay sprawled, his body deflated, his head resting comfortably on the towel in Amber's lap. Jimmy Maas knew the look on the boy's face. Once, traveling in Thailand, Maas had visited an opium den out of curiosity. In the clammy darkness, men had laid on bamboo mats on the earthen floor, their bodies inert, their eyes serene and glazed with a sheen of contentment.

Maas wished he felt the same effects, but his own heart was only just beginning to slow. He told himself again that it was age, and he knew again that it was a lie.

He looked out over the water, trying to draw from its quiet surface the peace it had always provided, but all he could think of were the strange sensations he had by no means left behind. Beneath the water a current had buzzed through his body. It hadn't hummed. It had screamed like an air raid siren. And there had been something else. It was that something that, even here in the bright sunshine, saw him still fighting to stamp out the crawling fear. Half of him had been on high alert, but at the same time he had felt a creeping lethargy. An opiate. As if he no longer cared. He had never felt that before. He had been a man divided. If something had happened, he wondered which half would have risen to the fore.

He was afraid he knew.

That night Justin sat alone in the dark galley. Today had been a farewell, and now, for some reason, it made him immeasurable sad.

Absently, he flicked on the computer.

The message was on the screen. It shocked him again. Why shouldn't it?

But the brief e-mail spoke like the man, not like the office.

I apologize for the intrusion. Would it be possible to stop over in Washington on your way back to Chicago? We would cover your expenses. I would like to meet with you. A little longer this time.

Of course they would know.

He looked at the time. Five minutes ago.

He typed back.

The response was immediate.

Thank you. And if you're startled, don't be. For better or for worse, I'm never away from my phone -- and you've become a bit of a priority for me. I'll explain when we meet.

The next e-mail arrived within two breaths.

I must apologize again, this time for our invasion of your privacy. I forgot to mention we will cover both your expenses. I was a college student.

Justin smiled at the screen. No doubt they already knew this too, but he typed it anyhow.

Three loans (and two small scholarships) between us. Thank you.

Our pleasure. In this case, tax dollars put to good use. We'll arrange everything. How are things in Palau?

Russell Shaughnessy stood in front of the world map on the Oval Office wall. He ran his finger across the blue, stopping when it rested atop Palau. Behind him the intercom issued its annoying buzz.

He looked down at his phone.

Quiet. But I have an uneasy feeling it won't stay that way.

After they logged off, Russell Shaughnessy continued to look at the map. He had never realized the extent of blue. It scared him a little. It made him feel like a stranger in a strange land.

The intercom buzzed again.

He walked to the desk, bent and pressed the button.

"Yes?"

"Mr. President. Congressman Arnold and Congressman Schmidt are here for your meeting."

Campaign reform.

Why did he feel like Nero fiddling as Rome burned?

"Thank you, Carole. Please send them in."

THE SEA.

The man, he does not dream. But he has a predator's instincts.

She was there, drifting where purple turned to black. Just deeper than the boy could descend.

Only the Bluefin left the reef. The other fish, all of them prey, they should have scattered.

But they did not.

She quieted their survival impulse. Smoothed it away. They no longer cared if they lived or died. She numbed this most basic instinct. Possibly abolished it. She put them at ease.

Astonishing. How did she do this? How did they allow it?

It runs counter to everything I know.

To subjugate the most powerful instinct is something else altogether.

Two things I do know.

She was invisible to the boy.

And she wants the man dead.

BRISBANE, AUSTRALIA.

As Jetstar Flight 343 lifted into the air, Lacey Goodenall absently fingered the manila folder. As soon as they leveled off, the tray table would come down and she'd go over her presentation again. Practice doesn't make perfect. Only perfect practice makes perfect. The words were from an old American gridiron coach. She searched for only a few seconds before she remembered his name. Vince Lombardi. American football was inane. Why in God's name did she retain such things?

Oh, she was a marvelous retainer of innocuous detail. Even now, four days past their parting at the airport in Koror, she could recall virtually every word of their conversation at the departure gate. Their parting had been more awkward than she imagined. She had been annoyingly nervous. No, not nervous. Schoolgirl besotted. But it had been nice too. It was nice to care for someone. She had almost forgotten. But caring was also a distraction. What was she accomplishing by daydreaming now, going over their conversation word for word, savoring each word like the last bite of the last supper. Christ, it was a curse being raised Catholic by people she didn't even know, people who certainly didn't care about her soul. And why, at the very last, had she belched the stupidity she had? Because she was nervous, that's why; and, if she was honest, punch drunk confused. She loved what he did to her. She hated what he did to her. Maybe she was just starved for love. So a dime store psychologist had once opined. An orphan, raised in a series of foster homes by parents inspired by monthly checks. Lacey wasn't even her real name, given to her out of twisted respect by the long line of boys who had suffered at the end of her fists.

One thing she wasn't was superstitious. Superstition was for frightened children, the ignorant and the rubber-minded. Still, she wished she hadn't said it. He had kissed her, a nice kiss, not too provocative given they were in public, but long enough to give her a definite tingle, and he had said, "I'll be back," and then he had laughed because he had realized how nervous he was and how stilted the phrase had sounded in both their ears. Nonetheless, if they had been holding an anxiety contest, she would have won, for she had looked up at him and said, "My men always come back."

She had meant it as a dark joke, but she hadn't yet told him of the darkness behind it, so she saw the puzzlement roll across his face and then they had both laughed because there was nothing else to do.

Now, after constant, unhealthy rehashing, what had begun as a confused blurt had become something sinister, a dark omen that breathed cold air on her heart. It ran counter to everything she believed in, the rational world she held up in the face of doubt like a talisman. Yet some ignorant, childish, quivering part of her half believed that, in caring, she had damned him.

"Miss?" The flight attendant gave her a vacuous smile. "May I get you a drink?"

May I get you another lobotomy? She reminded herself to be nice. The attendant had helped her find a row where she could sit alone.

"Scotch and soda. Thank you very much."

The woman smiled at her as if she had never seen her before.

The drink was good. When her friend returned she ordered another, and then a third. She rarely drank hard liquor, and she never drank when she flew. The head of the University of Sydney's School of Biological Sciences was meeting her at the airport. She'd have to buy Tic Tacs before she got to baggage claim, and, from the feel of things between her ears, plunge her head in a sink of cold water as well. She was glad she never wore heels. *That* would have made the airport rendezvous one for the scrapbooks.

The drinks didn't help. They only sprung the latch on her imagination. Placing her head against the window harder than she needed to, she cursed her idiocy as she again wondered if she had cursed herself.

My men always come back.

That had stopped with her father.

She closed her eyes and her mind rioted.

Sometimes she hated her mind.

THE SEA

North Carolina experiences a rash of shark attacks; seven in three weeks. So much conjecture. A perfect storm of conditions, your scientists say. A heat wave drives local water temperatures up, sharks from southern waters pursuing baitfish following the warmer waters. Combined with this, an extended drought with less rainwater flowing into the sea. This drives salinity up in the coastal waters; sharks like more saline waters.

I must allow, your species has become consummately skilled in conveniently explaining things away.

Might I suggest another theory?

Sharks are primitive, and so, more easily influenced. The merest flicker of anger from the right source is enough suggestion to inadvertently direct them. Dull foot soldiers of the Apocalypse.

Rage begets rage. Mob psychology. Of all species, you know this.

And now the intelligent ones are taking matters into their own hands.

Oh, and a small, but not unimportant aside. The perfect storm? There is no perfection. Imperfection is what Nature does. It makes us try harder. Eventually it makes us very close to perfect.

CURACAO.

The woman, she is actually little past girlhood but far past girlhood, lays at the edge of the enclosure, singing to the stars. Her voice is sweet, but she is not. The ground she lays on is hard and covered with tiny sharp stones that dig into her flesh, but this doesn't matter. She could be laying in a puddle of hot oil.

Where she lays, the ground is slanted slightly toward the water.

She smokes crack from the homemade pipe. Her boyfriend stands beside her. He can taste the crack, he is shaking, but he needs this night watchman's job so he lets her smoke alone. He consoles himself in knowing that as soon as she is properly stoned, he will stick his dick in her mouth until he comes. She only swallows when she is high on crack, and then she gobbles like jizz is champagne. He is looking forward to that. He looks down at the top of her head and notices she is going bald.

He hears a noise. Turning, he looks toward the three bunker-like buildings that house the Aqua Academy's indoor exhibits. The little girl has opened one of the doors. She knows her way. She has been here many times, wandering among the fish and the birds while her mother smokes crack and smokes him. From here, the girl is a smudge in the dark. He wonders if she might come to harm, and then he reminds himself she is not his child. The woman laying at his feet, he comes freely in her mouth, but he takes precautions when he inserts himself elsewhere.

"She is going inside by herself," he says.

"Good," murmurs the woman at his feet.

The word carries no emotion, no clue to feeling at all. Whatever feelings exist, they are drifting on unhinged clouds.

It makes him angry. He knows it may ruin his chances of getting what he wants, but he says, "She is only five. You need to be better about watching her."

"Fuck you and that brat." Even her anger has no hinge. It swings loosely. "Leave me alone," she says dreamily.

Looking down he sees the dolphin swimming slowly along the edge of the enclosure, looking up at them with their upturned smiles.

He says nothing as he leaves.

The little girl strides confidently through the half-dark rooms. Her mother's friend always leaves a few lights on for her, and she knows where she is going. Part of her boldness is pretend. The room's dark corners scare her. Sea beasts live in the darkness. In the light, that's where the pretty things live.

She finds the pink flamingoes. Placing her hands on the rickety wood fence, she stares, wholly content. They are the color of cake icing or a pretty dress. Maybe for her sixth birthday she will have a pink cake. When she turns six, she will be able to show her age with both hands.

The flamingoes are sleeping now. They look so funny. Like they were looking for something in their feathers, and they just fell asleep. Their long necks are like delicate flower stems.

The bad memory comes. She tries to push it away, but the bad memories never listen to her, so she lets it come and runs through it as fast as she can; her mother kicking over the rickety fence and kicking the flamingo so that it fell down, flapping its wings crazily. Her mother grinding her heel down on the long beautiful neck until the terrible wing beatings stopped. The wing beatings had made her want to scream, but she knew to keep quiet. When the wings stopped beating, her mother had laughed. Her mother's friend had come and taken her shaking hand and led her outside to the dolphins. That had helped a little. She loved the dolphins too. Her mother's friend had given her a piece of spearmint gum and told her that her mother was jealous of the flamingoes, and the dolphins too. The dolphins had drifted by with their smiles, and she had loved them so much she almost forgot about the flamingo.

Her mother's friend came to her now.

"Hello, Aurea."

She took his hand.

"Hello," she said.

They watched the flamingoes, sleeping with their heads tucked into their quiet wings.

"Is Mommy coming?"

"Not right now."

She was glad, but she didn't want to seem glad.

"Okay," she said.

But it is not okay. Out in the darkness beside the enclosure the woman's crack-fueled anger is rising with each passing dolphin. She knows what the man wants. She knows that the girl cares for these stupidly smiling creatures as much as she cares for her mother. Maybe more.

She takes the straw from the empty soda cup. Worming on to her stomach she inches out. Her hands dangle a few inches above the water. The straw is six inches long. She waits patiently. When the positioning is right, she jams the straw into the passing dolphin's blow hole.

The ground is sloped. She does not account for her lunge and the loose stones. She spills head first into the water.

It is strange, the sudden change. Darkness and cold. Like outer space. And chirps and clicks. Something streaks past her and the water shoves her rudely into something that scrapes her elbow. The enclosure is separated from the sea by a chain link fence. It is rusty and old. Many of the steel wires poke out like twist ties with clawed ends.

The injured dolphin's clicks reverberate through the enclosure and into the sea beyond. The dolphin streak from all corners of the pen. The first to arrive breaks six ribs. Blood bursts from the woman's mouth. It continues from there. She cannot scream. Most of the time she is beneath the water. When she is on the surface what air she has is crushed from her. The blur of gray shadows smashes her into the fence. Her arms and legs flap oddly. She lives for a surprisingly long time.

The dolphins continue after life is gone. Intelligence can assume madness. The dolphins put the rusted chain to good purpose. Again and again, they ram the body against the links. The links lacerate. The lacerations become deep gouges. Flesh is severed away.

Slowly, the madness subsides. Pieces of flesh are pushed through the openings. Some drift on the surface of the enclosure.

Eventually there is no discernible whole. Beyond the fence, the feeders have gathered. Those that can pass through the links help themselves to what drifts inside.

When the watchman finally takes the girl back to the enclosure, at first he sees only the plastic soda cup. Then he sees the t-shirt floating in the middle of the enclosure. In his onrushing panic, it looks like something he can't quite remember.

The little girl points.

"Jellyfish," she says.

THE SEA.

Terrible, you say? Yes, it is.

But may I ask, would you have had the patience? The dolphins in this enclosure have suffered abuse for years. This was not the first straw stuffed into a blowhole.

Sadly, it was the straw that broke someone's back.

Recall Hermes? Children dropped popcorn into his blow hole until finally he left. The wisest of the lot.

Hermes might have been the woman's savior, though now it is impossible to say.

On some occasions, intelligence can win the day.

But intelligence must be present.

KOROR, PALAU.

Miss Patsy woke, drowning in terror and sadness. She lay still, futilely trying to compose herself. It would be easier if they were just dreams.

When she was reasonably sure her legs would support her, she rose from her bed and went to the kitchen. She did not turn the light on. She opened the oven. She lived alone, but she still kept the bottle in the oven. Vodka was cheap and harder to smell on her breath. Not that anyone got that close.

She pulled the bottle out, noticing with disappointment that it was nearly empty. She poured a full glass and drank half of it in two swallows. It helped a little with her nerves. She knew she was well on her way to alcoholism and decay. It was where she wanted to go. The dreams had become too much. She was only a nosey busybody. She was not that strong.

She refilled the glass and put the empty bottle on the kitchen counter. The bottles emptied, but the glass never followed suit.

The kitchen smelled of burnt rice and fried pork. Even in the dark, she could see the dust and food bits on the counter. Once, she had been a fastidious cleaner. Above the stove, her grandmother's picture was spotted with grease. She had loved her grandmother with all her heart. She tried to resurrect the feeling, but nothing came. Instead she remembered the story of the alcoholic who got esophageal cancer because of his addiction. When it finally hurt too much to swallow, his wife gave him sherry enemas, sending the alcohol directly into his bloodstream. He died of alcohol poisoning. His wife was charged in his death, but later the charges were dropped. Cedar Mahoney had died of esophageal cancer. Sometimes her own throat ached. She wondered if she had esophageal cancer. She hoped it wouldn't come to enemas.

She drank into the morning and through the day. It had been a long time since she had been so drunk. When Nounpotu and Leonard arrived after work, she had already put herself to bed. By then her mind was at last going numb.

As she fell asleep she hazily prayed she would not dream about dolphin. But she knew now she had no choice in the matter.

They had packed their bags last night. The three of them were on the same flight from Koror to Manila and then on to Los Angeles. In Los Angeles, they would part ways, Maas for North Carolina and Justin and Amber for Washington.

They sat on the deck of the Wendell Holmes in the morning cool, drinking a last cup of coffee before Marty took them to the airport. Ernan had come down to the dock early. Fury had walked up from the dive shop.

Mist contrails rose from the harbor water, the last vestiges of a hard nighttime rain. Justin and Amber had made love to the music of water streaming off foliage. Now the jungle dripped. First light and last moisture combined to produce shy rainbows. Waxing and waning, they formed half arcs and dusky colors. The wet heightened the smell of plumeria.

"And why are we leaving?" asked Amber.

"Because you need to get an education," Justin said.

"I'm already smart enough to know when I'm being tossed under the bus."

Justin smiled at their surroundings, but they all saw the sadness in the boy's eyes.

"You're right," he said softly. "Chicago is going to be a shock."

Sitting on the railing, Fury asked, "Is Washington far from North Carolina?"

"Not too far," Justin said.

Justin had told them all about his correspondence with the President. They were all in this now. Each of them had absorbed the news with varying degrees of shock. Last night, he and Marty had talked long into the night. They had settled some things, but many things remained unresolved.

"If I had been invited to meet the President," said Fury, "I would have been able to try North Carolina barbecue."

"If he knew you, he would have asked you to come," Justin said. "And not just to cook barbecue." Justin glanced at Marty. "And now that it's empty, you're moving into the cabin."

Fury looked as if he had been slapped.

"You'll pay what you're paying for your current accommodation," said Marty. "Captain's orders, but not really."

Fury's lip trembled.

"If you refuse, he can keelhaul you," said Justin.

Fury did not look at either man.

"I did not believe him the first time," he said.

"It was a good trip," said Justin.

With this everyone fell silent. Each of them knew what he meant. They also knew that now things were largely out of their hands. They would do the small things they could, but it was the boy in front of them who mattered.

Marty thought, *He carries the weight of the world.*

The expression had once been an exaggeration.

"Wait," said Justin. "I almost forgot."

Reaching into the backpack at his feet, Justin pulled out a small gift-wrapped package. It was secured across the middle with duct tape.

Justin handed the package to Fury.

"Please deliver this to our friend, Mongkol. In a sense, it's for all of you."

Marty stood.

"Time to go," he said. "Some of us have to work today."

Justin and Amber hugged Ernan and Fury.

"You'll be back," said Ernan.

"We will," said Justin.

Fury held Justin a little longer. When he released him he said, "Tell the President I would like to be appointed Secretary of Barbecue."

"No one is more qualified. I'll see what I can do."

"You can do anything," Fury said.

They all stood silent again.

"No one can do everything," Justin said. "I know one thing, though."

"What?"

"If you're not sleeping on board tonight, I'll have the President send the Navy SEALs after you."

Fury grinned.

"Good luck to them," he said.

Marty dropped them at the airport curb. It was one of things they had resolved.

Reaching into the bed of the truck, Marty handed Amber her bag. It felt empty.

"You didn't buy any shoes while you were here," he said.

"Being here made me see the importance of fashion." She grew mildly serious. "Among other things."

Marty hugged her a last time. She seemed to radiate heat in the warming morning.

"Thanks for having me," she said.

"You can work with us any time."

Marty extended a hand to Jimmy Maas.

"The same applies to you."

"You may be sorry," said Maas.

Marty turned to Justin. It was harder than he thought.

"You," he said, "I'm not so sure."

Justin smiled.

"You're a wise captain."

"No I'm not."

"I think sometimes we don't realize what we are."

All around them people jostled and shouted and kissed. A bus belched black smoke and the driver leaned on the horn. Fathers hefted enormous packages, and mothers hefted enormous packages while carrying children. As if this sort of thing would go on forever.

Maas and Amber had stepped toward the airport entrance. They stood together pretending to talk.

Marty felt himself shaking.

Justin hugged him.

"I don't like goodbyes either," Justin said. "Thank you for making my mom so happy. She would be proud of you."

"You're not making this easy."

The green eyes sparked.

"Sometimes the hardest things turn out to be for the best."

All the noise and commotion seemed to disappear.

"Are we lost?" Marty asked.

A man carrying a crate of chickens stepped between them.

"No," said Justin. "I don't think so."

Mongkol was tinkering with the engine when Marty returned.

Marty retrieved the package from his cabin.

Reaching up from the hold, Mongkol accepted it wordlessly. Meticulously removing the tape, he produced a grin and disappeared from sight.

Marty, Fury and Ernan looked at each other in the morning silence, and then it was no longer silent.

When the first divers stepped on board, a raucous squalling rose to greet them.

Marty smiled at the divers.

"A little Nirvana to start our day," he said.

That night Marty took the bagpipes into the jungle.

WASHINGTON, DISTRICT OF COLUMBIA.

Justin and Amber arrived at the White House on Tuesday morning. Amber had ushered Justin to the hotel barbershop the afternoon before, but his hair remained shoulder length and sun-streaked. The Secret Service men watched him curiously, as did several interns. The Secret Service detail watched Amber closely too, though not solely out of professionalism. Justin and Amber had received the memo on White House protocol. After Justin's haircut, Amber had bought a dress and matching heels in Georgetown. The dress traced every contour.

They walked side by side down the carpeted hallway to the Oval Office, two Secret Service men fore and three aft.

Justin leaned close.

"Tell me why you got the longest pat down."

"*Stop*," she hissed. "Unless you want to be sorely embarrassed."

Nervousness made her laugh uncontrollably. She had rarely been this nervous. It felt like a tuning fork was vibrating inside her.

After a dozen more steps – she counted to distract herself -- Justin whispered, "Fine then. I'll tell you. Because men always misbehave."

She smiled at the Secret Service men. She knew it was a mildly hysterical smile.

"He whispers when he's nervous," she said.

Justin spoke in a perfectly comfortable tone.

"It's the dress," he said.

In front of them, two sets of ears lifted slightly.

"Told you," whispered Justin.

Russell Shaughnessy greeted them both warmly, but he got right to business.

"I cleared my morning calendar," he said, "but we have a lot of ground to cover."

A man and a woman stood in front of one of the couches. They had risen when Justin and Amber entered the Oval Office. They both recognized the woman, but the man with the dark eyebrows was unfamiliar.

"I'm sorry things are a bit stiff and regimented around here, but that's government for you. I believe you know our Vice President Margaret Cassiday, but you're not supposed to know Mike Neal. Mr. Neal is from the Office of the Director of National Intelligence. In layman's terms, he deals with secrets. And what we have here, we're trying to keep secret."

Russell Shaughnessy turned to his coworkers.

"This young lady, as you memo readers know, is Amber Giles. From my pen pal correspondence with Justin, I have been led to believe she is up to speed on the issues we will discuss. Quite likely, she knows more than we do. So, within this room, we may all talk freely. Thank you for coming, Amber."

"My pleasure," Amber said.

It was. The vibrating was already subsiding. She had also decided on her vote in the next election.

"And I believe you recognize Justin Mahoney from his speech. Based on that performance I'd like to make him my stunt double for every upcoming fundraiser, but as we can all see that won't likely work." Russell sighed. "First you're young, and then you're not."

Everyone exchanged handshakes.

"Please sit. I hope you'll understand if I don't. Looking across that prairie spread of desk is like being in another room."

Russell Shaughnessy's smile was different from the one at the fundraiser. It was slow and easy, and some of it reached down to touch the creases below his eyes.

"I want this to be as informal as possible because it's my humble belief that formality usually gets in the way of progress. Maggie and I go way back." He glanced affectionately at his Vice President. "Sometimes too far back for my comfort. And Mike has grown on me." He was already pacing. "Let's see. Where to start?"

"If it's a question of priorities," Maggie said, "I would like to ask Amber where she got her dress."

Everyone laughed.

"Now you see why Maggie should be president. You know it wasn't just ice breaking fatuousness, Justin. We were all impressed with your speech. Stunned, honestly. It's one of the best speeches I've ever heard. And I know nothing about octopuses and more than I'd like to about speeches."

Walking down the hallway he hadn't been nervous, but here in this office Justin suddenly felt a weight that hadn't been there before. So much history; so many history-altering decisions. Moment seemed to percolate up through the rug. It stole some of his ease, and made him forget for a moment his overriding task.

He couldn't do that.

"Thank you, Mr. President. Maybe you could see about changing my grade."

"Brilliant oratory and a quick study. Good." Russell Shaughnessy walked to the fireplace. He had his back to them, but his resonant voice still carried through the room. "The story you told about the octopus reminded me of my mother. She raised six boys alone." He turned back to them. "And it made me deeply sorry for your loss, Justin. Your mother sounded like a remarkable woman." He offered an apologetic smile. "We're very thorough in our background checks."

Justin felt the tension draining away.

"She was remarkable. She's the reason I'm here."

"A good mother never leaves us."

"No, they don't," said Justin. "The problem is we don't tend to recognize remarkable mothers outside our species."

"Different, but not so different."

Justin smiled his own easy smile.

"Yes. And that's exactly how we have to get people to think. For their sake. For our sake. As the oceans go, so we go. That's Sylvia Earle, not me."

The President rubbed his hands together.

"Now before we move on, I have to ask. Amber, you're familiar with the incident in the Malacca Strait?"

"Yes. Justin told me." *But not everything.* In her mind, he moaned in his sleep. Secrets. In this moment, she didn't care about the seas. She cared only about him. He was still barely a man.

She rested a hand on his knee. She felt the other man's eyes on her. When she looked at him, neither of their gazes faltered.

"I can keep secrets," she said.

"Good then," said Russell Shaughnessy. "We can discuss the Malacca incident freely. Freely speaking, I found it impossible to believe."

No one missed the tense.

"We are going to have to adjust to the impossible more and more," Justin said.

"So I've seen. You and I have discussed this via e-mail, but now the chosen few in this room," he tried to smile, "can hear the impossible directly from you. I want to hear it from you too. I'm still wrestling with all this. The refugees on the vessel, *numerous* refugees on the vessel, said the creatures that attacked the vessel were nautilus. Only they were much bigger."

"They were right."

Russell stopped pacing and slumped against the edge of the desk.

"Most of me wishes you hadn't said that. You're certain."

"Yes."

Maggie Cassiday spoke.

"The refugees said the creatures only took the crew."

Justin was quiet. He couldn't imagine.

"Why?" Maggie asked.

"Justice?" said Justin.

A deeper silence fell on the room.

"They're intelligent?" Maggie asked. "They can reason?"

"Yes on both fronts." Justin saw the look in three sets of eyes. "I said we have to adjust."

Maggie leaned forward.

"How do you know?"

The crossroad.

"I've seen some of their behavior. My mother saw some of their behavior. One of them saved my life."

Justin told the story.

When he finished Maggie Cassiday said, "Any idea why?"

345

"No."

It was an honest answer. That he was worth singling out was an adjustment he hadn't yet made. And no one was indispensable. This he knew.

"I'm glad," said Maggie softly. "Any mother would be."

Before coming into this room, Justin had decided not to decide. It was a strange feeling, especially to him, knowing more than some of the most powerful people on earth. It was a question of what to volunteer and what – maybe for the moment, maybe forever -- to leave out. He liked this man and woman. More important, he felt he could trust them. But too much, too soon might prove too much. And he was still figuring things out himself. It was like leading people across thin ice, and he had grown up in the tropics.

He felt their eyes on him. All three of them lived in a world of secrets. They would likely know lies. They probably knew half-truths. But whole truths might be too much, even for these intelligent people. *I communicate with these creatures. I can control certain creatures with my mind. I used that power to bully a bully. I have seen the end of the world.*

Justin chose his words carefully. They could see this. It didn't matter.

"As I told the President, there are four of them. A mother and three offspring. I've seen the mother twice, and once I saw her eggs. Now three of the eggs have hatched."

Justin stopped for a moment. He was beyond thin ice.

"Here's the rest, and it's even harder to digest. I'm certain there are three offspring, but not because that's what the refugees said. I know because the mother communicates with me through dreams. Or what seem to be dreams. It doesn't happen that often, but it happens often enough. And she did the same thing with my mother." His smile was carefully composed. He knew they could see this too. "I said we were going to have to adjust to the impossible."

Russell Shaughnessy released a gust of air.

"In spades."

"It's our midnight fear," said Justin. "A world beyond us."

Amber knew this.

Mike Neal leaned forward.

"You communicate with the mother," he said. "What about the others?"

Justin knew it might be the most important question of all.

He regarded the dark-haired man with respect.

"They don't reach out to me, at least as far as I know. I don't know…

"What they're thinking?" Mike Neal asked.

"By our definition, no I don't."

The drumbeat. Sometimes fast, sometimes slow. Like a heartbeat. What they're *feeling*.

"Should we be concerned about this?"

"Yes."

They all had the same question, but they looked to the President.

"And what do we do now?"

Here, Justin knew the answer.

"Pay attention. Pay very, very close attention and work very fast. We need to work together. As a nation. As nations. We need to make global changes, and we need to make them quickly."

"Are you familiar with politics?"

The feeble joke sat like ash in Russell Shaughnessy's mouth.

"We need to move beyond politics and self-interest," Justin said.

"When pigs fly."

"Soon enough they might."

Russell turned to Amber.

"Reassure me. He's not running in the next election? Though I'm not sure he's cut out for politics."

"Maybe a new kind of politician," Amber said.

"Maybe," said Russell Shaughnessy, but he had seen enough of politics to doubt it.

The President turned back to Justin.

"Someone recently sat on that couch and said that ninety-five percent of the ocean deeps are unexplored."

"They're right."

"Well then, that gives us some small basis for our vast pool of ignorance." Russell looked past the couches to the map of blue. "It's like something from Jules Verne."

"It is," said Justin. "But it isn't."

So very odd. Just the boy's soft voice made him feel better. He had spent his political life being browbeaten by messengers trumping their causes. My way or the highway. It was also odd to trust the boy without question or reservation. He had made a life in an arena rife with secrets, deceit and mistrust. Yet he was willing to rip the shirt of his back, and show this boy the scars. It was stronger than a gravitational pull. It was a siren call. He had felt it watching the speech. He was older and more world wise, but he knew now this didn't make him wiser. *What in the morning was true will at evening have become a lie.* Carl Jung. He remembered it from Introductory Psychology. Not so long ago, yet a different world now.

He told himself it would help their cause if he confided in the boy, but mostly he told him because he wanted to.

"The fishing vessel that rescued the first batch of refugees was called Rahmat Baru." He glanced apologetically at Maggie and Mike Neal. It was a small omission. "They didn't translate it in the report and I didn't think it was important. Rahmat Baru means "God's New Mercies.""

Mike Neal thought, *Justice*.

Justin simply said, "If there is a God, everything on this planet deserves equal mercy."

Russell Shaughnessy had no response for this. He needed a drink. He reached for his water.

He had one more item on the agenda.

"You're our second cephalopod expert," he said.

Mike Neal glanced at the President, but Maggie just smiled.

Russell Shaughnessy nodded.

"We have to work together and we have to work fast," he said.

He told Justin and Amber about Tom Browning's visit and the video they had seen.

He knew the answer, but he felt he should ask.

"Do you need to see it?"

"No," said Justin.

There was silence.

Mike Neal said, "You're not surprised."

"No. I'm not surprised."

"The scientist was," said Mike Neal.

"I think there are more surprises on the way. I think few of them will be good for us."

Beneath the dark eyebrows, the dark eyes narrowed.

"Is that just conjecture?" Mike Neal asked.

Russell Shaughnessy saved him.

"May I ask where this interrogation is going?"

"Nowhere," said Mike Neal, sitting back on the couch.

Russell knew his interruption was uncalled for. He was aware of his strange need to be the boy's protector. Yet at the same time, he felt as if the boy was far beyond him. He might need protection in the petty world they had constructed, but beyond this office Russell Shaughnessy felt the boy required no protection at all.

But we are all flesh and blood.

Maggie coughed.

"Mr. President. It's noon. You have an afternoon filled with postponed meetings. And they have a plane to catch."

"Right. Well then, that's it. Is there anything we didn't cover?"

This time Amber coughed.

He had already slipped back into officiousness.

"Yes, Miss Giles?"

"Caramel," Amber said.

Everyone looked at her, puzzled.

"The store where the dress came from."

Everyone but Mike Neal laughed. Russell Shaughnessy realized again why he admired women so much more than men.

"They had a few more in this style," Amber said. "The dress would look good on you, Mrs. Vice President."

Maggie actually flushed. He would be sure to remind her the next time they were alone.

"Well I'm glad we didn't leave that thread dangling," he said.

Everyone stood.

Russell Shaughnessy walked over and shook Amber's hand.

"Ahead of every good man, there's a better woman. And no, I'm not trying to win your vote."

"You already did."

"Well then, I'll try not to disappoint you. And I hope you won't think me rude if I ask Justin for a few minutes alone."

When everyone left, Russell told Justin about his dream. As he recounted the dream, the boy watched him with almost feverish intensity.

When he finished, Justin said, "It's almost exact."

"Help," Russell Shaughnessy said, though he wasn't entirely sure he wanted it.

The boy gave a brief smile.

"Right. Sorry. Have you heard of cyanobacteria?"

"No."

"They're primitive bacteria. And they're thriving and spreading through the oceans. In the Gulf of Mexico. Off Alaska. In the Adriatic Sea. Almost every summer now, off the coast of Sweden, there's a bloom of cyanobacteria. Locals call it rhubarb soup. Its stinks. And it turns the water yellow-brown."

Russell felt as if the yellow-brown water had poured into his lungs.

Softly Justin said, "Have you had many dreams like this?"

"No. Just the one." He heard the relief in his voice, but he wasn't sure if he should be relieved. "Is that a good thing?"

"I don't know," said the boy.

CHICAGO, ILLINOIS.

One of her roommates had bought a poster of James Dean and hung it beside the living room bookshelf. Other than that, nothing had changed. There were dishes in the sink and a bottle of lite salad dressing on the coffee table.

It made returning seem all the stranger.

Picking up the dressing, Amber asked, "Did we ever leave?"

"The only thing that's missing is a pair of briefs."

A gray ball appeared on the kitchen counter. The cat watched them both.

"Someone missed you," said Justin.

Amber crouched.

"Come here, Terror. Don't be such a standoffish grouch."

Dropping soundlessly to the floor, Terror went to Justin.

Amber regarded the cat and Justin with equal disgust.

"Well then," she said, "you can feed her."

THE SEA.

The boy is not removed, but he is removed from the sea. I know she sees this as an opportunity. It worries me. I wish I could see, but her intentions remain cloaked in fog.

One thing I know. She wishes to orchestrate your end. She may wish to orchestrate his end. And I am certain of this. If the boy and his kind do not survive, your kind will continue on in your madness and condemn us all.

She does not see that your madness is her madness. She wishes to destroy all of you, at any cost.

I will protect him. I will do whatever is required.

It is a matter of survival.

KOROR, PALAU.

The sun has been up for an hour. On this day it will rise, reach its zenith and set as it always does.

On the bridge, Ernan carefully wipes the salt-spotted glass with a paper towel. In the galley, Marty puts the last breakfast plate away. Fury, stepping aboard with two tanks, calls out to Ernan. Down in the engine room, Mongkol Songkhla finishes his work by lighting up a smoke. Holding the flaring match, fingers trembling, he doesn't know why.

The cloves pop. The sparks fall like pretty fireworks into the fuel puddled on the floor. The flames run about the engine room like excited children, and then the Wendell Holmes goes up in a mushroom of flame. No one has time to think any thoughts.

Death is nothing at all. And everything.

Pieces of debris drift from the harbor. Each charts its own course.

Beneath the full moon something like a small branch floats on the ocean's dark skin.

A splinter of bagpipe.

THE SEA.

She was responsible. Ash and man were only puzzle pieces.

Yet another unforeseen turn.

Yet not wholly unforeseen.

Remember. Change is only truth.

KOROR, PALAU.

In the midnight lake, the blacktips turn on each other. When it is finished, the last blacktip gobbles the drifting cornucopia.

Miss Patsy wakes and goes to the kitchen. She opens the oven door.

It is an old fashioned coal gas oven. Ten percent carbon dioxide. Roughly ten times the requirement.

She turns the oven on.

She leaves the vodka bottle where it is.

ABOUT THE AUTHOR

Ken McAlpine is the author of ten books; fiction, non-fiction and selected essays. His books and magazine articles have received numerous awards. Ken lives in Ventura, California with his wife Kathy.

Other Books by Ken McAlpine

Fiction:

Juncture (Book One of the Ship of Pearl Series)

Together We Jump: A Journey of Love, Hope and Second Chances

Fog

Rise of the Mooncusser

Nonfiction:

Islands Apart: A Year on the Edge of Civilization

Off Season: Discovering America on Winter's Shore

West is Eden: Reflections on this Gift Called Life (life stories)

Salt on Our Lips: Stories of Humor, Humanity and Mysteries Happily Unresolved (sea stories)

Lightning Strikes of Loopy Giddiness and Other Bucket List Travel Tales (travel stories)

For more information, please go to…

www.kenmcalpine.com

www.facebook.com/kenmcalpineauthor